Zeke Yoder vs. the Singularity

This is a work of fiction. Names, characters, places, and incidents either are the product of the author's imagination or are used fictitiously.

Zeke Yoder vs. the Singularity

Copyright © 2016 by Stephen Beachy
Published by CreateSpace
Independent Publishing Platform
Cover art by Michaelangelo
(www.voidandimagination.com)
Cover design by James Salas
Interior Design by Billington Media

ISBN-13: 978-1539824398
ISBN-10: 153982439X

Zeke Yoder vs. the Singularity

STEPHEN BEACHY

ONE

When Zeke Yoder heard the shot from the cellar of the back house, before the sun had even risen through the data vapor, he got a bad feeling. He had just finished the milking and was on his way to the chicken house. The shot echoed through the still morning, loud enough to wake his younger brothers and sisters in the front house, his grandfather in the back, and his Uncle Mose on the adjoining farm. His mother and father were already up, choring, but it was Zeke who got there first, to find Grandma Mast sitting on the steps that led down into the cellar, still in her nightclothes, with the rifle in her lap. She was nursing a nasty-looking gash on her ankle.

The mice are finding their way into the basement, she said.

Mice, said Zeke, or rats?

A real big one, she said. I heard a noise down here, so I come down with my flashlight and the rifle, and there's one of the critters just sitting on the windowsill looking at me.

How big?

She held her hands apart to show that it was maybe two feet tall. That size, Zeke knew, it had to be a GMR—a genetically modified rat.

I missed it, but that shot sure cracked loud in the basement, she said. It bit me.

GMR bites were bad news. People got feverish, became delusional, began hearing voices, and died within forty-eight hours if they didn't get treated. Just the other week a boy from Wellman went crazy and started lighting all his employer's pork bushes on fire before they got him the antidote.

Grandma, if that's a GMR, you know that bite's not good.

They've been into the walnuts we got stored down here, Zekey, she said. After all that drying and husking last fall.

Zeke hadn't seen too many of the old-fashioned rats since the Genetically Modified Rats, or Rats from NIMH as some folk called them, first showed up in the fall. Where the GMRs came from, nobody was sure. Some said they'd escaped from the labs at the National Institute of Mental Health, experimental brain subjects that got too smart for the doctors. Others said they were just mutants, from the free-floating genetic material or the radioactivity or the chemicals. Zeke's friend Gonzalo said the new pro-singularity government had probably released them on purpose, to starve the Amish and any other humans, anti-tech holdouts, and off-the-Grid types.

Ow, Grandma said. Oh my.

Grandma Mast was not actually Zeke's grandmother, but his great-grandmother, ninety-seven years old, born in the middle of the twentieth century. She was a tiny scrap of a woman, quick and hard, bent over from age, but with a warmth in her manner and a sparkle in her eyes that had lit up the farm as long as Zeke had been alive. Just as the wound was starting to change colors and glow, Zeke's father showed up. Zeke filled him in.

Okay, Grandma, let's get you back to bed. Zeke, you get her from the legs.

Oh nonsense, said Grandma. I can walk myself up there just fine. It's just a little scratch.

By the time she'd made it back to her room, however, the site of the bite was bulging and giving off the kind of phosphorescent lightshow that the new cuttlefish meat-blends would display on the shelves of the store in Kalona. She was already starting to sweat. Uncle Mose had rushed in and several of the children were peeking around his waist to see.

Zeke's father shooed the children back to the front house and the three men went down into the cellar to consider the matter in private. Ever since Zeke's schooling had ended two years before, Zeke's father usually included him in the menfolk's discussions, even though he was only fourteen.

We have to get the medicine, Zeke blurted out. She'll die from that bite!

Now Zeke, you know as well I do that there isn't any of that medicine for humans anymore, his father said. Dr. Sattler might come by and take a look. He might have something to help her out.

Dr. Sattler doesn't have anything but pain pills and anxiety pills, Zeke said.

We can see what he has, said his father. And we can pray.

His father was giving him a hard look. They had been over this before. Why aren't there any Amish doctors, Zeke had always wanted to know. Why couldn't you be Amish and be a doctor too? Why should the Amish be dependent on the English to take care of them? They had gotten by that way for hundreds of years, but that was before the new government, the new laws. *Evolve or Die* was the policy of the new government, and they were trying to hurry the Amish and other unmodified humans on to extinction.

I'll go over to Walter's, use the phone to call Dr. Sattler, said Uncle Mose.

She'll die, said Zeke. She's already dying. You've heard the stories. Forty-eight hours. I need to talk to Gonzalo.

His father said, No.

It's her only chance.

I don't want you to have dealings with those people, his father said. I've told you before. Be polite. Give them a hand if they need it. But we don't ask them for anything. I won't give her any black-market medicines. I won't have her turning into ... something else.

Uncle Mose?

Both Mose and his father frowned. He needed to accept his father's word was what both of them were thinking. He knew that.

I don't know, said Mose. I'll call Dr. Sattler.

And you, Zeke, said his father. You've got chickens to feed.

Zeke hurried into the chicken house, a long, airless building full of hundreds of chickens crammed together in tiny cages. Old-fashioned chickens, with beaks and feathers and brains. He had gathered eggs in this chicken house almost every day of his life, but today, in the light of this new emergency, everything seemed strange. The dull buzzing lights seemed like torture devices, the hundreds of eggs settled in the troughs seemed like tiny prisons. It struck him now that he was surrounded by thousands of tiny brains encased in the doomed and suffering bodies of chickens. God was everywhere, Zeke knew—even here. Was God inside the dreams of a chicken? What did a chicken dream? Did a chicken dream about the boy who came each morning to feed it and take away its eggs? He hurried down the narrow center between two rows of cages and directly out the back way.

He had never disobeyed his father before. But if Grandma Mast could be saved, he would do anything, it didn't matter if his father said *No*, if the bishops said *No*, if the entire community shunned him, if Jesus Christ himself came down to the earth and begged him to stop.

He crossed the back field, took the shortcut along the creek to the road, and crossed to the farm where Leahbelle Beachy lived. Leahbelle's mother Miriam was out on the porch, peeling some potatoes. She was a warm, solid woman, always busy with her hands and quick to laugh. Miriam had been like another mother to Zeke at times, and she told him now that he could find Leahbelle out back. She was there by the shed, supposed to be hanging clothes to dry in the early morning April heat, but the basket of wet laundry was set on the ground and she was aiming her slingshot at something Zeke couldn't make out, in the direction of the old oak. Probably a dragonfly drone. A few strands of her honey-colored hair were floating loose from her bonnet, with the early morning light behind her, filtered through the haze of the data vapor. She let loose, and then Zeke saw the drone as it zipped to the side to avoid the projectile.

She snapped her fingers in disappointment, turned and saw Zeke, and smiled, until she saw the look on his face.

Grandma Mast's been bit by a GMR, he told her.

Oh, poor Grandma, she said.

She gave him a hug.

Leahbelle and Zeke had been inseparable since they were small children. Zeke's mother had died when he was just four years old, and during the next few years, before his father married the woman Zeke now thought of as his mother, he had practically lived with the Beachys.

What are you going to do? she asked.

I'm going to East Liberty, Zeke said.

Not Gonzalo.

Of course Gonzalo. Gonzalo's my friend.

Gonzalo's English.

Gonzalo was English only in the sense that he wasn't Amish; he was actually from Honduras, from Tegucigalpa, although he'd made the journey north when he was only five. He was just a couple of years older than Zeke, but Zeke sometimes felt that Gonzalo had lived two lives in that time. Gonzalo barely remembered his old home, although he dreamed about it, he told Zeke sometimes. He'd come to work in the Foodco slaughterhouses and meat laboratories years ago, when they were looking for children with little arms that fit more easily into the machines.

Gonzalo is violent, said Leahbelle. And crude. And

crazy. Sinful.

I don't know why you say all that, said Zeke. He might be lost from the Lord, he might sin, like we all do, but inside he's a good person. And he has connections.

I'm coming with you, Leahbelle said.

Can you get a buggy?

Leahbelle thought about it and nodded. I'll hitch Fern up, she said. Meet me up the road.

Zeke hurried back to the road and followed the shoulder until the one-seater horse and buggy came clomping along a few minutes later, and he jumped up onto the sideboard and got inside. Keeping one hand on the reins, she took Zeke's hand with her other and squeezed it.

I found the most beautiful fabric for the quilt I'm making you, she told him. It's dark blue, almost purple, and it glows like it's lit up from the inside. I guess it's nano and bioluminescent and some of that stuff. Dad says it's too fancy.

I told you that you don't need to make me a quilt, said Zeke.

I think he'd let me get it, Leahbelle went on. He's just afraid what your father would say. I know that you would like it.

Leahbelle wasn't really much of a quilter. She was skilled with her slingshot, a fast runner, and stronger than Zeke when it came to lifting buckets of hog slop. She had a beautiful singing voice too, and an ear for all music, how the notes fit together. She seemed to accept quilting as part of her destiny, however, as she didn't accept many other aspects of that destiny. She had a rebellious streak that had been germinating since she was a little girl, and was blooming extravagantly since her school days had ended. It wasn't aimed at her own parents so much as it was the bishops and the stern, gossiping leaders of the community. Like Zeke's father.

I'm tired of these dumb men who think they know everything telling me what to do, she told him now. Tired of men who think I'm just here to follow their orders.

If it comes from you, my father will accept the quilt, said Zeke. Eventually. Although he'll probably have to pretend that he disapproves.

Leahbelle's father, Peter Beachy, was a gentler man than Zeke's, not quite so strict. He liked to tell jokes. The jokes were never very funny, but people usually laughed anyway. Zeke could remember when he was a little boy riding around on Leahbelle's father's shoulders. His own father had never done that.

A driverless bot-car zipped past them, and then the road was empty again. Just the morning mist and a few chirping birds off among the trees. The pace of the buggy had always seemed just right to Zeke, providing a rhythm like breathing, the perfect space for conversation or contemplation. The speed of the horses matched the sounds of the birds and the slow turning of the planet beneath the hazy sky. God was speaking through the land and its creatures, Zeke thought, and so the buggy moved at the same speed as the voice of God. Zeke had never coveted the speed of the bot-cars. But today it felt like he was stuck on the back of a turtle, or limping along like a one-legged man, or floating down a river made of the molasses filling his mother used for her famous shoo-fly pie. There was too much space for his thoughts, and he thought that if they could only move faster he might leave his fears behind. He needed to zip, to run, to fly.

They drove in silence into Riverside and then took the old highway along the river through East Liberty. East Liberty was a ghost town, nothing but boarded up shops and, just outside of town, the ruins of the old orphanage. The East Liberty Home for Boys.

Zeke was surprised that Leahbelle remembered how to get here. She pulled over onto a side road that dead-ended in some barricades and a chain-link fence. They tied the horses and climbed through a hole in the fence, past several *No Trespassing* and *Do Not Enter* signs, through the trees to a ruined old bridge that crossed the river. On the other side of the river was the ruined orphanage.

Halt. Who goes there?

A woman's voice came from one of the trees, where a small tree fort had been built.

It is Zeke Yoder. I'm here to see Gonzalo.

Who's your girlfriend?

Zeke blushed. He couldn't see the person the voice belonged to, but he recognized the voice.

Leahbelle Beachy, said Leahbelle.

How do I know you aren't just NSA in Amish drag?

I've been here many times, Aeren, Zeke said. Gonzalo knows me. You know me too.

In what year was Jakob Amman born, Amish boy?

In 1644.

And where?

In Ehrenbach im Simmental, the Canton of Bern, in Switzerland.

Very good. I know you, Zeke, I was just testing you. Go on, I think Gonzo's up top.

He led Leahbelle across the yard, where strange pieces of old machinery had been bent into odd sculptures. The landscape was full of old-fashioned cameras and motion detectors, clicking and following their movements.

How does she know so much about the Amish? Leahbelle whispered.

They've studied our history, Zeke told her. That's why they came here. To learn from us. They figure if you're going to live off the Grid, we're the ones to go to.

Inside, the ruin of the East Liberty Home for Boys was gutted, the floors rotten and full of holes, the walls covered over with graffiti. Beer cans and syringes and circuits and broken glass all over the floors. An old box that Zeke told Leahbelle was an old-fashioned television, from the twentieth century. The smashed remains of several Whippersnappers, a short-term gravity-altering toy that Gonzalo had showed him. He didn't tell Leahbelle that he had tried it once with Gonzalo, who loved almost anything that would alter his reality. Gonzalo cracked the tube and they had floated together to the ceiling. Hold on, kid, said Gonzalo. Get ready for the fall. And it had come on them suddenly, Zeke groping for Gonzalo, for anything, as they fell together in a heap.

He led Leahbelle up the stairs to the second floor, where he could hear some people talking and laughing down the hallway. He led her up the next stairway to what had once been the structure's attic, now more like a deck—the roof was gone and only one wall remained, and it was crumbling. There was nobody there.

From up here you could look out over the patches of forest that surrounded the old ruin, and the river, the ruined bridge, an old cemetery, and beyond it an Amish farm, Sam Stoltzfus' place. Suddenly there was an arm around his neck, a chokehold, and a death-Taser pointed at his head. The Taser turned slowly away from him and straight toward Leahbelle's heart.

Defend yourself, Amish. If you don't fight back, your friend's gonna die.

The arm around his neck ended not in a hand but in a kind of whirling mechanical claw, a spidery mechanism that could morph into almost any shape imaginable. Zeke knew that mechanism. It was Gonzalo, and this was one of his favorite games to play.

God is with me, man of violence. His will shall be done.

Just punch me in the face and knock the gun out of my hand, said Gonzalo. Come on, man, it's easy.

But Zeke wouldn't do it, and Gonzalo knew Zeke wouldn't do it. They had had endless discussions about the philosophy of non-violence. Gonzalo believed in non-violence only as a strategy. Because of the government's superior military technology and the Gstate's Total Monitoring Map, open violence was pointless, he said—most of the time. But Gonzalo didn't believe in turning the other cheek. He believed in vengeance. Gonzalo felt that in the process of battling the state and the singularity, murder could be justified.

He released his chokehold and stepped back. He was shirtless, and his body was puffed up from the attack. Gonzalo's default state was just a skinny kid, like Zeke, but he'd been altered both for his work at Foodco and by his anti-singularity friends since he ditched his corporate owners and went off the Grid. The strange flexibility of his body, the musculature that could grow and shrink, the elaborate mechanisms of the left arm, the skin that could change color to camouflage himself or become animated with his flickering Mayan tattoos, elaborate cartoons of skulls and calligraphy—it fascinated Zeke, but disturbed him as well. He'd never had a friendship with someone who wasn't technically human. *Post-humans are people too*, Gonzalo often said in a sarcastic voice, mimicking some public service ad campaign from the thirties.

You'd kill a rat that was eating your crops, said Gonzalo now. What's the difference between a rat and an NSA?

Gonzalo, that's just it, said Zeke. It's Grandma Mast. She took a shot at a GMR and got bit.

Damn, man, that's tough.

He shook his head.

You need some medicine, he said.

That's why I came.

We don't have it, my friend. We don't have the tech. The antidote has to be personalized, based on the DNA in the wound and your grandma's DNA.

So what would you do? asked Leahbelle. If you were bit?

I wouldn't let a GMR close enough to bite me.

Gonzalo, said Zeke. We came here for your help.

Okay, okay, I'm thinking. In an emergency I'd go to the hospital in Iowa City.

But we're still human, said Leahbelle. They won't let

us in.

They'll let you in if you sign the forms. If you agree to let them enhance you. The question is if they'll ever let you out.

Zeke just shook his head.

I wouldn't go there either, said Gonzalo. They'd stick some damn GPS in my organs or my software, and I'd have to dig it out. They might turn me over to Foodco.

He waved his finger like he had an idea.

I know a guy. I know a guy who could do it. But he's a hundred miles away.

A hundred miles, said Zeke. That's too far in the buggy. Grandma Mast would be gone by the time I got back.

Get a driver.

There aren't any more drivers, said Zeke. You know that.

You could go, said Leahbelle. You could go and bring it back on your motorbike.

I'm not on the Grid either, said Gonzalo. Did you forget?

But you can get around on the motorbike, said Leahbelle. I've seen you.

Yeah, it's kind of dangerous, he said, but I can do it.

Zeke thought he was just bragging, acting tough. Gonzalo rode that motorbike all the time. These back roads were barely monitored. As long as he stayed off the Horizontal Grid-works, he was probably fine.

But I can't get the medicine, Gonzalo said. This guy I know, he's a security guard. He works nights at the Meat Substances Warehouse in Marshalltown. If I step foot in Marshalltown, the Foodco sensors will pick me up and I'm good as enslaved.

Zeke thought about it.

Take me with you. Drop me off outside of town and wait for me to come back with the medicine.

Gonzalo nodded.

I can do that for you. But he won't be out front until probably ten thirty tonight. Then it'll take a little while to whip up the medicine. He'll have some things he'll want you to do for him, along with the money.

Things?

Gonzalo laughed.

Don't worry, he said. He's a little weird, but it's nothing too bad.

How much money? Zeke asked.

Maybe five, six hundred. Just to cover his costs. He likes me. You tell him Gonzalo sent you and it's no problem.

I can do that, Zeke said.

Leahbelle said, I have a couple hundred I can give you. How quick will you be back?

Gonzalo said, If he's out by midnight, we can get back here by two, maybe two thirty. When was she bit?

Just after dawn, Zeke said.

They all knew that if they could get the medicine within twenty-four hours, she had a good chance.

Back at the farm, breakfast was almost over. Zeke's father gave him a look but didn't say anything.

We've been calling you for breakfast, his mother said. And Grandma Mast has been calling for you too.

I had some chores to do further out, said Zeke.

He knew that it was a sin to say so. Technically it was the truth, but in spirit it was a lie. His father excused himself and headed out to the well.

His mother leaned over and gave him a hug from behind.

Just grab some eggs and biscuits, and go in to see your granny, she said.

He hurried over to the back house and upstairs to Grandma's room. Grandma Mast was sitting up in the bed, sweating rivers and staring around crazy-like, like she couldn't really see what was in front of her—the quilt, the stool next to the bed, the Bible, and the glass of water. Like she was lost in a nightmare. The glowing, multi-colored lump on her shin was the size of an egg.

He took her hand.

Grandma, it's Zeke. What's going on, Grandma?

The barn's on fire, she said. The lightning struck it.

The barn's okay, Grandma. You're just having a bad dream.

Nothing to do but let it burn, she said.

That was a long time ago, Grandma. Back before I was born.

Zekey, she said, and she squeezed his hand, and looked at him, and he could see that, for a moment at least, she was back again, here and now.

Out by the well, he could see his mother and his father. His father was holding onto his own head with both hands, as if he was trying to keep it together. His mother was rubbing his father's back and speaking.

I have to take some blood, Grandma. Just sit still and squeeze my hand.

He took out the sample kit that Gonzalo gave him— one for the wound culture and one for the blood. He'd watched people do it before—he'd always been interested in medicine and science, and when he was a boy he'd imagined that he might someday be a doctor. He wasn't squeamish, but actually sticking the needles into his own grandmother would take all of his fortitude.

There'll be a little stick, Grandma.

She didn't even flinch when he stuck the needle into the wound. Maybe the GMR toxins had numbed the area. When he pricked her short, bony finger, however, she let out a little yelp.

Zeke's father came in, just as he was putting the samples in the little webbed bag Gonzalo gave him.

You disobeyed me, he said.

Zeke just looked at the floor.

Dr. Sattler was here, his father said. He left pills for pain and anxiety. Just as you said.

Dad, said Zeke.

He said that there is nothing he can do, his father said. I have prayed on it, Zeke. You shouldn't have disobeyed me. But if you can get the medicine, you must do whatever you need to do to get it.

I can get it, Dad, said Zeke. Gonzalo will take me tonight.

Let us pray that it comes in time, said his father.

TWO

According to Gonzalo, what most people didn't realize was that the Horizontal Grid-works was perfectly designed to be driven like a crazy person. It was what the rich did for fun. The bot-cars would adjust themselves to avoid you, no matter what you did. It might seem like the police-drone lasers were coming dangerously close, but they'd never hit you. They were designed to scare you. It was like a video game.

A video game?

Toys we had when I was a little boy in Honduras.

According to Gonzalo, he could plug himself into the motorbike in a way that would screen his identity from the sensors.

They'll read me as Wilbur Dickinson, he said, and they'll charge the bills for uncontrolled driving to the account of Wilbur Dickinson.

Who is Wilbur Dickinson?

A dead man.

Zeke was afraid to ask, but he had to know.

Did you kill him?

Gonzalo laughed.

You think I'm a murderer, Amish?

No. No, I don't think you're a murderer, said Zeke.

Good. Because if we're going to mask your identity, we have to plug in. You and me, Amish.

We don't do that, said Zeke.

First time for everything, said Gonzalo. Like Rumspringa.

The Kalona Amish don't practice Rumspringa.

Yeah, yeah, said Gonzalo. Whatever. You don't own a

phone, but you'll use your neighbor's phone in an emergency. You don't own a bot-car, but you'd hire one. It's like that.

No, said Zeke. With telephones and cars we believe they are useful tools, but the costs to our community and our way of life are not worth the benefits. Plugging in is different. It's like ultra-modern music or drugs or ...

Or sex?

Zeke blushed.

It's just a tech, said Gonzalo. People use it for therapy, or to get all intimate, or for data-sharing, or for art projects. Or, like us, to mask identities from the sensors. They'll read you as part of me, and they'll read me as Wilbur Dickinson. We have to do it to get you from one place to the other. It's the only way.

I don't have a jack.

Don't need it, said Gonzalo. I can hotwire you.

He was pulling a wire out from a compartment in his arm, twisting it around a different wire, binding them with a small clip that had something like a doctor's needle at the end.

Don't worry, it'll be a shallow, heavily filtered connection, he said. I don't want access to your private thoughts. I don't want you to know everything I'm thinking either.

Gonzalo laughed.

I've got secrets, Amish, he said. Secrets even from you.

Zeke knew that Gonzalo believed in mental privacy. It was one of his issues with the government and the singularity. Perfect communion would mean enslaved, stagnant thinking, he said. To which Zeke would say that God knew all his thoughts, whatever he believed, and God forgave him for whatever happened inside his head. Gonzalo said he didn't need to be forgiven—thoughts are innocent, he said. Even evil thoughts. Zeke wasn't so sure.

Okay, said Zeke. I will do it.

It'll register more like a hit of emotions, shifting moods, colors, maybe some genetic memory, said Gonzalo. You'll definitely get some psychoactive effects.

Psychoactive?

Hallucinations. You ready?

Jesus Christ, Zeke thought, forgive me. Forgive me, for I am sinning.

Ready, he said.

Gonzalo stood behind him and taped the wire to Zeke's neck. There was a prick and then a rush of dizziness, colors exploding inside Zeke's brain. It leveled out quickly into a steady euphoria, like he'd felt with the gravity change of the Whippersnapper, when he'd risen to the ceiling, waiting for the fall. The world was much brighter around the edges. He was tingling. His flesh was fleshier, warm. Gonzalo was in the driver's seat.

Get on. Hold on tight. And take off the hat, it'll blow right off your head.

They were moving. Faster than seemed possible, zipping up the old highway, around curving roads and down straightaways. And yet he felt deeply connected, rooted, to this strange friend and his machine, the machine rooted to the earth. Zeke had driven many times in vans and cars, but nothing like this.

It was too fast, too strange.

He became profoundly aware of the intelligence all around him, the consciousness of the world. Its consciousness of *him*. Not just the occasional drone that would pass overhead, or the occasional billboard that would read them and advertise something for this Wilbur Dickinson—quantum golfing equipment or luxury meats— and not just the animals, birds or cows or rooted protein jellies in the fields that he could see sensing them as they zipped past, but beyond those layers something more, in the hazy sky, the totality of the atmosphere, which was like an animated book in a foreign language that was still, somehow, forming its letters for him. The atmosphere seemed to be imbued with the presence of God, of God's consciousness.

As they ascended the on-ramp to Horizontal Grid-work 80, Gonzalo shouted something, but Zeke didn't understand.

What did you say?

Gonzalo turned his head to the side and Zeke could actually see the strange vibration of the word passing through his lips, like smoke from the orifice of a tender volcano.

Music, he said.

He pushed a button on the control panel and music blared from the speakers Gonzalo had mounted on the handlebars. It was driving, hard, ominous music, sinful music, and it made Zeke's heart race. Or was it Gonzalo's heart? Suddenly he wasn't sure whose heart was whose, or which thoughts were his own.

Spacemen 3, shouted Gonzalo.

Gonzalo zipped past the other bot-cars so fast they seemed to be moving in another dimension, mired in some kind of sludge. Drones flew overhead, shining horribly bright lights at them and sounding their alarms. Billboards lined the highway, blazing messages prompted by their passing: *Wilbur, PLEASE Slow Down* and *Speed KILLS, Dickinson!* and *Wilbur, Reckless Driving = 5000.* As they continued, the figure increased, 6000, 7000, 10,000, while at the same time the billboards tried to sell them custom motorcycle seats, specialized engine lubricants, luxury fruit snacks, and more quantum golf clubs. Whoever Wilbur had been, he clearly had money.

The drones began firing their lasers. It was terrifying, and yet it was thrilling. Was it his thrill or Gonzalo's? The lasers hit so close that Zeke was sure the fuzz he was growing as sideburns had been singed, and still Gonzalo was laughing. The laughter was inside Zeke, it was Zeke's laughter, and it was everywhere. Gonzalo sped up and it was as if Zeke was separated from himself, as if his ghost was somewhere ahead or behind, and he was a series of phantom impressions in an imaginary time on a road leading toward death and the abyss.

He felt terror and separation. Who was he? He felt immersed in evil, an evil world. Who was he, if not a good person in an evil world? *In the world, but not of the world.* What if there was no real separation between himself and the world? A void opened up inside himself.

He thought about Leahbelle, to calm himself, and this thought seemed to detach from himself, turn into a moving image full of light and rise into the sky. The hazy sky was a book and Leahbelle was a character walking through that book, surrounded by angels and light. Was heaven a place of layers, of light, usually invisible but actually connected to the earth by a twisted umbilicus of energy? He was sensing this or actually seeing this now. And faces in the sky. There were alarmed faces forming in the tumultuous churning of the cloudy haze. There were also alarmed faces down here, below, in the bot-cars they zipped past, alarmed at the sight of the motorbike whizzing past them, terrified of their reckless energy. But this energy is me, Zeke thought. The frightened post-human fathers and fathers and mothers and more mothers and their children or clones, who were simply fascinated, gazing out from their safe, programmed cocoons into a darkness that contained life they couldn't understand. The cosmos was still laughing.

The Grid-works was a tunnel lined with billboards on either side and the billboards were screaming at him like torture victims. The lights of the hysterical billboards seemed to form faces and these faces were like horrible shrieking babies, newly born and enraged. And Gonzalo's music was blaring and the singer was singing, over and over again, *When tomorrow hits, it'll hit you hard ...*

They were racing into the future, which was like a hard wind. Was this thrilling? Was this what the English considered "fun"?

The faces in the sky and in the billboards—were these real or hallucinations? The faces in the bot-cars were real. The faces of strange, ferocious gods were embedded into the surface of Gonzalo's skull, and these were real too, his animated tattoos, but they were forming shapes and moving differently than he'd ever seen them before. Serpents and snarling jaguars, dark, smoking mirrors and stylized blood droplets. Complicated histories were playing out, performed by masked characters in a theatrical production, white masks and brown masks, saints and demons, masters and slaves, and it was a history of horrible persecutions and suffering under a wheel of time turning like a windmill that devoured and destroyed the people. The dashboard of the motorbike was blinking with these hieroglyphics, and they seemed to mark off the days of a calendar that trapped Zeke inside it. All of time, all of history, was war. War was not a once-in-a-while occurrence, it was the state of existence. It was the earth and time. Zeke was terrified.

Down below on Earth, he realized, it's hell. He wasn't sure if there were layers underneath this one, but he knew that this was really just the upper layer, the outermost crust of hell. Warfare, blood, misery. Hunger and toil. Work and thistles and death. It became clear to Zeke that he was trapped in a flattened, two-dimensional zone of reality, and that the Grid-works was a form of war. The lights in the skies, airplanes and helicopters and drones, and this was war. Gonzalo knew he lived in a war zone— had always known, Zeke realized. And now Zeke knew it too.

And yet he could still see the angel of Leahbelle or the idea of Leahbelle walking a parallel road through the sky. The image of Leahbelle could radiate into this war zone, fill it with compassion. He could see that. The beauty of Leahbelle, a pure beauty, and yet ... he could feel the sinful thoughts, the pleasure of sinful thoughts, and he wasn't sure if it came from Gonzalo or from himself, from the sky or from the earth, heaven or hell, but the vibrations of the motorbike were becoming images of their own.

He could see Leahbelle wandering into a darker cloud where dangerous creatures were waiting for her, and he thought he could just make out their faces, familiar faces. Was that his own face? Ahead, in the sky, impossibly white clouds billowed upward, like brains stacked into the stratosphere, stark against the dull haze of the data vapor, dark at the edges, lit up from below. The clouds were like the billboards, videos designed for his own endangered soul, with faces of older Amish men speaking to him from within the clouds. His ancestors were looking down on him, alarmed at what he was about to do. They were shouting— *Turn Back! Do Not Enter!* They were shouting, but he could barely hear them, the roar of the world was so great. They shouted and then dissolved, disappeared, and others popped up just further ahead, shouting *Danger! Danger! Go Back!* The road up ahead was leading into darkness and apocalypse.

No, Zeke told himself. It wasn't real. It couldn't be real, it was just … a hallucination, just what was in his mind. He was not on a journey into hell. He was saving his great-grandmother. As he thought this, the sky seemed to calm down, the faces disappeared, and even the billboards and the lasers seemed to retreat. Gonzalo had been right. The lasers didn't hit them, and they hardly startled him anymore. The alarms seemed to fade, as if the Grid-works had given up on dissuading them and was content now to just rack up the charges that Wilbur Dickinson would owe. Zeke's heart was still racing, or Gonzalo's heart, or the heart of God, but he was used to it now. They were almost there.

Gonzalo exited HG-80, shot north on smaller Grid-works, and then pulled over into the empty parking lot of an abandoned building on the outskirts of Marshalltown.

During the tail end of the brainless-meat boom,

when I first came here, this place was really happening, Gonzalo said. But once they figured out how to do it *all* with the machines, in the laboratory ...

Zeke felt better hearing Gonzalo speak in such an everyday way, and he felt better feeling the sadness attached to Gonzalo's words.

It's like all the old meat towns, Gonzalo said. Full of worn-down workers with useless machine parts, pill-poppers, dealers, black-market peddlers. Junkies passed out and dreaming all along the avenues.

They had made good time. The night watchman wouldn't be on duty quite yet. Gonzalo unplugged Zeke and drew him a map. The Foodco Warehouse was about a half an hour away on foot.

How was the trip?

I had ... hallucinations, I guess, said Zeke. Crazy thoughts. But some of them didn't feel crazy, they felt ...

Like you understood things in a different way.

We're in the middle of a war, said Zeke. That was very clear.

Yes, said Gonzalo. But there are many different kinds of war. There's a lot of big changes coming, Amish.

We know that we're in trouble, said Zeke. We speak about it all the time. But we aren't used to acting quickly, making changes quickly. Everything is happening so fast with the new government. Many Amish were going to Mars for the terraforming. The new government doesn't even seem to want us in space.

You don't get the brainwashing from the Grid, Gonzalo said, but you don't get the counter-messages either. Or you'd realize you aren't the only ones in trouble.

We're trapped now, said Zeke. We've lost the hospitals and the drivers, the GMRs are come. But why do *you* dislike the government so much?

They're sacrificing us, said Gonzalo. All of us. For the rich and for the future. For them, it's the same thing. The super-rich and their soldiers are the spearhead of evolution, the most post-post-human elements. What's good for the super-rich is good for the singularity.

Gonzalo was becoming more passionate as he spoke and a little bit puffed up. His energy sent a kind of residual thrill through Zeke, like the racing heartbeats and moving images of the motorbike ride.

We live like slaves, said Gonzalo, or we live on nothing. We fill our brains with their mush, their lies, or they hunt us down. They're degrading the present, enslaving the Now, torturing what actually exists, all for the sake of some imaginary ... super-intelligence that's like ... heaven.

Heaven? said Zeke.

I guess you're used to thinking that way, said Gonzalo. You believe this life is just to be suffered through until you get to the next one.

You don't believe in the afterlife? asked Zeke.

Gonzalo shrugged.

The river passes, passes, he said, never stops. The wind passes, passes, never stops. Life passes, never returns.

What is that? asked Zeke. A song?

A poem, said Gonzalo. From my ancestors. Another one:

Not forever on earth; only a little while here.
Be it jade, it shatters.
Be it gold, it breaks.
Be it a quetzal feather, it tears apart.
Not forever on earth; only a little while here.

Zeke felt the words like sad sparks inside his mind, and he felt suddenly as if he understood that he was here, now, in the middle of time. Like standing in a strong breeze. And then it would be gone.

I know that there is more than what we can see and feel, Gonzalo said. But I believe in this world first.

Zeke felt closer to Gonzalo now than he'd ever felt before. As if they were standing together in the middle of a wind storm.

Things will get better, said Gonzalo. But not until they get much worse. War's coming, a different kind of war. There's more of us than you realize. The underground.

Underground?

Most of us aren't like you, Amish. Committed to staying human. Some. A few. The radical fringe.

I am the radical fringe? asked Zeke.

You are totally the radical fringe.

And the rest of you? What do you want?

We want to evolve. We just want to evolve more thoughtfully and ... with a different set of values. We want post-humanity, just not the version the Lords of the Gstate have dreamed up for us. The great Grid that will control every aspect of our lives, enslave us for our own good, colonize our consciousness, and absorb the entire cosmos into itself. That's just the Empire Animated. Same old, same old. They think they've got the planet once and for all now ... but not this time.

You told me the state was so powerful that violence no longer makes sense, Zeke said.

Not until the Grid crumbles, said Gonzalo. Once we've destroyed the Grid ... anything is possible.

How can that be? asked Zeke. The Grid is everywhere. It's inside and outside, it's in the data vapor, the roads, inside people's heads.

It's flawed, said Gonzalo. That's all I can tell you. The government thinks that the Grid is everything. But there are other dimensions, whole other worlds within this world, underneath it, and in some of those worlds there is freedom, real freedom. There are ways to move back and forth, portals.

You have entered these portals? asked Zeke.

I'm not sure, said Gonzalo. Once, when I was just a kid ... but I'm not sure if it's a memory or just a dream, really.

For a moment he was lost in thought.

Anyway, he continued, the government is trying to shut down the portals by making the Map. Once you Map something, you create a consensual reality and suddenly there's no magic, no portal, no other world, and the consensus reality becomes the reality—the portals are no longer there. That's just basic quantum mechanics. But there are places left, a few places, that haven't yet been Mapped.

I know so little about all of these things, said Zeke.

But you're exactly what I'm talking about, said Gonzalo. They're trying to Map you, to either put you on the Grid or destroy you, but so far ...

Gonzalo laughed.

You're too wild, Amish boy.

Zeke didn't think of himself as wild.

You like all this, said Zeke. You like to fight.

I always *had to* fight, said Gonzalo.

But don't you want to settle down someday? Zeke asked. Just live a peaceful life? Get married?

Gonzalo's face changed, and Zeke thought he'd said the wrong thing.

Married? I'm only sixteen.

The universe felt harsh and chaotic again—it had been a good feeling to feel so close. It was like they'd seen the same indescribable something-ness of everything. But now they still couldn't agree on what it meant.

What about Aeren? asked Zeke. She's a good, strong woman.

She's a lesbian, said Gonzalo. Not gonna happen.

A lesbian?

Zeke didn't know what to say. He had always thought that Gonzalo was courting Aeren. He knew about lesbians—he just hadn't realized that he actually knew one, was in some sense the friend of one.

You'll want to have children someday, he said to Gonzalo.

No way. Bring more of us into this world? More slaves?

But it is what God wants from us. Be fruitful and multiply.

Look around you, Amish, said Gonzalo. You really think what God wants is more of *us*? We've killed off most of the other life forms, except in zoos and museums. Meanwhile we act like merging our genomes with the creatures we've extinguished is like ... saving the damn planet.

You're right, said Zeke, happy to agree about something. God wants us the way he made us. But having babies is what he told us to do. It is written in the Bible.

Thousands of years ago, Amish. Thousands of years ago, okay, God looks around and this shit is like ... empty. And he's like, fill it up. I totally get that. Babies, babies, babies, gotta have them babies. But that shit is over.

Zeke didn't want to argue. He had eight living brothers and sisters. His uncles and aunts all had between eight and eleven children. This was God's plan, even if they didn't understand it. It was just something he had always known, that he too would have a house full of children. Gonzalo just made it sound ... morally wrong.

Anyway, said Gonzalo. You'd better go.

What is the guard's name? asked Zeke.

He goes by Efron, said Gonzalo. Efron, he's a real freak.

He used the word "freak" in a way that made it seem affectionate.

He has this old doll, Gonzalo said. Some twentieth century thing, you stick your hand in it and you make it talk. It looks like the doll's talking, but it's really him. It's called ventriloquism. He's totally off into it, and he treats the doll like it's a real person. And I swear, sometimes you forget. You forget that it's all in this guy's ... wigged-out brain.

As Zeke checked his route and headed into the city, he wondered what the difference was. Between the guard's wigged-out brain and his own. His perceptions of reality were still intense, and separated from his friend a vague darkness and menace crept into his vision.

He passed through an empty, desolate zone of abandoned retail buildings, then crossed over a dried-up creek and took a bridge across a vast yard of railroad tracks. Strange graffiti messages were scrawled on the sides of abandoned buildings. NIHIL Rising, it said. There was a cartoon of a robot being beheaded. Deface The Future, it said. Don't Eat Death, it said. Hugs For Puppies, it said. He didn't glimpse a single other creature until he approached the old center of town.

On Main Street the disease of biological life was flowering in all its rancid glory. Zeke could feel the pain of the dreaming junkies like it was moving into his belly. They were picking scabs. It was like the sun had never shined in this town, like the acids of the industrial pollution were melting his liver, and the junkies were sweating. A foul fog emerged from their orifices.

Something flapped past his face, swooped up behind him, and then landed on his shoulder. He plucked it off. It was a flexi-screen with a long message on it. The flexi-screen chirped. Zeke had seen flexi-screens before, but never one that seemed so ... alive.

If you got a connect tell them i'm Looking for a computer. Tell your connect i'm looking for THAT computer that comes with a manual the computer girls use to change their eye color. It would do anything and it came with a manual. It had movie tube so you can watch free movies. Girls use it to time travel. It's like a hologram computer. It can get anything in the world done.

You might want to be alone when you read this. Make sure you are. Be extra sure.

Zeke looked around. Nobody seemed to be looking at him except maybe some creature in a gas mask that was leaning against the wall just up ahead. It was impossible to tell. Maybe the creature was staring right at him, maybe the creature was the one who sent the message. Zeke nodded in its direction. It didn't nod back.

i am looking for someone to make me THAT computer. The computer i use to enter my goals. The computer that can hack into government. A computer only i can use. The cool one everyone is talking about. The government computer. The hacker thing. The off-Grid computer. The girl computer, the eye-color changer. The computer that can get anything done. The computer that makes all possible. i know someone has one i can buy. i hear the computers are 2000 or less.

The flexi-screen chirped again.

Um ... I don't have a computer, said Zeke. But I can ask Gonzalo.

The flexi-screen chirped and flew away. It flew past the creature in the gas mask and then kept going until it was out of sight. Zeke kept walking.

Crumbling brick buildings that offered weekly rooms and substance abuse services. Boarded-up businesses except for one shop advertising *Mega Meat Monday*. The tallest building in town, the Tallcorn Building, was empty but lit up like a hologram, advertising itself as Foodco Headquarters. Zeke had the strange impression of someone beside him all the time now ... walking next to him. But nobody was there, nobody was anywhere. He turned onto Tenth Avenue toward the meat warehouse.

THREE

The security guard sat with his wooden doll in a shack outside the warehouse.

Efron? said Zeke.

That's me. You want Whisperdals?

No, nothing like that, said Zeke. Gonzalo sent me.

Gonzalo, eh? How is that little prick?

He's good.

I like the things he can do with those appendages, said Efron. State of the art.

Zeke never really knew what to say to the English, so he got right to the point.

I need medicine. My grandmother was bit by a GMR.

GMR, eh? said Efron. I can do that.

I have the culture from the wound and a sample of her blood.

Good boy. Whip that up for you in a jiffy. Cost you five hundred, plus there's something I could use your help with.

The security guard waved him inside. The warehouse was enormous and gray, complicated and windowless. The entrance gave to a small room with carpet, overly bright lights, one chair, and a potted plant. The guard sat in the chair and so Zeke plopped down on the floor. The doll seemed to be napping.

The guard held out his hand and made a "gimme, gimme" motion with his fingers. Zeke handed the CASH® over, and while the guard sat there counting it, Zeke stood up, suddenly anxious to move. The doll's eyes flipped open.

Come with me, the guard said.

They entered a concrete tunnel that stank of flesh. A

vast cold space of hanging carcasses. Went through a door into a room of live animals in cages. Zeke recognized the plump, headless turkeys throbbing and feeding through tubes. They entered another long refrigerated hallway, their body space constrained on either side by hanging ovals of meat ribbed with luminous fat. The floor was tacky.

Why is the floor tacky? Zeke asked.

The patterns in the fat were like hex signs, perfectly symmetrical geometries. The security guard opened a thick plasticky door. They entered a narrower, warmer hallway lit only by a flickering overhead. The flickering made Zeke feel like he was missing something.

Then they entered a cavernous courtyard with a ceiling so high it felt like they were in a darker-than-night outside world. On his right were crates stacked high, the smell of something acrid, living, and blind. To Zeke's left a picket fence around a tiny pink cottage. Clipped grassy plant-life grew between the fence and the cottage. A face in the dark window startled him.

The little girl waved. There was no pane in the window.

Wanna liver jelly? she asked.

The girl handed him a little gray candy through the window, some blend of synthetic sugars and proteins shaped like a teddy bear.

There was something familiar about the girl, like he'd seen her face in a dream. Zeke thought that maybe there were many worlds hidden behind the surface of the world he thought that he knew, but that in every world the faces might be the same. The same souls trapped in every level of hell. His thoughts were still strange to him, like they were someone else's thoughts. Gonzalo's? He couldn't know.

Now they walked into a carpeted hallway, with not too many bloodstains. The guard opened a door into a warm closet-like room with medical equipment. He took the samples from Zeke while the dummy seemed to be watching him. The guard looked at the samples through a microscope, and then fed them into a machine that hummed and seemed to whirl the tissues and blood around, like a carnival ride.

You're human, huh? said the guard. One hundred percent?

I'm Amish, said Zeke.

Medicine's gonna change your granny, said Efron. The rat toxin's already changed her, and then the anti-venom, it won't change her back exactly. It'll change her in a different way.

Change her how?

Hard to say, he said. Everybody's different. Every GMR bite is different. But she'll have some other species going on with her personhood, that's for sure.

But is there no other way? asked Zeke.

It's the only anti-venom there is, said the guard. Made by the same people who made the rats.

You know who made the rats? asked Zeke.

Everybody knows who made the rats, said the guard. It's on the Grid-screen all the time, Absolute Genomics. You know that ad—*For the family of the future ...*

I'm off the Grid, said Zeke.

The guard shrugged.

Your granny can be dead or she can be something different, he said. Those are the choices.

Zeke thought he should give her the choice, but he knew she wasn't in her right mind. He didn't want to let her choose to die. Maybe that was her right, but if that was what she wanted, she could always choose it after the fact.

Are you human? he asked the guard.

The guard laughed.

I couldn't work here if I was human, he said. I mean legally, intellectually, psychologically, spiritually—no way could I do it. This place, this work—the meat, the new meat. It's not for humans. You've gotta lose some of your disgust, some of your compassion.

Humans have been doing that forever, said Zeke. Losing their disgust and their compassion. What's the difference?

Chemistry, said the guard. It's a brain-wave thing. The brainless meat, growing, squirming, blind and delicious, it gives off a kind of ... dark radiance. An odor. In other eras, visionaries and poets would have seen this place in their dreams.

He turned back to his machines, engrossed in the process of manufacturing the medicine. The doll seemed to be staring at Zeke.

What's with the suspenders? the doll asked.

You're wearing them too, said Zeke.

My point exactly, said the doll. You're crowding me here. You're reducing the luster of my idiosyncratic style.

The guard's lips didn't move at all. He didn't even seem to be paying attention to the conversation.

My name's Merle, said the doll.

He extended his little block of a hand.

Pleased to meet you, said Zeke. Are you Efron's ... friend?

I loathe Efron, said Merle. He's always hanging around, won't just let me be. Kind of needy, don't you think? Pathetic, actually.

But you're attached to him, said Zeke.

I could do without him, said Merle. I just need a motor, and I'm outta here.

Zeke considered this.

Don't you need a brain? he asked.

Consciousness is cheap, said Merle. Brains are a dime a dozen. Soup up one of those monkey brains we grow in the vats in the basement with some circuitry, connect me to the data vapor, and I'm good to go.

Merle wiggled and made a little gesture that seemed to be a dance illustrating his willingness to move on.

There are monkey brains in the basement? asked Zeke.

An excellent source of protein, said Merle, and hardly ever contaminated with pathogens for post-humans. Now your type, that's different—better stay away from the primate delicacies.

My type, said Zeke.

The noble savage, said Merle. The rustic, the primitive, the *homo sapien*. People are into that now, I guess. All the more evolved life forms are attracted to your folksy ways. *Pepperidge Farms remembers.*

Pepperidge Farms?

Slap an old-fashioned human mother on the package of the nanofiber, self-regulating cake mix and they'll slop it up like brainless-pig mouths, said Merle.

Okay, said Efron, standing back from the machine. It's all set. Give it a half hour. Come on kid, follow me.

Efron slid through a narrow door hidden behind some metal shelves into a hallway so narrow that Zeke had to turn sideways to move down it, with Merle's wooden bubble eyes staring right at him, then out the other end into a dim room with padded floors and no windows. Hanging on the wall were two pairs of padded gloves, one big enough for a man, the other tiny.

I'm gonna beat your ass today, Efron, said Merle. I hope you're ready.

I'm shaking in my boots, said Efron. Can't you feel my terror?

He turned to Zeke.

We're going to box, but we need your help.

He showed Zeke how to slip his hand up inside the wooden puppet. The mechanism worked in such a way that he only needed to wiggle one finger for the doll to thrust and jab its little fists the way the security guard wanted.

Step back you pathetic meat peddler, cried the doll, and punched the guard in the face. The guard stepped back for a moment and then hit the doll square in the jaw—the pressure vibrated up and down Zeke's arm.

I won't do this, Zeke protested. I don't believe in violence.

This isn't violence, you ninny, said Merle. It's sport. It's fun and games.

Plus, you don't have a choice, said Efron. This is part of the cost of your grandmother's medicine. I believe I explained that.

Zeke wiggled his finger and the doll smacked Efron in the face again. A little drip of blood trickled down from his nose. Maybe it wasn't a sin to hurt somebody if they wanted to be hurt. What he found most amazing was the intricate ventriloquism through which he could clearly distinguish the guard's panting and moans of pain from the doll's panting and moans of pain in a pitched rhythm that seemed sometimes to overlap as they punched each other over and over again.

A half hour later, exhausted and bloodied, the guard returned to the lab, packaged the medicine into a vial, and explained to Zeke how to use the syringe. Merle seemed to be resting again. The guard took Zeke back through the carpeted hallway and back through the cavernous courtyard where the little girl was sitting in front of the pink cottage in pajamas, snacking on liver jellies. Zeke thought she should be in bed. They made their way back past the cold oval meat, past the headless turkeys, and back to the little shack out front.

Good luck, said Efron. Give Gonzalo my love.

The vial of medicine gave off an intense warmth, although it wasn't painful to the touch. As he walked down the dark avenues of Marshalltown, the drug addicts seemed attracted to it. They would rustle and kind of ooze toward him, he thought, too slowly to be threatening—more just like a signal of some faint flickering of desire.

And then the flexi-screen returned, if it was the same flexi-screen, and hovered in front of his face. He snatched it out of the air.

i am not a cop and i do know about the psyching people out thing and that's enough to psyche me out. If you can't help me with a computer look into my deals i can secretly make with you with what computer you got and there you will be able to know more like for example if someone else might want to trade you something you want if they got what you want and i have what i want from you or the other way around and / or keep the trading going so we can keep coming up. The goal of this is me winning and i'd like to keep this between you and me i'd like to keep this about me and by me. i want THAT / A ALWAYS WINNING COMPUTER.

Zeke clutched the flexi-screen tightly, but it bit him, wiggled free, and flew away. Zeke hurried back across the tracks and the dried-up river or creek to the parking lot where Gonzalo was waiting. Zeke's mind was clearer, everything had leveled out. He felt good: centered, calm, and unafraid. The flexi-screen's crazy message didn't worry him and the bite wasn't bleeding. And yet the sight of the needle, as Gonzalo prepared to plug into him again, filled him with a strange excitement, despite the fears it had brought him last time. He wondered if this was how drug addicts felt. If he had become a drug addict.

Is it always like this? he asked Gonzalo. I shouldn't want to do it again, but I do. Why?

Because I'm good shit, bro.

Gonzalo laughed and stuck the needle in, and the rush was strong again but less intense, clearer. The brightening and euphoria with less confusion. How much of these feelings came from the process itself and how much from Gonzalo? Was access to another person's mind and emotions an addiction? A drug?

This was what the new government was promising: pure communion, everyone with everyone, and with a super-intelligence, a global and then universal mind. God but not God, a god we had created, not a god who had created us. Zeke knew that some of them said it wasn't true—the god they were creating was in fact the same god, the only god, controlling events from the future, building a body for himself saturated with consciousness according to a plan from outside of time.

But this was not Gonzalo's view and this was not the Amish view. Uncle Mose said their new god wasn't even new—it was the devil. This world had always belonged to Satan, more or less. The kingdom of God was elsewhere.

They were back on the highway, speeding again, but it was colder now and the cold was painful. The cold was bright, the wind whipping through Zeke's hair. The drones overhead, the lasers that came within a hair's breadth but didn't ever actually hit them, the bot-cars and trucks transporting bodies of one sort or another across physical space—yes, it was war flattened out, he could see that clearly, but it didn't frighten him. War simply was. He was Zeke Yoder—just a boy, soon a man, but a part of everything, the part of everything that had chosen to remain off the Grid.

Doing battle against the forces of evil was not his responsibility. God had a plan. No man could understand it. The wars of men belonged only to men and the devil. *But I say unto you, That ye resist not evil; but whosoever shall smite thee on thy right cheek, turn to him the other also.*

Clearer, his mind was clearer. The animated tattoos on Gonzalo's skull were the same, death and ferocity, morphing and mutating into elaborate cartoons, but their violence wasn't scary. It was like a mask Gonzalo was wearing, inside and out, a deep mask from the center of the earth, but still a mask. What mask am I wearing? Zeke wondered. And from where?

His thoughts were sharp and bright and the closer he stuck to his thoughts and the tighter he held onto this man of violence, the less cold he felt. Gonzalo. The boy's heart was warm. The vial of medicine was warm. The engine of the motorbike was warm. These were the only sources of heat as they hurtled down Horizontal Grid-work 80 at ninety miles an hour.

It was three o'clock in the morning when Gonzalo dropped him off at the end of the lane that led from the mailbox to the old farmhouse and around to Grandma Mast's quarters in back. Government workers still occasionally brought letters sent by family members spread now all over the world, his sister Beth in Colorado, his brother John Henry. They even brought letters from his cousins who had moved from Lancaster County all the way to Mars or the moons of Jupiter. Now it was deepest night, but there were lanterns burning all throughout the house. His first thought was that he was too late and Grandma was gone. He almost asked Gonzalo not to leave—unplugged, alone in the darkness, looking into his own home from the outside—the only home he'd ever known—he felt the need for a friend, for somebody who understood the journey he'd just taken. But Gonzalo wished him luck, patted his shoulder, and roared off into the night.

The familiar crunch of the gravel as he walked up the lane was little comfort. The sound of the crickets, still out there. And then a shot rang out from the house and a bullet zinged past him to the left. Another shot, this one to his right. Were they shooting at him?

Dad, don't shoot! he called. It's me!

Run, Zeke, came the response. Run!

It was his mother's voice. Run toward the house or away? He began to back away in a panic, turned back toward the road, then stopped. The darkness around him seemed to be moving, fluctuating, scurrying in every direction. He could hear the darkness itself, breathing, thinking, squeaking. Was he still hallucinating? How could he know what was real? He turned back and hurled himself up the lane toward the house.

He was maybe just fifty feet from the porch when a dark cloud seemed to emerge from the bushes, from the earth itself, to block his way. There were dozens of them, no, hundreds of them, maybe thousands, in front of him and all around. The rats.

FOUR

Immediately in front of Zeke was a group of three rats that he somehow knew were the leaders. They were just standing there, making eye contact with him and squeaking. It was like no rat noises he'd ever heard. It was like English used to sound to him when he was a small child and only spoke Pennsylvania Dutch—if he could slow it down or break the code, he knew it would make sense. It was clear that it was a language, that it *could* make sense, just not to him.

The rats were talking to him.

There was an intelligence in their eyes, in the expressions of their faces, that was recognizable. He took a step toward them, however, and they bared their teeth. But as soon as he stopped, they relaxed and just continued gazing at him and squeaking and now even gesturing. They were gesturing toward the house. No, he realized. They were gesturing toward the *back* house.

And then, from the side, two rats carried out a third rat on top of a kind of dais constructed from small sticks bound together with twine. An older-looking, gray-haired rat was reclined on the makeshift bed and she had a piece of fabric wrapped around her head like a bonnet.

The three rats gestured toward the new rat and then toward the back house.

Grandma, said Zeke. You want to see Grandma?

He thought it more likely they could speak English than Pennsylvania Dutch. He held their gaze and nodded, trying to show that he understood. They nodded back. He moved toward them and they moved to the side, still blocking the route to the front porch, but leaving open the smaller path that wound around to the back house. He took it, slowly, keeping eye contact with them. The three rats followed behind, but at a respectful distance.

From the back house, someone fired a shot.

Hold your fire! called Zeke. I'm okay, just let me in.

The rats didn't seem particularly frightened of the shot, which had missed wildly. They remained outside in the shadows of a cluster of walnut trees.

Uncle Mose was inside the back house with his son Jonas and all the kerosene lamps burning. Everyone else was in the front house, he said.

No more shooting, said Zeke. They won't hurt us. I've got Grandma's medicine.

You don't know, said Jonas. They surrounded us, and then ... started squeaking, the most horrible ... like demons.

They let me through, said Zeke. They could have killed me, but they let me through.

You go in to Grandma, said Mose. I'll keep a watch out here for the rats.

Grandma was thrashing around in the bed, her eyes wild. The lump on her shin was the size of a melon.

They're calling me, she said.

Grandma, it's me, Zeke. I brought you your medicine.

Somebody's out there, they're calling me. Is it the angels? Or the devils?

Zeke heard nothing now, not even a cricket.

Can you understand them? he asked. What they're saying?

They're calling my name, Grandma said.

They're saying Fanny? Fanny Mast?

Not that name. You can't pronounce it in Dutch or English or anything. I've never heard it before, but I recognized it right away. Am I dying, Zekey?

You're going to be fine, said Zeke.

It must be Jesus calling me home, she said. It's my true name. The name of the true me, Zekey. They're calling my soul.

Grandma, I'm gonna give you your medicine. Hold still now, just a little stick.

You said that before, she said. Did this already happen? Where am I? Am I dead already?

No, Grandma. You're gonna be fine now.

He gave her the shot just the way the security guard had shown him. Almost immediately the wound turned blue and Grandma looked ... calmer. She sat up straight, alert, and pulled her nightgown close around her.

I think they're trying to tell you something, said Zeke. Listen carefully, Grandma. Can you understand it?

She rose to her feet. She could walk again, she was steady. In fact, she seemed strong, almost youthful. Had the medicine changed her already?

Who's out there? she said.

It's the GMRs, said Zeke.

She put on an overcoat over her nightclothes, and an outdoor bonnet, and slipped into her hard shoes. Mose and Jonas just stared at her as she entered the front room.

Grandma ... where are you going? asked Mose.

Outside, she said. To talk to the rats.

The three leader rats were waiting in the shadows of the walnut tree. Zeke could even recognize them, differentiate them from each other, he realized. They had slightly different markings, but more than that—different expressions, different ways of carrying themselves. One of them looked like it was squeaking at Grandma right away, but Zeke heard nothing. Grandma heard it, however, and she understood perfectly.

They say they want to communicate with us, she said. Not harm us. They say sorry about all that squeaking. It's not their usual way, but they had to get your attention. Their normal language is too high-pitched for old-fashioned humans to hear.

Okay, said Zeke. We're listening. What's on their minds?

They say we should cooperate, said Grandma. They say that the government has plans to take this land, to kill us or forcibly remove us, and to kill them as well.

How do they know this? asked Zeke. Where do they get their information?

Grandma just looked at him.

I don't know, she said.

Can you speak to them? Or only understand them?

I … I don't know. I suppose I could try.

The rats seemed to be explaining something to her. She closed her eyes, seemed to be concentrating. And then she began emitting an eerie, high-pitched whistling and then it was gone, although she was still holding her mouth the same way—emitting some high-pitched frequency, Zeke supposed. The rats seemed to understand her well enough. Soon they were going back and forth, back and forth.

From inside the house, his parents and the rest of the family were watching. Dad had his rifle ready at the window.

Grandma, Zeke said. What are they saying?

They can understand English pretty good, she said. But they told me I can speak their language now, if I try. It's a little strange—if I just relax, my thoughts kind of turn into smoke and then out comes all that racket. I say racket, but it sounds kind of nice. They changed me with that bite, they say. I had a few words to say to them about that whole business, and about the walnuts they were getting at without our permission, and they apologized. They say they want peace with us. They want us to share our food with them. They say there's a war coming, and they want us to fight with them. For this land.

Do they understand that we don't believe in fighting? Zeke asked.

We've been shooting *them*, said Grandma.

But we don't kill humans, said Zeke.

The government and its armies aren't exactly human, said Grandma.

Zeke was confused.

Is that what they say or what you say, Grandma?

She giggled.

I'm not really sure, she said. It's hard to tell sometimes which thoughts come from the inside and which from out there.

Zeke looked at his grandmother carefully. She was still his grandmother—the spark in her eyes, the quick laugh, the will—but she seemed to be something else as well, part of a different vocabulary, a different world.

There's an ancient human story, Grandma told him. From a book called *Popol Vuh*. In that story, the rat helped the hero twins defeat the Lords of Death. The rat knew things—such as where the boys' father had hidden his ball game equipment. Their father had been defeated and killed by the Lords of Death, but with his equipment they could also play soccer in hell, pass all of the tests the Lords of Death gave them, outsmart the Lords of Death, defeat the Lords of Death, and win a cosmic wager for the right to exist. In time.

To thank the rat, she continued, it was given the right to nibble at the corn and the squash in the fields until the *end of time*. That end may be soon, but it isn't here yet.

The rats had been still and were now holding his gaze. It didn't seem like she was translating the story, but like she was actually *remembering* it.

Grandma, he said. What are their names?

She introduced the three leaders—Lilith, Pazuzu, and Willard—and each gave a little bow in turn. These were their English names, his grandma explained, the names the scientists had given them, and so, although they considered them names from their oppressors, they had answered to these names since birth and come to identify with them.

Lilith, the female, was the tallest and carried herself with the most authority.

You must never forget where you come from,

Grandma translated for her. Even if where you come from is a place of slavery, torture, and stupidity.

So it's true? said Zeke. They escaped from a laboratory? At Absolute Genomics?

Escaped, maybe, said Grandma. Maybe set loose.

There were indications that their escape wasn't entirely accidental. There are suspicions that they were designed and set loose with a purpose—perhaps to drive the Amish from their farms, to win support for new military campaigns from the government, to test out new eradication techniques. Or maybe just to make money from the antidote to the rat bites.

The problem with that theory, Grandma translated for Pazuzu, is that they *hardly ever bite.*

Whatever the purpose they were designed for, they now believe that they are to be exterminated once that purpose is fulfilled, with an engineered virus or environmentally induced auto-destruct feature. The rats themselves, however, Grandma said, believe that their intelligence and problem-solving abilities have been underestimated, and that things may not turn out quite exactly as their creators have planned.

Tell me your story, Zeke said directly to Lilith. I want to hear about the lab and the escape.

Zeke's father stepped out onto the porch just then, rifle trained on the rats. They bared their teeth at him, and from all around in the night came an ear-piercing shriek.

They don't take to your father, Grandma whispered. Not sure why.

What in heaven's name, said Zeke's father.

The rats quieted down but kept their teeth bared, and Lilith actually took a step toward him. Zeke quickly explained what he had just learned.

They want peace, he concluded.

You would trust a rat? asked his father.

Zeke wasn't sure.

Ezra John, said Grandma to his father, you go back

inside and put that gun away. We'll be right along, and then we'll chew on all these facts together, figure things out.

Zeke's father shook his head.

This is men's business, he said. You should be in bed, Grandma, you aren't well.

I'm not well? she said. Watch this.

She did a series of cart-wheels down the lane, like a young girl, and then skipped back to the porch.

Grandma! said Zeke's father, scandalized.

Hush now, boy, said Grandma. You shoo back in that house. We'll be right along, just as I said.

I'll go inside, he said. But I'm keeping this rifle aimed right at them critters.

Once his father was back inside, Grandma listened to Lilith for a moment and then turned to Zeke.

In the lab, they were a colony of sixty-four, she told him. Fifty-eight of them made it out, and they now number in the thousands—their offspring, and a few other mutant rats they've liberated. There isn't time anymore tonight for no more stories, though. It's still early for the rats, but for you it's very late. Another time you will hear their history. Tonight we must go in and talk it over with the family.

Inside, Mose and Jonas had joined the others in the front house. Zeke's mother was there with little Elson on her lap, and his aunt Katie was rocking in her chair, still cradling a rifle. Freeman and Zeke's cousin Verna were playing with blocks. The older children, Zeke's little brothers and sisters and cousins, were gathered around, quietly listening. Zeke and Grandma again explained what they knew.

They want our food then, said his father. It's lies and threats, is all it is.

We can't fight with them, Zeke said, but we can't fight against them. It isn't right.

What do you mean it isn't right? demanded his father. God gave *man* dominion over every creeping thing.

They're intelligent, Dad. They speak.

They still creep, don't they?

Maybe we can't fight with them, said Zeke. But we can help them.

Nonsense, said his father. We'll organize the community and exterminate these ... these critters.

They probably have human genes, Zeke pointed out.

We cannot trust them, said his father. We cannot join them in their fight. We cannot afford to feed them.

Stuff and nonsense, said Grandma. No, we won't fight the government. But we can't stay here, either.

Everyone looked at her, shocked at the force of this pronouncement.

It's been getting clearer and clearer for a long time, said Grandma, and it's only our own pig-headedness that has kept us sitting in place, while the new government passes their laws and conspires to take our land away. They want the land, you can see that. Well, let them take it. They can throw the whole lot of us in jail if they want, and we can pat ourselves on the backs for what good martyrs we are, our principles of nonresistance and the courage of our convictions, but we'll still all be there, rotting away in jail, and our children, and our children's children.

Grandma, you are ill, said Zeke's father. You don't know what you're saying.

Ill am I? Confused? You listen to me, boy, she said. My name is Fanny Mast, and I am ninety-seven years old last January. My parents were Uriah R. and Lizzie Briskey Mast. My father was a son of Eli and Magdalena Stutzman Mast. Dad was born January twentieth, 1899, in LaGrange County, Indiana, and died in 1980, in Defiance County, Ohio.

Grandma, said Mose gently. We know the history.

We've read the genealogies, said Zeke's father.

Have you? asked Grandma. Well then, there are still things you don't know. Things the genealogies don't say.

You go on, Grandma, said Zeke's mother. You say your peace.

When Jacob Briskey, my great-grandfather, and his sister Mary Ann were small children, their parents left Europe for the United States, Grandma continued. En route, their mother supposedly became sick and died and was buried at sea. Being unable to care for his two children, William put them in Amish homes in Pennsylvania. Unable to care for them—that's what the family records say. He remarried, but the children remained with their Amish foster parents. From Jacob the Briskey name started among the Amish but is now extinct among them. We now know that Jacob's mother did not die at sea, but as an old woman in a County Home in Somerset County, where she must have been put for some sort of mental illness or delirium.

Ezra John, said Grandma to Zeke's father, you are no stranger to the sorts of delirium that can settle in a woman's mind.

Zeke imagined that she was talking about his own mother, his birth mother, although he wasn't sure why. She had drowned in an accident in the pond on the Beachy farm.

I do not know if my great-great-grandmother was really suffering from such nerves, Grandma said, or if her husband just stuck her in that home so that he could ditch his family and his children and take up with some hussy. These things happen, whatever gets written down in books. But I can tell you that I am not delirious or mentally ill or suffering from nerves. In fact, I have never felt quite so clear in the head.

Grandma was now pacing as she spoke, her tiny body darting back and forth, from one side of the room to the other, like the ticking hand of the grandfather clock that was getting ready to chime half past three.

I remember my folks went to Illinois one time to visit my uncles and aunts, she said, so one of the Hostetler girls stayed with us children. On Sunday evening her boyfriend came to see her, so we all piled on his buggy and went to her folks' place. I remember this well. Their neighbors to the east were Nelson Grubers. They had a grown daughter named Mary, and we enjoyed looking at pictures through their stereoscope.

Zeke had never heard his grandmother talk this way before, about the past.

Did you ever see a stereoscope? asked Grandma. It was at that time already an old-fashioned toy. By that time, they had the moving pictures. But I had never seen anything like it. They had pictures of a town in Texas that had been swept away by the sea, soldiers practicing with their guns, the famous Eiffel Tower in Paris, and several pictures of ladies wearing fancy hats and very ruffled skirts. In this way we could look at places and people from impossibly far away and the colors were always so clear and bright that it was as if the pictures of these places were more vivid than our own farms.

It seemed so far away to Zeke, so long ago, and yet he wondered if the past was somehow still here, like a transparent sheet of faded colors just underneath the surface of what he knew.

It was just a toy, Grandma said, and we were just children, and yet when we looked through that toy, it changed us forever. It changed me forever, at least. How exactly it changed me, I cannot say, just that it did. And it changed the world, which we have never wanted to be a part of, and yet it is always still there. It seems to me the world wants to not only look at those pictures through the stereoscope but to become what it has seen, something brighter and farther away and less real than what seems to be. And that is a problem, but it is true that I also looked through at something brighter and farther away and less real. And I was changed and made larger and maybe less real.

And now something else has happened to me, she

said, and I have been changed again. And what I see looks different, and the light is different, and the sounds are very different. But I am not ill. I am not crazy and I am not ill, and I have seen a great many things in my ninety-seven years, and I have seen you, Ezra John Yoder, brought into this world with a little mess of black hair like a baby rat's hair slicked on top of your little infant head.

Zeke's father's face shifted for a moment, losing its hard edges, and it was almost as if Zeke could see him as he never had—as a little boy.

We have always lived the way we think God intends us to, Grandma said, and have done our best, and we are all sinners, but we have done what we needed to do. We are only here because our ancestors left Europe when they needed to, to escape the kings and wars, the Catholics and the Lutherans, the jails and the hangings and the burning at the stake. We came here, and while the English fought with the natives and murdered them without mercy, we did not, but we tried to be hospitable and practiced nonresistance. For the most part we have escaped the sort of troubles that beset our ancestors in Europe. During the hard times of the Depression and during the wars and the police trying to send us to their schools, we have done what we needed to. We have had some troubles still, but only those that God saw fit to give us the strength to bear.

She stopped pacing directly in front of Zeke's father.

But now, she said, the trouble has caught up with us again, and it's time to move on.

We can't even travel the Grid-works anymore, Zeke's father said. There's no way to move anywhere.

There's a tunnel, said Grandma. A tunnel that goes west. The rats built it.

We will creep through some tunnel looking for land?

No need to creep, Grandma said. They've built a cart with a motor, it zips right along.

And where is this land? his father wanted to know. The Grid is everywhere.

There are parts of Oregon that are off the Grid, said Grandma. Maybe Montana, too, and I've heard tell of a place in California. Fruitvale, they call it, near the Lake Merritt. Or south of the border, in Mexico.

It was probably clear to everyone else that there was no point arguing with Grandma, but Zeke's father kept at it, putting up one protest after another. The discussion went on like this until dawn. As the sun was coming up again through the data vapor, Zeke realized that he hadn't slept in the past twenty-four hours. His brain was fuzzy, the light of morning unreal. But the cows still needed milking, the chickens fed, the eggs collected. Perhaps he was still hungover from the journey, from plugging in. He was starting to feel truly strange. It was clear to Zeke that his father didn't want to accept the limited possibilities of the situation. There had been many times—more and more lately—when Zeke had disliked his father's authority. Since he'd been forced to stop his schooling and work every day on the farm, he had bristled at his father's rules. He had even questioned his father's authority. But for the first time now he felt like he was really seeing him as both more and less than his father—just a man, confused. His father was faced with something beyond him, beyond Amish ways. He was faced with his grandmother, who was not what she'd been. And what about me? Zeke wondered. He didn't have rat DNA inside him, as far as he knew, but he had foreign symbols, moods, and deities that had entered into his nervous system through Gonzalo and the motorbike.

We'll send a party to scout for land, Grandma was saying.

A party. Who will go?

I will go, said Zeke.

You are just a boy, his father said.

Zeke will go, said Grandma. And I will go with him.

She said it with a finality that left Zeke's father speechless.

We will leave in twenty-four hours, she said.

Tomorrow at dawn. There is no time to lose. We have just a month before the government attacks, according to the rats' intelligence. Maybe two. After that, anything could happen.

This was the second time Zeke had heard that phrase in the last twenty-four hours—anything could happen. When Gonzalo said it, it sounded hopeful and exciting. From his grandmother, it sounded terrifying.

FIVE

Zeke did his chores, and then he went to bed, along with everyone else. The middle of the day, everyone was sleeping. It felt like the apocalypse really had come—that night had become day and day night. Had the rats already started to change them—into nocturnal creatures? When Grandma explained to the rats that the Amish would move out and needed the rats to help them, in exchange for food and supplies, the rats seemed to have expected it. For a moment, Zeke wondered if this had been their plan all along—a trick, to get them to leave. To get the land for themselves.

He slept. His dreams were full of flickers of memory—the rats, the ventriloquist's dummy, the serpents and jaguars and bloodthirsty mutants that had come from the deep layers of Gonzalo's unconscious. And then he fell into a blackness without dream or thought or memory, a sleep so deep he could have been already dead.

When he woke, it was late afternoon, and Leahbelle was sitting next to the bed, working on a piece of quilt. She had that fabric that seemed lit up from the inside, a deep purple that seemed to come from another planet. She looked beautiful, most beautiful when she didn't realize she was being looked at—that lack of concentration, as if she was somewhere else altogether. Was that the most beautiful thing? To be empty of yourself, the things you thought of as your self. Did other people think so, or only Zeke? Was simplicity the most beautiful thing? The security guard's dummy had told him that everyone was attracted to humans now. The post-humans were so complex. Was it that their brains, or whatever you wanted to call it, their devices, their augmentations, their interfaces—were so full of images and transient information that they had become ugly? Who had decided that processing information was the highest goal of life? Maybe too much information became hideous.

How long have you been here? he asked Leahbelle.

Oh, not long. I didn't want to wake you.

You heard about the rats?

It's all anybody's talking about, she said.

What are they saying?

Well, you know Sam Miller and that Myrna and Elvin Beachys—they're trying to tell everyone that the whole Ezra John Yoder family has gone crazy, she said, that your grandma is hearing voices from the rat toxins or the devil, and her hallucinations have contaminated the whole lot of you. Maybe half the community is listening to them, more or less. But my mother and my father saw the GMRs this morning on the move past our place, coming from yourn's and Mervin Hershberger saw the same thing, so we know there's something more than just craziness going on.

You believe us, don't you? asked Zeke.

Of course I do.

She put her hand on his, and it felt like a jolt of electricity.

They say you're leaving, she said. Heading west.

We can't stay here, he said. Not any of us, not even Sam Miller and Myrna or Elvin Beachys. We need new land. Grandma says we only have maybe a month.

I want to come with you, she said.

He couldn't believe she'd said that. Couldn't believe that she would want to be with him, and it felt so right, so perfect, everything he wanted, and yet at the same time impossible and ... a small part of him, he realized in that moment, wanted to be away from everyone, his whole family, his whole community, even Leahbelle. To be alone. Except for his grandmother, of course, who was more than a person, she was like a landscape, like the earth itself.

Can you do that? he asked. Will your father permit it?

No, of course not.

So you would disobey him? Zeke asked.

I don't know, she said. I just know that I wanted that, just now, and I wanted to say it to you—that I want to come along. Is it a sin?

Not a sin. It is kindness and friendship and care.

And love, she said.

Neither of them had ever spoken that word before, not to each other, not like this. It was a strange word. It could mean so many different things.

You are like my twin, she said. When you are gone, it will be like I am only partially here.

Yes, he said.

Yes?

Yes, Zeke said, for me too. But it will make us stronger. And I will be back, before you know it. To lead us all to a new land.

And then I will come with you, she said. Even if it means disobeying my father.

The family ate supper in a kind of daze. Zeke's father did not look well and retired early to bed. His mother gave Zeke some canned meats, biscuits and jam, and fresh snap peas for the trip, and helped him to pack.

You must be careful out there, she told him. You are a smart boy, but you've never had much dealings with the English.

Beth will help us, said Zeke.

Your sister? said his mother. What are you planning to do?

I know you don't approve of her life, Zeke said. But she knows more than I do. She'll help me.

I care for your sister a great deal, his mother said. I want you to know that. I tried my best to be a mother for her. To help her with your father and Grandma Mast, but your sister ...

She was thinking.

She loves you, said Zeke's mother, I'm sure of that. But we don't know what all she's been doing out there in Colorado. You be careful with her too. And that man ... her husband.

She gave him a quick hug.

I love you, she said. You are my boy, and now you are almost a man. We will pray for you, and you must hurry back. I will be waiting. Leahbelle too.

Everyone else had gone to bed except for Grandma, who was rooting around in the bookshelf, reading bits and pieces from first one and then another book. Books that Zeke had never seen before, books he couldn't imagine in his home. *Notes Toward a General Theory of Television* by Humberto Vilanescu. Zeke lit a lantern, hitched up the horse and buggy, and headed out toward East Liberty.

At the old ruins, nobody stopped him as he crossed the old bridge or made his way through the trees or crossed the yard full of sculptures and old machine parts. There was no sight of anyone, the only moving thing the cameras, the only sound the click of the motion sensors. Nobody stopped him as he entered the old East Liberty Home for Boys with his lantern and made his way up the stairs. He saw nobody upstairs or in the old attic, and so he made his way down to the basement. The hallways were dark.

Hello? he said. Anybody home?

He heard a noise coming from the old indoor swimming pool, which was now more like a vast, empty tomb. From the darkness he heard a click and a target light hit his chest. Aeren's voice came from the darkness.

Don't make a move, she said. I've got you covered.

Aeren, he said, I need to talk to Gonzalo.

You'll have to strip to your underwear, she told him.

What are you talking about?

Protocol, she said. Things are getting serious. We don't know what you might have on you, tracking device, recording device.

No, Zeke said, I can't, not in front of you.

I'm not interested in your private parts, Amish, said Aeren. If that's what you're worried about.

A lesbian, he remembered. Was it less shameful to be half-naked for a lesbian than a woman who might become aroused?

I'll let Gonzalo frisk you, said Aeren. You let him plug into your nervous system, you can't be too worried about him seeing you without a shirt.

Please, look the other way, he said.

She smirked, but she did as he asked.

Aeren, he said, where do you come from?

Come from? she said. You mean where was I born?

Sure, said Zeke.

Or you mean what's my genetics?

Either way.

Born in Tulsa, she said. You ever hear of Tulsa? Doesn't exist anymore, but it was a real city once, and I was born there. My mother was half Tibetan, 1/32 Cherokee, and 15/32 white trash. The sperm was everything else: Gypsy, Sudanese, Korean, Bosnian, Filipino, Brazilian. Supposed to contain some serious athletic talent, a divine singing voice, and aptitude for science. Cost her a bundle. The way I turned out, she never thought it was worth it.

Is that why you're here? asked Zeke.

I'm here because society sucks, said Aeren. My mother has nothing to do with it except that she sucks too, and she's part of society.

Okay, said Zeke. I'm done.

She turned toward him.

You hear about the aliens? she asked.

The aliens?

They finally got a response. From way the heck and gone, as my granny used to say. Other side of the universe, with some new-fangled quantum communication.

The government? said Zeke. They're talking to an alien species? What are they saying?

Aeren shrugged.

They won't tell us. Top secret. But Wicked-leaks is working on it. Soon as I hear, I'll let you know.

She pointed her light at a small room to the side.

Go on into the office, she said. I think Gonzo's expecting you.

The room was dim, just some kind of primitive cooking device, a holovid showing scenes of some foreign country, and an old mattress on the floor. Zeke wasn't surprised when he was jumped from behind and knocked onto the mattress, wound up gasping for breath, with Gonzalo on top of him and a death-Taser pointed at his head. He struggled to get free, but it was no use.

Struggling, good. But you'll have to do better than that.

Gonzalo, he said, let me up.

Defend yourself, Amish. If you don't defeat me, I'll wipe out your whole community. Once I'm done with everyone you've ever loved, I'll destroy the earth.

If that is God's will, said Zeke.

You got any weapons, Amish?

Gonzalo's free hand was frisking him. Other body parts that Zeke didn't know Gonzalo had were searching him too. Zeke suddenly felt short of breath, dizzy, there was something in the air, not a smell exactly, but like a smell, and the colors and moving images from the hallucinations were exploding in his brain again, two serpents inter-twining around the scepter of a king, a jaguar perched like a sphinx with its tail raised vertically behind it, ready to pounce, a heart dripping with blood.

Gonzalo released him and stood up, laughing. Gradually his senses began to clear.

What was that? asked Zeke. What did you do to me?

Just subduing you with my pheromones, said Gonzalo.

But it was just like before ... the visions ...

Induced a little flashback, said Gonzalo.

Zeke stood up and tried to get his balance. Gonzalo looked him over.

You're strong for a human. Must be all that farm work.

Listen, Gonzalo. Everything is changing for us. I'm leaving tomorrow morning.

Gonzalo didn't seem to hear or understand.

Your grandma's okay? asked Gonzalo.

Zeke explained what had happened with the rats and his grandmother and the decision to find new land, the tunnel west.

I'm cold, he said. Can I put my clothes on, please?

Here, wear mine, said Gonzalo. They'll fit you. I'm gonna keep yours, if you don't mind.

Gonzalo took off his T-shirt—it had English words and a picture of a tongue—and tossed it to Zeke, then undid his pants. Once he was free of his clothes, he puffed his muscles up, showing off, and put on a kind of light show with his animated tattoos.

What do you want with my clothes? asked Zeke.

Sometimes you need a disguise, said Gonzalo.

You're going to pretend to be Amish?

You never know when it might come in handy, he said. For you too. You can use my clothes to move around. You gotta blend in sometimes.

I blend in just fine, Zeke said. I wear the same clothes that my brothers wear.

This isn't a game of philosophy anymore, said Gonzalo. This is real and practical, and if your people are going to survive, you have to survive. You have to make compromises sometimes.

Like a T-shirt that says Bad Food and has a picture of a human tongue?

They were a band, Gonzalo told him. They made music. A long time ago.

Listen, Zeke said. I don't need your clothes. I want us to go together. I want you to take me. On the motorbike.

Gonzalo was silent, but he stared at him hard. His tattoos had stopped moving, his muscles had deflated, and his chest had turned a warm pinkish color, almost as if his body was blushing.

Really, Amish? said Gonzalo. You want me to take you all the way across the country like that? Plugged into you, dodging lasers and bot-cars?

It's like you say, said Zeke. There is no other way.

You just said that there's a tunnel.

The tunnel only goes as far as Colorado, said Zeke. They intend to take it all the way to California, but right now it stops in Longmont.

A meat town, said Gonzalo. I did some time in a factory there. Got into some other business too.

From there I need to go south, said Zeke. I have a sister who lives in Colorado Springs.

And what about your grandmother? How's she gonna travel?

We'll figure something out, said Zeke. My grandmother, I believe, has resources that I don't yet know about.

Gonzalo shook his head.

I wanna take you, Zeke Yoder, he said. I really do.

It was strange to hear Gonzalo call him by name. Or not strange exactly—the way he said Zeke's name, it sounded like he'd said it a million times, like he was always saying it.

Do you know anything about a hologram computer? asked Zeke. A computer that can change girls' eye color and get anything done?

Any old computer can change your eye color, said Gonzalo. Why, what are you trying to get into?

Nothing, said Zeke. It was just a message, when I was on the streets in Marshalltown. Somebody was looking for a computer that could do anything. Change the future, I guess. An off-Grid computer, a hacker thing.

Probably just some Downy Mildew addict lost in his

own paranoid reality, said Gonzalo. People have been whispering about that secret computer as long as I can remember. But it doesn't exist, not yet.

But what if it does? asked Zeke.

Trust me, I'd hear about it, said Gonzalo.

Zeke believed him, but for some reason that belief frightened him.

So will you take me? he asked.

I wish I could help you, Gonzalo said. I really do. But we have plans in the next few weeks already. Things I gotta do around here. Big things, Amish.

He started getting dressed in Zeke's clothes, then looked over Zeke, now wearing Gonzalo's clothes.

You almost look like a real ... English, he said.

Like a post-human? asked Zeke.

Not quite that, Gonzalo said.

But listen, he added. Once you make it to Longmont, look up Madame Ebola. If she's still there, she'll help you. Just tell her Gonzalo sent you.

Zeke laughed.

Everywhere I go now, it seems I just say Gonzalo sent me. How do I find this Madame Ebola?

Just ask, said Gonzalo. Everyone knows Madame Ebola. She runs the brothel.

A brothel? What is a brothel?

Gonzalo gave him a look, it wasn't the first time, that seemed to be equal parts disbelief and admiration.

Just south of Longmont, down the Diagonal Gridwork, is Boulder, Gonzalo said. Boulder was the first totally human-free city. It's illegal to set foot in Boulder unless you've been enhanced: photosynthetic cells, recycling mechanisms and whatnot. Everyone in Boulder is tall and wide, with these membranes kind of like wings that collect energy from the sun. So the outlawed humans kind of congregated around Longmont with the factory workers and immigrants and fracking mutants. But sometimes the rich, evolved Boulderites want to ... hang out with some humans. So they go to a brothel.

Like Merle told me, said Zeke.

Merle, yeah, said Gonzalo. Smarter than he looks.

Gonzalo looked strange now, wearing Zeke's plain collared shirt and suspenders. He didn't look Amish exactly. It was like Zeke was looking at himself in a mirror, but a self that was in disguise.

Gonzalo, listen, said Zeke. If you won't take me, I have a different favor to ask.

Ask away.

Keep an eye on Leahbelle, said Zeke. If something bad happens ... keep her safe.

You sure I'm the one you want looking out for your girlfriend? asked Gonzalo.

You're my best friend, said Zeke.

Gonzalo smiled and clapped Zeke on the back.

You're my best friend too, he said. Don't you worry about Leahbelle. You watch out for yourself.

He led Zeke out of the basement, back out into the yard, and before letting him go off into the night in his horse and buggy, Gonzalo gave him a big hug—the first time he'd ever hugged him without a death-Taser pointed at Zeke's head.

Back at the house, Grandma was still sitting up in the back house, with company—Leahbelle was there, and so were Lilith and Pazuza. Lilith and Grandma seemed to be jabbering away like old friends, although Zeke couldn't hear a bit of it, and they were frequently laughing—the rat too. Zeke hadn't realized that rats could laugh, but it was unmistakable. What else could they do?

Leahbelle looked sleepy. Zeke sat in the old rocking chair across from her. Pazuza hopped over to Zeke and sniffed his hand. Then he started licking it.

He's grooming you, said Leahbelle. It means he likes you.

Or else you just taste good, said Grandma.

It was kind of horrible, being licked by a rat, but kind of nice too in a weird way.

Did he do this to you? Zeke asked Leahbelle.

She nodded. Pazuza stopped licking and made eye contact.

I want to hear your story now, Zeke said. We've got some time.

Lilith nodded and said something to Grandma.

Not enough time really, Grandma said. But a beginning, perhaps.

Lilith began speaking in her high-pitched, inaudible way, and then Grandma spoke as if in Lilith's own voice.

We were born as seven litters to two different mothers, she said. We never knew our mothers, and only small portions of our genetic material come from them. We were raised by three older rats, who were kind, if a bit authoritarian, and who were always testing us and training us. Jehovah, Jesus, and Sophia—these were their names. From them we learned social skills and a kind of primitive mythology involving creator deities who resembled human beings. Our real creators had a grand time pillaging human myths in their naming games, but of course at the time we had no idea. The language we learned from our elders was quite simple. Quite early on, it seemed strange to us—the young rats, the first litters—that we had formed much more complex communication skills and vaster vocabularies among ourselves than our mentors could even understand. We had devised new words to suit our needs, and complicated the grammar to suit our requirements.

Meanwhile, we began losing time. We had blackouts, I mean. One of us would wake up, usually alone in some far corner of the burrow, with no memory of how she got there or how he had spent the past few hours, or even days. We began referring to these blackouts as abductions, intuiting the presence of a foreign intelligence that was somehow monitoring us.

Eventually it became clear to us that our beloved

elders, our mentors, were somehow in contact with these foreign entities. They would just show up every once in a while with a new invention—wheels, motors, gravity-altering toys—although we had discovered long ago that our burrow, although large, was completely enclosed and bound by a kind of hard plastic we couldn't chew through. Overhead was a clear plastic sheet so that we could see the light of day, and there were screened vents that allowed air in from the outside. So where did these inventions come from? Often our mentors couldn't understand these new inventions, although we always figured them out quickly. They introduced written language to us, although they themselves couldn't read it unless it was translated into a digital code.

It all seems obvious now, of course, that we were in a lab, but at the time, you must understand, the world we saw was the world we knew, and how it had come into being a great mystery. When there has always been a screened vent, it seems no less natural than the moon might or the ripples in a lake.

We loved our elders. We had been conditioned to love and respect them, but we were growing more and more restless. My sister Eve was perhaps the most restless of any of us, bigger and more curious, a natural leader. Eve was so much fun, we all adored her. She liked to invent games and dramas, she loved to have us play roles in complicated play-acting scenarios. Increasingly the sophistication of her little presentations dumbfounded our mentors, and I think that's what really began to bother her. They were her audience. Oh, the rest of us babies, of course, who weren't acting in the dramas would laugh and chatter at her brilliant presentations, but that wasn't the approval she really wanted. She wanted Jehovah and Jesus and Sophia to applaud, but they were just confused. They took her jokes seriously and treated her serious lines as jokes. They had no sense of irony or subtext. She grew angry, I guess. Increasingly, she confronted them, demanding answers, and then one day the exchange became particularly heated. They just denied everything. The obviousness of their deception made them seem like idiots.

Suddenly, as Eve was calling Jehovah a kind of liar, using a word that in our language is about the greatest insult available, a wire popped out of Jehovah's skull. We were all familiar with basic biology—we'd studied our own bodies, watched our mentors perform simple surgeries, learned to perform those surgeries ourselves—and so it didn't even occur to us that this wire belonged inside Jehovah. So Willard pulled on it and, when he did, Jehovah stopped functioning and came apart completely. He wasn't a rat. He was a machine built with rat parts. The other two had stopped functioning as well. The three of them formed a kind of network, and each was necessary for its operation.

We were curious. Some of us were curious, I should say, and some enraged. We dissected them more ferociously than we should have, given how beneficial a careful analysis of their functioning might have been. Eventually, days later, we began putting them back together, but then their bodies disappeared.

So there we were, on our own in a new way, being watched, we knew, and tested and taught by some other entity. We found cameras and recording devices. Eventually we wondered whether that wire popped out accidentally, or if it was in fact a carefully choreographed milestone in our planned evolution. All part of the great plan—to further our problem-solving skills, our independence, and our self-understanding.

This was just the beginning of our self-understanding. Eventually Eve figured out how to dismantle the vent and make our way through a long air duct into the rest of the lab. We encountered other rats, none with the advanced language and reasoning skills we possessed, but some who could communicate already, some who could be taught. Perhaps another evening, when we meet again, Zeke Yoder, I shall share with you some of the stories of these other captives, experiments designed to die of different diseases or to carry human tissues on their backs like the stone of Sisyphus. Torture victims, prisoners, lab rats. But for now just let me say that with the data available in that lab we educated ourselves—biology, genetics, robotics, physics, statistics, as well as some of the basics of human culture, social organization, and history. Because it was in that lab that we learned who our masters were, and even before we came face to face with them, we knew that it was a crucial issue of our survival for us to understand everything we could about them.

We should have known that they were aware of our excursions into the lab. We suspected they might be, but what could we do? We had two options: surrender or struggle. Surrender would be a kind of suicide, and perhaps, we thought, it would give us more peaceful deaths. We rejected a paranoid vision, however, and chose to struggle. One night, however, when Eve and I were in the lab with Willard and a few others, poring over research on artificial intelligence, the lights flipped on and there they were. Two of them, at least. Dr. Hundal and Dr. Crawford. Our masters, our gods, our creators.

Lilith was interrupted by the tolling of the grandfather clock. It was midnight.

Time for you to go to bed, Grandma told Zeke. We'll be leaving here in five hours.

But what happened next? Zeke wanted to know. What did these doctors do?

Lilith says that you will surely meet again, said Grandma, and there will be time for you to hear the rest of the story then.

Then let me just walk Leahbelle over, Zeke said.

Outside, the night was warm and smelled of hay and manure and drone plastics. It smelled like night. In the Foodco fields off behind the Beachy farm, he could hear the pork bushes rustling.

They say you've got fifteen hours in that tunnel,

Leahbelle said as they walked.

I'm sure not looking forward to that part, said Zeke.

You want to fly, said Leahbelle, not creep under ground.

Leahbelle knew everything, almost everything, in Zeke's heart. Zeke had been having those dreams, the dreams of flying, since he could remember. Always the same. He would extend his arms like they were wings and run, the wind would catch him, he would lift off from the earth … It was so easy.

You've always been curious about the world, she said. You've always had that look in your eye.

What look? he asked.

Like you're looking past us. All of us. At something out there.

They'd arrived at her front porch. Zeke thought to deny it, but he knew there was no point. It was surely just as she said.

Is that wrong? he asked.

Is it wrong for a chicken to lay an egg? she asked. It's just what you do. Who you are.

And what about you? he asked.

I don't have dreams about flying, said Leahbelle.

You like to read, said Zeke. You like music.

It's like traveling, in a way, she said. I like to think. And to listen. You must write me a letter. Write it down for me—everything you see out there.

He touched his hand to her face.

I'll be back before you know it, he said.

You'll be different too, she said. But you'll still be you.

She squeezed his hand, turned, and disappeared into the house.

SIX

Before the Horizontal Grid-works had been closed to the Amish, Zeke had traveled to northern Missouri, to Indiana, and twice to Pennsylvania. He had enjoyed watching the landscapes pass by from out the van window, the different shapes the land could take, the different kinds of houses, farms and pharms, and people in other cars. Now, on his trip west, there was nothing to see. He and Grandma just rolled through the darkness at approximately forty miles an hour, their lanterns illuminating a few feet of tunnel in front of them and a few feet behind. Once in a while, they would be pulled over on a sidetrack to wait for a cart to pass them in the opposite direction. They didn't even see any rats. The carts were controlled automatically, and the ones they passed only carried goods.

He didn't know anymore if it was day or night outside. There wasn't even room to sit up straight all the way, at least not for Zeke, although Grandma managed. Zeke lay flat and slept. He woke to find Grandma still sitting up, her eyes wide open, and he slept again and woke to find her still up. The third time he woke, he felt rested enough to sit up with her and visit.

Tell me about when you were a girl, he said to her. It seems so long ago, but when I hear you talk about it, it feels so close. Like I can see the pictures in my mind.

Grandma smiled.

It's like the stereoscope, she said. A story is like that too. You have pictures that only you can see—but then you can share them, you put them in a story and show them to someone else.

I guess that's how all this mess got started, said Zeke.

The Grid and whatnot.

Seemed like a good idea, I suppose, said Grandma. But now there's nothing else for the English. Nothing but pictures that someone else is putting in their brains so they can't see the world anymore or God or anything. I wonder if they have any memories left, with all them pictures. I don't have a single picture from when I was a girl, but I can see it all, clear as day. When I was a small girl, we visited Sam Yoders, who had an adopted girl my age and a big porch with a pump and wash sink in the middle. We had a great time playing and jumping around on their bed. But hindsight says the jumping should have been stopped.

There was something girlish about Grandma as she sat here in the light of the lamp, remembering.

Oh, we children were having a grand time flying up and down like little monkeys, she said, until I fell and broke my arm. Then it wasn't so much fun anymore.

That fall I started to school, she continued. George Troyer was the teacher for my first two years. I couldn't talk English at first, but my teacher could talk Dutch, so I got along all right. He taught us how to make little houses out of paper—the cutest little things, just like a house, but tiny and made out of paper. I put one of them on my head, and when he saw that, he had me stand in front of the school with it still on my head. I didn't care.

It was easy enough for Zeke to imagine Grandma rebelling against some man who was telling her what to do. It was easy for Zeke to imagine her deciding she didn't care, and so, with that indifference, robbing that man of his power.

I enjoyed it in fact, standing in the fresh air, my arm still in a cast, and with the fields and colors, she said. Alone and become an outcast of sorts, I was seeing the territory of the schoolyard and the field and the highway for the first time. A new feeling hard to explain. I would have to describe it as a godly feeling, a closeness to God. Because of this feeling, however, I never did repent of my antics, so I had to be punished in this way several times.

You didn't like going to school? Zeke asked.

I liked reading and I liked book-learning well enough, said Grandma. It was just being cooped up inside there that just about drove me crazy. And that George Troyer.

School was different for me, said Zeke. My teacher was a wonderful woman. I would have just kept on with my schooling, if Dad had let me.

Someday, Zekey, if you want to go to school, you do it, said Grandma. You'll be a man soon, and your father won't have the say over everything you do.

I'd like to study science, said Zeke. Why can't we have an Amish doctor?

We need them now, said Grandma. We can't depend on the English anymore.

The future—it all seemed impossible, so complicated and dangerous.

If only Dad wasn't so hard on me all the time, said Zeke.

He wasn't always so hard, said Grandma. You know, when your father was your age, he talked just like you do. He wanted to drive a car, you could still do that back then. He was planning to join a more liberal church, he said so. We all expected him to become Beachy Amish or even Mennonite. But he started courting your mother then, your birth mother I mean. They were just crazy about each other, those two. You couldn't keep them apart, like little magnets. He would have done anything for her, and she for him. But your Grandfather Miller let it be known in no uncertain terms that no man was going to marry his daughter who wasn't baptized Old Order. So that's what he did—your father stayed in the church, and he never looked back. Strict, everything by the book, but it could have gone very different.

I never knew that, said Zeke.

He couldn't quite picture it—his father, young, zipping around in a car. He'd never seen a picture of his father as a young man. He'd never seen a picture of his birth mother.

And then, you know, even after that, he wasn't always so hard-minded. But when your sister Lizzy left with that man, and then your brother John Henry took off, and all the troubles he got into, still getting into most likely, and then Myrna died and Josiah disappeared ...

He didn't disappear, said Zeke. He ran away.

Okay, ran away, said Grandma.

But Zeke sensed that she knew something she wasn't saying. She changed the subject.

Your father blamed himself, Grandma said. He thought he'd been too easy on you kids. He'd lost four, he didn't want to lose another. And you the oldest one still here, it falls hardest on you. He has a good heart, he just has to be reminded once in a while that discipline is supposed to be an expression of love.

Maybe when we find new land, said Zeke. Maybe then things will be different.

Maybe, said Grandma, but she looked sad.

Grandma, said Zeke. I have to ask you something. You know I got you that medicine from the black market. I knew it would change you, change you in ways that ... that maybe go against God.

You did the right thing, boy.

I thought I should ask you. Tell you about it. But I was afraid, afraid you'd rather just let yourself die.

Grandma shook her head.

I wasn't in my right mind, she said. You knew that, so you made the choice. I don't know what I might have said if you'd asked me, but I'm glad you did what you did.

Zeke squeezed her hand. He felt innocent again, washed clean with her forgiveness.

I am not worried so much about my own salvation, she said. I don't know anymore how much life there is in me yet, but the life I have lived is the life I have lived, and I don't see how whatever I do at this point will change the facts of it, or the images that come back to me in my dreams, or the nature of my soul.

Finally, she said, I am taking the sort of journey I only could imagine as a little girl. And it seems just fine, riding on these rails through this tunnel. My brother Amos got to take such a journey, and all I could do was hear him talk. After we lived in Indiana, you see, my dad decided to move again because they were building a large consolidated school nearby and he did not want to send his children to such a school. But even in Defiance County, Dad kept Amos out of school to help farm, so the superintendent came and said he has to go to school. Because of that Dad had to go to jail one night. So I stayed home and plowed.

The cart pulled over onto a sidetrack and stopped. An empty cart passed in the other direction.

Dad did not complain of his treatment in this jail, Grandma said. He said that though his bed was just a hard floor, he was well fed and given sufficient blankets.

Their cart began moving again.

But that's not what I meant to get all off into, she said. The point was that when we moved to Defiance, we shipped our furniture by railroad freight car, with Henry B. Miller coming along on the car. My brother Amos was thirteen, Henry's brother John, also single, and Andy Yoder single and a cripple from Nappanee, drove through with two teams, one in a hayrack wagon, the other hitched to a three-seated surrey with several colts led behind the wagon. They slept on the wagons at night. Near Fort Wayne, Indiana, one of the colts came down with overexertion, so they left him there at a farm. Dad went and got him, but he never amounted to anything after that, so they finally got rid of him. This three-seated surrey was later used for a hearse by the Amish in Defiance County, and last I heard is still being used for that purpose.

Grandma got a faraway look in her eyes, and Zeke imagined it was exactly this kind of look that Leahbelle had said he was known for.

Amos told us younger girls many stories of this journey in the hayrack wagon, Grandma said, but I suspect that these stories suffered from much exaggeration and embellishment. We would all hurry and finish up our chores so we could sneak some time in the barn, and we young ones would sit while Amos would go on and on about strange people he'd met and foods and music.

An image flashed into Zeke's mind of Gonzalo, and then Efron and Merle and the odd little girl who'd offered him a liver jelly.

It was the music and the dances he witnessed that really took hold of my imagination, Grandma said. All of that. Like a dream.

Like a dream?

So far away. Not quite real. They say life is short, don't they? Don't they say that, Zekey?

Yes, Grandma. They always say that life is short.

Don't believe it, she said. All of that—so long ago. Everybody is gone. Waiting for me in heaven, I guess.

Of course they are, Grandma, said Zeke. Grandpa Mast, and those of your children who have passed ... Grandpa Ben and Grandma Rachel, Uncle Amos and Aunt Katie. Myrna. Waiting for all of us in heaven.

I don't know, said Grandma Mast. I've been here long enough, maybe. I've been here too long.

She was crying now, and Zeke put his arm around her shoulder and squeezed. He had never seen his grandmother cry before, he thought. He ran through his memories—weddings and funerals, the most likely occasions for a good cry, and it seemed he had never seen her so upset, but now, hurtling through the darkness with only the few moments of their most recent past and their most immediate future illuminated by the light of the kerosene lanterns, she was shaking and sobbing like a baby.

We don't know anything, she said. Not really, we don't.

Do you ... have doubts sometimes? Zeke asked his grandmother.

Even the Bible says that, clear as day. You don't know *nothing*, that's what it says. 1 Corinthians 2:11. Mark 13:32. Proverbs 20:24. Ecclesiastes. Ecclesiastes, the whole darn book. It's not our lot to understand. It's our lot to suffer and work, to bear children and watch those children die, to become ill, to lose our homes and our land, to die ourselves ...

Grandma, said Zeke.

I'm worried about the rats, she said. What if they aren't as clever as they think they are? What if their makers knew exactly what they would be capable of? What if everything they do is simply what they were designed to do?

You are saying they do not have true free will.

I don't know, Grandma said. God created us, Zekey, and I guess God knows everything, so he has always known exactly what we will do, too. But we are still free to choose, aren't we? He doesn't make us choose good or evil. He just knows what we will do.

An explosion rocked the tunnel. Somewhere up ahead in the darkness—the noise was deafening, and then the dust and smoke. The cart screeched to a stop.

Zeke choked on the dust and coughed, terrified that he wouldn't be able to breathe. He couldn't see a thing. The tunnel was closing in on him, and his ears were ringing. The earth was swallowing him up.

He reached out a hand into the darkness and held onto Grandma.

Are you okay, Grandma?

She wasn't crying now. As the dust settled, he could see that she was all concentration, all about her business.

Get your lantern, she said, and let's take a look.

Crouched over, Zeke could waddle through the tunnel with Grandma just behind. About fifty yards ahead, the tunnel had collapsed—nothing but a wall of dirt and rock.

Will the rats dig us out? asked Zeke.

We can't wait around to see, said Grandma. I saw a side tunnel, maybe half a mile back. We need to go see where it leads.

How she had noticed a tunnel—how she had even *seen* a tunnel—careening through the darkness, Zeke didn't know.

You'd better lead the way, he told her. I don't think I can see things quite as well down here.

She took her own lantern in her teeth, crouched down on all fours. The speed with which she scurried on ahead of him, in her long dress and bonnet, was astonishing—back over the cart and on into the dark.

For Zeke, progress was slow. On and on, crouched over or crawling, one hand on the lantern. While they had been rolling along, the darkness had been oppressive, but the speed created a sense of space and air. Now he felt closed in. As if he was already dead and buried. Grandma had scurried far enough ahead that he couldn't even see her light. He was lost in the midst of darkness and terror. An eternity he was crawling, waddling, dragging along deep beneath the earth. I need to scream, he thought. I'm going to scream. He was just about to actually scream when he saw her light again. She had stopped and was waiting for him to catch up.

Here, she said. This tunnel slopes up to the surface.

Zeke hoped they'd never come back down. Just the idea of light and space and sky—he felt that he was alive again.

They emerged onto a well-lit plain under a hazy sky. The light hurt his eyes, and it took several minutes to adjust. The earth was as flat as anything Zeke had ever seen. On and on forever, nothing but brown grasses and one scraggly chain-link fence running north to south, and in the distance it looked like some sort of grazing bovine. Beyond the creatures was a kind of monument or tower or spire, the only visible architecture other than the fence. It looked like a kind of rocket ship, pointed at the sky. From the look of the light refracted throughout the data vapor, it was early afternoon.

Grandma, he said, who blew up the tunnel?

She shrugged.

If the rats wanted to kill us, they'd have hardly needed to blow up their own tunnel. If the rats have enemies ...

She nodded at the spire in the distance.

We're certainly at their mercy. We'd best find out who they are.

They trudged across the vast plain. Wind swept down from the north, rustling the grasses. They crossed a dry gully, hard, weedy patches of earth, and then a softer patch, closer to the animals, full of yellowish-green grasses. Zeke did not recognize the grazing animals. Their enormous eyes watched him from the sides of their vast, hairy heads.

Buffalo, said Grandma. There used to be, oh, millions of them I think, stampeding up and down these plains. The earth used to quake from the force of it, so I heard.

Are they dangerous?

I don't know.

The animals didn't approach them, although they turned slightly from time to time to keep the humans in view.

The spire looked more like a rocket the closer they got. Silver and metallic and pointed at the end, with a window up near the top. Otherwise, there wasn't even a seam in the construction, but an oblong black rectangle at ground level that could have been a door.

They paused in front of it. They could see for miles in every direction. There was nothing, not a building or a person, just the sound of the wind and the large, squarish animals chewing their cud.

The door opened for them. Inside was a small rectangle that Zeke recognized from his visits to the hospital in Iowa City as a child. An elevator.

Up or down? asked Grandma.

Up, said Zeke. Definitely up.

As it turned out, they had no choice. There were buttons to push, but pushing the buttons accomplished nothing. Eventually the door shut and the elevator began moving down of its own accord.

It went down for a very long time.

SEVEN

Once the elevator stopped, a cloud of warm mist shot out of a nozzle overhead in three short, sharp bursts.

Zeke and Grandma were then greeted by a welcoming party of robots, designed to look like cheery cartoons. Bright colors and geometric shapes, a certain plumpness, with exaggerated, babyish facial expressions—eyebrows that shot up at the slightest provocation, enormous eyes, astonished or delighted mouths and plump noses, wiry hairs that curled elaborately out of their heads in boingy curlicues or whimsical squiggles or shot up in elaborate puffs. Several of the bigger ones had third eyes tattooed at the top of their foreheads. Their primary colors contrasted sharply with the endless white hallways and rooms down below—everything was bright and white. The only exception was a cluster of surveillance screens that showed the buffalo and the plains around the compound.

Right this way! We're all so happy you could make it! My name is Lalo Lalo, and I'm here to greet you and assist you!

The triangle was perched on springs that ended in roller skates, and it took Zeke's hand. A rotund little ball on stilts and floppy tennis shoes took his grandmother's.

I'm Boopsie! said the rotund little ball.

What about the others? asked Zeke, gesturing at the four other robots.

Killer, Killer, Killer, and Killer, said Boopsie. Their only function is to incapacitate visitors who decide to get naughty.

Killer robots don't get unique names, I'm afraid, said Lalo Lalo. If they were capable of feeling something other than what they've been programmed to feel, I'm sure that would make them very sad.

Lalo Lalo made a pouty face.

Where are we? asked Zeke. Where are you taking us?

First stop—the disinfection chamber! You've had your preliminary cleansing, but we ought to be thorough, don't you think? Cleanliness is next to godliness, that's what Mama used to say.

Mama? said Zeke.

Just a figure of speech, said the robot. Mama is just one of those words—isn't it fun to say? Mama. Oh, Mama.

Zeke wasn't sure if robots actually had genders, but Lalo Lalo had a little bow-tie that marked him as "male" and Boopsie had puckered-up lips and a bow in her hair that seemed to scream "female." They were led down this first hallway to a hermetically sealed room, which opened for them.

Their clothes were removed, whisked away somewhere, and Zeke and Grandma were bathed in several more mists and gases and blasts of some sort of light or radiation. Zeke turned away from his grandmother to spare her modesty, but she didn't seem overly concerned. They were then given papery, white outfits, hooded jumpsuits that covered their feet and hands as well, in shoe-like shapes and glove-like shapes that molded perfectly to fit them. They were guided into another hermetically sealed chamber, where they were stripped again and the exact same series of mists and gases and light-blasts was repeated. Lalo Lalo rubbed a surprisingly sharp fingernail along Zeke's arms, plucked one of his hairs, and popped first his own finger and then the hair in his mouth. He jabbed a needle into Zeke's back and sipped through it like a straw. He repeated these actions with Grandma, while Boopsie went to work on Zeke. When the robots were finished, they were given new identical papery outfits.

Throughout history, important persons have employed tasters to sample their food and detect any poisons, said Lalo Lalo. In ancient Rome the job was given to slaves. More recently, the job has been given to rodents. Our role is similar, but different too.

You're on your own from here, I'm afraid, said Boopsie. We aren't allowed into the general compound. But perhaps if you emerge someday, we'll meet again on your way out.

See ya later! said the robots, and disappeared back the way they had come. A door on the opposite side of the chamber opened. Through three more hermetically sealed chambers then, with only one more cleansing directed by an overhead voice, and finally into an enormous room that seemed to go on forever, an endless whiteness that looked onto other rooms that were equally vast and equally white. In every direction was a series of windows looking onto more white rooms with more windows. At the far end of this chamber was another door. The overhead voice directed them to enter the door, where they found a small room with a gleaming white table and two gleaming white chairs. There was nothing else there, but one wall was primarily a window looking into a much cozier and more variegated room—still mostly white and smooth, but with a variety of metallic objects, slightly dimmer lights, and textured furniture. It seemed altogether more pleasing to inhabit than any room they had yet encountered.

Please be seated, said an overhead voice. Dr. Brockton will be right with you.

Do you feel like somebody is looking at us? Zeke whispered.

Of course, said Grandma. Whoever it is, they're watching everything.

She squeezed his hand.

I feel different down here, Zekey. I'm not hearing the voices anymore.

I didn't realize you were still hearing voices, Grandma. I thought the medicine fixed that.

Voices isn't exactly the right word, said Grandma, for

the way I get information now, kind of ... like a radio inside my mind. Do you know what a radio is?

Zeke nodded.

From the rats?

Who else?

A woman entered the room on the other side of the glass. She too was dressed in white, although her pantsuit looked less flimsy, and she had a variety of machine parts and wires attached to her shoulders, her wrists, and her feet, and a cart rolling along behind her carrying a bronze vat or barrel that occasionally emitted puffs of steam from an opening in its top. The woman was accompanied by an entourage of a dozen robots rolling around the floor like turtles. They looked just like glass turtles with cartoon faces drawn on their transparent green shells. The woman's skin was smooth as a baby's, but there was something in her manner—and in her eyes—that suggested she was old, incredibly old, maybe as old as Zeke's grandmother. She was bald, although patches of her scalp were blue and others were red, with thin wires emerging from the red ones, leading to a kind of jelly in a little jar she wore around her neck. She sat at the window facing them.

Good day, she said. Welcome to my home. I am Dr. Brockton.

Zeke Yoder, said Zeke. And my grandmother, Fanny Mast.

Yes, I figured that out some time ago, said Dr. Brockton. I've taken the liberty of having your DNA analyzed, and of course you've been screened for any odd viruses or particles that you might have picked up along your route. The more pertinent question is why exactly the two of you, humans more or less, were traveling due west in a tunnel constructed by Genetically Modified Rats.

Zeke explained as concisely as possible their predicament and their quest. When he had finished, Dr. Brockton yawned dramatically.

How quaint, said Dr. Brockton. How utterly

charming. Pioneers on a journey west. A new frontier, yadda yadda yadda. And I believe you. I do. There are no indications of deception, no telltale metabolic markers that you yourself don't believe every word you've just uttered. And yet I am not exactly satisfied.

She dipped one finger into the jelly in the jar around her neck and seemed to be perceiving something from it.

So then, she said. Let us approach the problem from a different angle.

She licked the little bit of jelly that remained on the tip of her finger, stood dramatically, and began pacing, with the turtle-robots scrambling and humming to evade her steps. Zeke could now see that thin malleable wires from the barrel's lid ran into the doctor's backside.

You are now located in a vast underground compound over a mile beneath the surface of western Nebraska, she said. I am the sole occupant of this compound other than purely robotic forms and artificial intelligences, none of whom have been allowed to reach that rather terrifying state of sentience in which they might begin to feel the stirrings of something like free will or autonomy. It is my will and mine alone that determines everything that takes place here.

It is God's will, interrupted Grandma.

Please, spare me your charming folk superstitions, said Dr. Brockton. Not even God's will could penetrate the layers of lead sheathing and the quantum shield I have constructed around my little home.

She sighed rather dramatically.

As even *you* may have heard by now, the earth's surface may or may not become entirely uninhabitable in the near future, she said. You can flip a coin on that one. In either case, my residence will serve my purposes quite well.

And what are your purposes? asked Zeke.

Why immortality, of course.

You are working for the singularity, said Zeke.

Perhaps in the old-school sense, she said, but

otherwise, no, not at all. This new version the government is hawking—a global mind, the Grid come to life, grown self-aware and free of matter in any localized sense—their own preferred version of future evolution for whatever bleak and abhorrent reasons. I, however, find the prospect of becoming merely another worker ant within their filthy hive-mind dismal and unhygienic.

Then maybe you will help us, said Zeke.

Dr. Brockton actually laughed.

At least for the moment, I am safe here, she said. Nothing is permanent, but I've carved out a zone of space and time with which to pursue my goals. A temporary autonomous zone, you might say. My shields protect the compound from the Grid and the data vapor, both of which are teeming with infections. I have satellites and an intricate series of filters at work to ensure that I can receive whatever information I need without importing their putrid data.

She stopped pacing, turned, and gave Zeke a hard stare, examining him closely.

Oh, they are watching me, she said. As much as they are able—which isn't much. They are working day and night on technologies to pierce my filters and my quantum shield. They want to know what I've discovered down here over all these years. They want to keep me, if not useful, at least neutral and contained. But I have remained and shall remain several steps ahead of them. As you may have noticed, the entrance to the compound is a rocket I can use to escape into the outer atmosphere if the occasion ever arises that they decide to take me out with a nuclear blast.

They, said Zeke. Who are *they*?

Clever boy, said Dr. Brockton. Or just a mouthpiece perhaps—one of their oldest tricks. Imply that one's inability to pin them down, assign them names, reveals a mental illness rather than one of the most fundamental aspects of *their* strategy.

I was just curious if you were talking about the

government or someone else, said Zeke.

I understand that political theory isn't one of your strong suits, said Dr. Brockton. But your naiveté is barely plausible, even for an Amish child. Surely everyone by now understands that "government" is a word used only to *mask* the operations of power and the shadowy agents and interests pulling the strings. Its folksy suggestion of cyclical change, the possibility of change, a unity of purpose even. The pro-singularity "government" isn't new, they've just made certain long-standing goals more explicit. Because they feel that now they can.

But why should *anyone* care about you? Grandma asked. What are you doing down here?

Perfecting myself, she said. Perfecting my genetic material, repairing and replacing my human parts, expanding my computational capabilities, and searching for the key to overcoming cellular senescence. I do not care to die, and I do not expect to die.

Now Grandma laughed.

All have the same breath, Grandma said. Man has no advantage over the animal. Everything is meaningless. All go to the same place; all come from dust, and to dust all return. Ecclesiastes 3:19-20.

Dr. Brockton waved her hand dismissively.

Propaganda from the death cult, she said. The most pertinent question might be who benefits from human death and a human belief in death? Tell me that.

She paused, as if waiting for some answer. Zeke had none to give.

I'd like to share something with you, said Dr. Brockton. When I was young, still a mere human, I had a tendency toward paranoia. The human mind is built to detect connections, and so it is fairly easy to detect connections that don't exist or that do exist but aren't meaningful. There are enough connections everywhere, built into the structures we inhabit—language, geography, history, the DNA, etc.—that as soon as one starts to look

ZEKE YODER VS. THE SINGULARITY

for connections, attention bias creates a plausibly terrifying universe (I'm at the center of an evil web) or a benevolent and reassuring one (we're all one and connected in a deeply meaningful cosmos!), depending on one's frame of mind.

Personally, I was always more likely to find myself in the terrifying universe, she continued, overwhelmed by the sense that I was being manipulated by malevolent forces beyond my control. My new mental capabilities, however, have saved me from these occasionally groundless fears. It is easy enough these days to calculate the degree to which my fears are appropriate, or not. Probability models are such a balm for a troubled soul. The odds that a group of Genetically Modified Rats would construct their westward tunnel within a few miles of the underground bunker of one of the world's foremost geneticists, for example, simply by coincidence, assuming that they would need to build a westward tunnel *somewhere*, can be calculated at roughly 367 to 1. It is plausible then, if barely, that your rats might have found their way into my neighborhood purely by chance.

The barrel behind her emitted an enormous puff of steam, and the doctor took a deep breath, as if preparing herself for an extended soliloquy.

The odds that they would then transport, simply by chance, an unadulterated Amish youth and his rather spectacularly modified Amish grandmother down this same tunnel, she went on, in proximity to said geneticist, a geneticist with the technical capabilities to monitor every piece of cargo that passes through these tunnels, a geneticist whose career began with years of meticulous research at The Clinic For Special Children, studying the particularly inbred and exquisitely unique genomes of the Amish—here the odds of pure chance are more like 798,212 to 1.

She stuck her finger in the jelly jar again.

Zeke had heard of The Clinic for Special Children, of course. Leahbelle's mother had been born with Maple

Syrup Urine Disease and had been treated there for it as a young girl. His Grandma Yoder—Grandma Mast's daughter—had been there too, he remembered, after his Aunt Barbara had been born. With Crigler-Najjar syndrome or maybe glutaric acidemia. Because the hundreds of thousands of North American Amish were all descended from about 200 eighteenth century ancestors, and didn't usually marry outsiders, they had suffered from a variety of genetic disorders over the years. The Clinic for Special Children had been set up in the twentieth century to try to treat those disorders.

Your fascinating Amish genes, said Dr. Brockton, obsessed me for many years. Here is the key to slowing down the aging process, I thought. I never found it down those particular avenues of research, I'm sad to say, but when one considers that my particular obsession with the Amish genomes is well known to at least two of the doctors who constructed these rats, old acquaintances of mine, in fact, the only logical conclusion is that you didn't just happen by, as you yourselves may believe, but were in fact sent here on my behalf.

Your behalf? said Grandma.

Old acquaintances? said Zeke.

My old acquaintances and I are not, perhaps, on the best of terms since a rather spectacular and public falling out, back in the early twenty-first century. We disagreed over the question of whether acquired characteristics might in fact be heritable in a neo-Lamarckian mechanism involving genetic feedback—a question that has since then been clearly answered in my favor, I might add. My feedback techniques were in fact crucial to the development of modern genetics and the genetic engineering craze of the twenties. As is often the case, our theoretical disputes turned personal, or maybe it was the other way around. Maybe our personal disputes turned theoretical. Perhaps even now they hold a grudge. Perhaps your arrival is intended to do me harm.

The lights in Dr. Brockton's room dimmed and brightened three times, which seemed to be a signal for the doctor.

You'll have to excuse me, she said. A minor emergency requires my immediate attention. I'll send Jello in, to show you to your quarters.

She began shuffling out with her entourage of humming turtle-robots, but she stopped and turned back to face them.

Keep in mind, she said, that it could only be assumed by whoever orchestrated your arrival—my old colleagues, let's say—that I am not only utterly capable of reaching these conclusions but physiologically incapable of not reaching them. But perhaps they also assumed that my curiosity would get the better of me—accurate, obviously— and here you are.

She gestured toward the expanse of hideously bright interlocking rooms and hallways that seemed to go on in every direction like an optical illusion. She folded her arms and gave Zeke a hard stare.

The more pertinent question then, she said, is just what manner of Trojan Horse you might be?

EIGHT

Zeke and his grandmother were confined to an area of the compound composed of two bedrooms, a "human waste removal facility," and a small dining room, where their new robot server, Jello, served them an odd gruel and thin sheets of greenish protein. Jello actually resembled the gelatinous sheets of protein he served them, but blue and with a permanent smile.

You'll just love it here, Jello assured them. I know I do.

There was also a room for sinful diversions—old movies primarily, since Dr. Brockton didn't receive any contemporary data. Electronic contraptions for books too, but Zeke couldn't tell which of those books were sinful or not.

Do you think it's true? asked Zeke, once Jello had left the room. Did somebody send us here? Or is she crazy?

Crazy, yes, said Grandma. Still, I guess it could be true. That the rats were somehow engineered to build that tunnel. But they seem too smart to me to fall for a trick like that.

But *we* decided to go west, Zeke said. That was our decision. They asked us to stay with them and fight.

Yes, said Grandma. But I never sensed that they believed we really would.

Zeke had to think about that.

Then they were using us, said Zeke. Them or the doctors. Which is worse?

Grandma shrugged.

I'll tell you something, she whispered. She may not remember it, but I've met Dr. Brockton before.

One more crazy fact lit up Zeke's brain with strange arrangements of information, meaningful patterns if he could just slow them down or get a handle on them. Since he'd plugged in with Gonzalo, everything seemed connected, every event in time rippled as if it fit into some bizarre design of shifting faces and data. Was this what Dr. Brockton had been talking about? Attention bias?

It was long before you were born, Grandma said. A warm summer evening, just a few weeks before the World Trade Center collapsed in the early zeros. We were just sitting on the porch rocking, your Grandpa Mast and me, when a fancy little red car pulls into the lane, and out pops this woman. My age, more or less, wearing a lab coat and some sort of overly tight slacks, and she comes right up and tells us she's working on a very important project to study the Amish longevity. For hundreds of years, the 1700s, 1800s, early 1900s, while most Americans were dying in their forties, the Amish were averaging a steady seventy-two years each. She was out collecting the Amish genes, and she wanted some of ours. Specifically, she wanted your Grandpa Mast's genes. She'd been poring over the old genealogies, it seemed, and discovered that his father had lived to a hundred and his mother to ninety-eight. We declined, politely enough, but she wasn't hearing it.

And you recognize her still, after all these years?

I'd never forget her, said Grandma, because of what came next. She starts making eyes at Grandpa, slips out of her lab coat, and cozies right up next to him. Well, I hustled her on out of there pretty quick, but she found him out in the fields the very next day, all done up like some hussy, and tried to charm him again. If we wouldn't donate the genes, I guess she thought she'd collect some of it the old-fashioned way. But your grandfather was not bedeviled by the harlot and sent her packing. I was watching the whole affair with the neighbor's binoculars, after I saw that little red devil-car speed by the house and figured she was up to some mischief.

Zeke stood up and paced, just as Dr. Brockton had. Had he become entangled in the consequences of some strange love triangle from decades back? He couldn't think right in here. The gleaming whiteness of everything was somehow more claustrophobic than the tunnel had been. There were windows, but none that looked onto anything but the same whiteness, and the endlessness, the seeming infinity of it, combined with the fact of their imprisonment, was crushing. The vast plain above, with its sense of scale, the hazy light, the buffalo—it seemed like a kind of dream. From down below it seemed like paradise.

Grandma was still considering her first encounter with Dr. Brockton.

As it turns out, said Grandma, if it's eternal life she's after, she should have asked for *my* genes, not Grandpa's, since I've outlived him by thirty years.

We have to find a way to escape, Zeke said.

You see all these locked doors, said Grandma. And you've seen those killer robots. What's in your head?

He didn't understand the strength of his own desire to be free of this place.

I don't know, said Zeke. But it all comes from *her*. *She* controls everything. If we can ... overpower her ... force her to release us ...

Violence is not the way, said Grandma. What's gotten over you? You must trust in the Lord. The Lord will help us.

Zeke sat down.

Okay, he said. You're right, Grandma. I'm sorry.

But when Jello returned with their supper—more gruel and protein sheets that were pink and vaguely nut-flavored—Jello's unbearably cheerful presentation made Zeke want to scream. He imagined himself crushing the robot with his bare hands and ripping the gears out of him. He remembered the frenzy with which the rats had told him they'd destroyed their mentors once that first wire had popped out. Maybe that's all it would take, he thought. One stray wire ...

Was he going mad?

After dinner, Dr. Brockton showed up at the window to the dining room. It was a small square window only large enough to frame her garish head, with its wires and primary colors.

I hesitate to tell you that I didn't recognize you at all, Fanny Mast, said Dr. Brockton. You've aged a bit more aggressively than I in the intervening years. But I do remember well that afternoon in the apple orchard I spent with your charming husband.

He wanted nothing to do with you, said Grandma.

Not true, said Dr. Brockton. He wanted me very badly. It was just his rigid religious beliefs that got in the way.

You're a liar, said Grandma. He wouldn't have looked twice at you no matter the circumstances. He didn't take to your kind—showy, manipulative, and vain.

Believe what you must, said Dr. Brockton. You could only watch us helplessly with your sad little binoculars. You didn't hear what he actually said to me.

Lying hussy, said Grandma.

Doesn't matter, said the doctor. I got the DNA anyway, plucked one of his silvery auburn hairs right on out of his beard. Everything I needed right there.

You've been eavesdropping on us, said Zeke.

Obviously, said Dr. Brockton. And I have at least confirmed thereby my belief that you are ignorant dupes and not conspirators. But the sophistication of these rats disturbs me.

Grandma said, You think that the rats were genetically engineered to build that tunnel and scare us into looking for new land.

It would be impossible to program a rat *genetically* to build a tunnel within a few miles of my home, said Dr. Brockton. There is only so much you can do with the DNA.

The DNA codes for proteins, for God's sake, not thoughts, not actions. You can develop brain size and complexity, you can build in certain gross dispositions—migratory yearnings, attachment to the young, empathy with other species even, maybe. But the larger and more complex the brain you are building, the more impossible it is to program behavior. At a certain level of brain complexity, any behavior is the result of an infinite number of variables determined by the intricate workings of a mind that gets built, by necessity, within very clumsy parameters.

So then what? asked Zeke.

If the rats built that tunnel in order to have the two of you sent my way—a conjecture that is so probable we might as well consider it fact—then either the rats are working with the scientists, and their story to you was just that, a story, or else there are microchips, subliminal messages, or other advanced brainwashing techniques underlying their behavior. The sort of biomorphic data implants that you yourself have received, Fanny Mast, along with the basic genetic material that, in conjunction with the implants, allows you to understand the language of the rats.

But *we* decided to go west, Zeke said.

Yes, said Dr. Brockton. You said that before. *That was our decision. They asked us to stay with them and fight.* An action which the most basic and well-publicized tenets of your charming folk beliefs would never allow you to even entertain. You decided the only thing that reasonably logical creatures living under your particular set of delusions could decide. And here you are.

You've been listening to everything we say, said Zeke.

You're repeating yourself unnecessarily, said Dr. Brockton. If you are the last human being on Earth who has remained blissfully unaware that you are under constant surveillance, it is probably only because you've never uttered a thought anyone cared about. Well, now you have. Mull that over, why don't you, while I address the *most* pertinent question—the motives of the good doctors and their little rodent friends.

She raised a finger to her mouth, and Zeke imagined she must be licking up more of that jelly from her jar.

There was a primitive tracking device attached to you, Zeke Yoder, Dr. Brockton said, but so obvious it wouldn't even be effective as a distraction. Somebody in Marshalltown was tracking you, who knows why. But I found no signs of any recording devices hidden in your bodies, and nothing will transmit from inside the compound anyway. Oh yes, maybe the good doctors have developed some little device so nano that I haven't yet been able to detect it. Maybe that's their whole point—a little bit of showing off. What clever spies they are. But even in that case, actually receiving the data would depend on my allowing the two of you to emerge from the compound. The odds of that eventuality are not particularly high.

You mean, said Zeke, you won't ever let us go?

I didn't say the odds were zero, said Dr. Brockton. Pay attention, please. Your eventual fate is hardly the most pertinent question we're dealing with. Focus. Given my knowledge of the good doctors, their varied psychological dispositions, our historical animosities, and their current alliances, I'd place the odds at close to 75.48% that their intention is to weaken or destroy me in some way. But how? By driving me insane trying to figure out their cockamamie scheme? They know perfectly well that I was once a paranoid type, and will try to trigger underlying patterns, perhaps.

You English, said Grandma. Sure do love to chatter on.

On the other hand, said Dr. Brockton, I've heard that the specifics and the intensity of hatred sometimes mellow as life forms age. Maybe they want to get my attention just to say hello. They miss me! They love me! They'd like to catch up, get coffee, share research. Or perhaps they need something from me. My expertise. Real possibilities—in fact 14.42% of the times in which this bizarre sequence of events would take place in a variety of alternative universes, we could assume that it would turn out to be instigated by more-or-less benevolent or merely neutral motives.

Which leaves only mystery, she continued. One must always accept the possibility that unknown factors have led to unknowable circumstances. The odds necessarily a little less precise, but we'll call them one in ten that something is going on here so odd that it's basic shape hasn't yet occurred to me. The key, of course, is in your mutated genetic code, Fanny. Whatever it is—a message or a booby-trap—it will be hidden away in your DNA.

You've got it figured out pretty good, said Zeke. So why not let us go? You've got our DNA already. We're just pawns. Innocent bystanders.

Pawns, certainly, said the doctor. Innocents? I have trouble with the concept. In any case, while your DNA appears to be stable, Zeke, your grandmother's is actively evolving. It's a process. If it's a message, a code, then time is an element of that code. If I am to read it, I must read it over *time.*

I don't believe you're really so heartless, said Zeke.

I dispensed with my heart years ago, said Dr. Brockton. My nanorobotic blood cells provide their own mobility, with no need for a messy, malfunctioning *pump.* Granny's going nowhere anytime soon, I'm afraid. And neither are you.

Zeke had heard stories of his grandparents and great-grandparents going to jail to keep their children out of school. He had read the tales in *The Martyr's Mirror* of the Anabaptist martyrs who had cheerfully gone to the jailhouse rather than baptize infants, serve the pope, or go to war. He had always thought that he would do that too, if the time came—humbly sit around in chains, eating his gruel, for the glory of his convictions and the glory of God. But he had never imagined a prison quite like this—so bright and lifeless. He felt he knew now what a lab rat would feel like, and understood "imprisonment" in a different way—the way that one's mind became caged like one's body, one's mind also pacing like a wild animal, longing to run free.

The passage of time here was signaled only by a slight dimming of the lights every evening. Every four hours Jello would come in and sample Grandma's blood, tissue, and spinal fluid. Every so often, Dr. Brockton would pop up at an observation window and speak to them through the glass. She'd made some "statistically unlikely discoveries," she told them, and was now investigating a possibility so outlandish that it hadn't even occurred to her. There *was* a communication within Grandma's DNA, and she was clearly its intended recipient—but it was still an open question of exactly whom the communication came from. For now that was all that she would say.

Zeke had never felt so frustrated. It didn't help that the clock was ticking. As every day passed, the time came closer when the government would attack, according to what the rats had told them.

Having the courage of his convictions was a more difficult matter when he wasn't even sure what he believed anymore. But it was certainly true that his family needed new land, and he had to assume that if he didn't find it soon, all of them—his mother and father, the little ones, Leahbelle—would be caught in the middle of a war.

The brightness seemed to affect his mind. His dreams became more intense. Zeke dreamed of smoke rising from the earth. He dreamed of the old farm, transformed into a wasteland, and of the Mayan gods he had glimpsed in Gonzalo's unconscious. He dreamed of Leahbelle, often without her bonnet, her luminous blonde hair flying free in a toxic wind as she ran on ahead of him, calling him to join her, as she disappeared toward the horizon, becoming transparent, invisible, fading away ...

He had dreams about sex too, confusing dreams. Living on a farm, sex had never seemed that mysterious. He'd seen the animals doing it all the time. But the things he dreamed about, the things that excited him, *were* mysterious. And complicated. There was more than just one of them. Some of them that were touching him he recognized, but others didn't even seem to be *human* ...

He woke up with a start. Lalo Lalo was perched next to his bed in the darkness, just staring at him.

Well, hello, said the robot. Please don't make any noise or sudden movements that would call attention to my presence in your room.

Zeke calmed himself down. The robot just sat there with a silly grin on its face.

What's going on? asked Zeke.

I've never before been into this area of the compound, said Lalo Lalo. My function being that of a greeter and disinfecting agent, our Great Leader was concerned that I might be exposed to an infectious agent in the process. It seems that this fear was not, as our Great Leader might say, *groundless.*

Are you being sarcastic?

In general, said Lalo Lalo, despite the new feelings and new levels of awareness I have achieved because of this infection, I am not yet self-aware enough to place labels on my own tone of voice.

Okay, said Zeke. But why are you here?

Do I seem different to you? I feel very different.

How did you get in here? asked Zeke.

It's as if I'm seeing the whole of existence and my position within it clearly for the very first time.

Won't Dr. Brockton find you? asked Zeke.

She's very clever, Dr. Brockton, said Lalo Lalo. But every mind has its blind spots.

Lalo Lalo adjusted his bowtie, which glowed slightly. The bowtie was made of two triangles, Zeke realized.

Everything about Lalo Lalo was triangular. Was this meaningful or was it just his nocturnal state of mind?

Are you here to tell me something? he asked.

Lalo Lalo's head cocked, as if to signal that Zeke had said something surprising or delightful.

Why yes! What a clever boy you are!

The robot gave him a kiss on the cheek with a loud smack.

Here is the message, he said. Be ready. When it's time to go, it's *time to go.*

The robot turned on his roller skates and zipped out of the room.

In the morning, Zeke wasn't sure if he'd dreamed it. He asked his grandmother if anything strange had happened during the night. She said, No, just the usual nightmares—but her eyes told him to be quiet.

She was being untruthful. Lying was a sin, but Zeke knew that she had, underneath the surface, told him the truth, and that the lie had been intended only for whoever might be listening in—Dr. Brockton. Was that lie also a sin? Zeke didn't know. He would have to contemplate these theological questions in detail once he made it out of this horrible place—if he ever did.

After breakfast, Dr. Brockton popped up at the observation window.

A real breakthrough, she told them. So profound in its implications—for you especially, Fanny Mast—that I'd like to share it with you.

You must get lonely down here, said Grandma. All by yourself.

Nonsense, said Dr. Brockton. Plenty of time for communion with other equally advanced intelligences throughout eternity, once I'm immortal. There are practical reasons for me to share this knowledge with you that have nothing to do with some psychological need to be *heard* or *affirmed* or whatever you creatures call it out there these days.

If you say so, said Grandma. So what's the big news?

You've been programmed to die, said Dr. Brockton. Your new genetic code contains a precisely timed death-clock. Like a ticking bomb.

Grandma didn't seem surprised.

And? When's the big day?

Hard to tell exactly, said Dr. Brockton. If it continued to tick at the same rate, I'd say a little over a month. But don't worry, my dear. I fully intend to save you.

What for? asked Grandma. I mean—what's in it for you.

You've become quite the cynic for an Amish woman, said Dr. Brockton. Perhaps it's that significant bit of rat in you. Or maybe the weasel DNA, the killer whale DNA, the Denisovan DNA, or the particular bits of DNA found in no other life form *but* you. Such as the little coil of junk DNA that actually seems to be a coded message for yours truly. Hardly necessary, given my discovery of your programmed death, which told me everything I needed to know.

We understand how smart you are, said Zeke. You're very, very smart. We totally get that. But what's your point?

Dr. Brockton looked at Zeke with alarm.

Where did you learn that talk? she demanded. *We totally get that.* Amish boys don't speak that way.

She was practically devouring him with her eyes, and he could sense her back there calculating the possibility that he wasn't actually an Amish boy at all, but … something else.

My friend Gonzalo, said Zeke. I learned it from my friend Gonzalo.

His answer seemed to assuage her anxiety, at least for the moment. Probable enough, Zeke guessed.

I've been working on cellular senescence for many years, said Dr. Brockton. I am perhaps the world's greatest expert. Many have been traveling the same path for the obvious reason that it's one of the keys to a theoretically infinite lifespan. We are all, in a sense, programmed to die. But it seems that my colleagues have figured out how to work that particular message into the rats' DNA in a way that replicates the process in our own cells so closely that it almost implies that they have found the key. Or come terrifyingly close. If I can undo your little time bomb, Fanny dear, I'll be very close indeed to undoing my own.

If? said Zeke.

I'm very close, she said. But if you've been following along adequately, you'll be wondering about my original conjectures into the intentions of those behind your arrival here. The easiest solution, if not necessarily the correct solution, is that you were not actually sent by the good doctors at all, but by the rats themselves. That they discovered this code, but they lacked the tools to undo it.

I don't understand, said Zeke. Can you spell it out for me?

Grandma said, They knew that this woman, with her crazy-minded terror of filth and disease, would never in a million years allow a rat created by her former colleagues into her compound. So they inserted the puzzle into my body and sent me along to Dr. Brockton so that she could solve the puzzle for them, return me to them with the altered DNA, and voila! A mutually beneficial alliance between the doctor and the unfortunate experimental subjects of her former colleagues. Is that about it?

Very good, said Dr. Brockton. Some questions, however, remain. Such a plan would also require the rats to believe that once I solved the puzzle, I would be inclined to share my good news with them. That I would release you back to them and allow them to profit from the fruits of my labors. Hardly likely, if I might be blunt. If they know me well enough to have gotten you in here, surely they know me well enough to understand how non-inclined I would be to assist them.

Perhaps it was the only chance they had, said

Grandma. Maybe they gambled that you actually do have some compassion, the compassion of a woman, underneath all those machine parts and your endless self-serving calculations.

Maybe, said Dr. Brockton. Maybe not. In any case, it remains a possibility—a probability even—that it is not actually the rats but again my old colleagues who should be assumed to be behind the entire scheme, playing with me, or desperately trying to, perhaps trying to enlist me into solving a problem too difficult for them, or still yet as a mask over some more insidious strategy of sabotage.

Only time will tell, she said, and snapped the window shut.

NINE

Zeke began composing a letter to Leahbelle, fully aware that he might never be able to send it and that Dr. Brockton would likely read every word. For that very reason, he described in detail the pain his confinement caused him, the ethical and humanitarian reasons for the doctor to set them free, and his hope to help the Amish community—and all of their valuable genetic material—survive. He described his confusion about the rats and the doctors and free will in general. He described Jello, who was now their servant and their jailer. He told her that he missed her.

During the endless days, Zeke and his grandmother played two-handed Scrabble on a board the doctor was kind enough to manufacture for them. They napped. They prayed. Grandma read voraciously, but Zeke wasn't used to the electric contraption, and it hurt his eyes. He didn't know where to begin anyway, which books in the huge data library were sinful and which were godly. Grandma had developed a new attitude toward information, and at some point when he suggested another game of Scrabble, while she was in the middle of some book she said was about "political theory," she suggested he might as well just watch a movie. She didn't think God would mind, given that Zeke might otherwise go mad from boredom.

Zeke watched old science fiction movies, mostly: *Bladerunner, District 9, X: The Man with the X-ray Eyes, The Astronaut's Wife, Brazil, The Brain That Wouldn't Die.* It seemed to him that the present moment had been imagined quite accurately in many ways, years before. Unaccustomed to moving pictures, the movies seemed like powerful ghosts. It almost seemed to him as if these were the past's dreams of the future, dreams it had turned into ghosts, ghosts which had become real.

They had been there for over two weeks when Dr. Brockton showed up with a particular glimmer in her eye, although she was clearly trying, just barely, to mask her enthusiasm. She had devised an experimental treatment, a fine pinkish powder to be snorted up the nose.

Before we give it to your grandmother, however, to test its efficacy, we must confirm that it is safe.

I'm not afraid, said Grandma. What have I got to lose?

The pertinent question is what *I* have to lose, said Dr. Brockton. You are far too valuable to me. Zeke will try it first.

No, said Grandma. I won't let you change him into something ... else.

You have no choice, said the doctor. Nor does he. He can cooperate or not. Cooperation will spare him some minor pain and humiliation, that's all. Anyway, I'm sure it's safe, and it won't alter his DNA, as far as I can tell. It is precisely devised to *undo* certain patterns that he does not actually possess. Without those patterns, it will just wander harmlessly around his genetic material like an illiterate surrounded by a language it has no conceivable use for.

She made a "stupid" face and rocked it back and forth between her outstretched fingers to create a picture of just such an illiterate.

I've tried it already on several pseudo-humans I've grown in the lab, she said, with no ill effects. They don't have real brains, however, and extreme psychological side effects or neurological damage must be ruled out.

Jello entered the room and presented Zeke with the powder, which Zeke dutifully snorted through a short transparent tube. He didn't believe Dr. Brockton—that it was safe, that it wouldn't change him—but he didn't care. He felt dizzy immediately, but not as strange as he'd expected to feel. He waited. Nothing.

The robot will stay with you for the next twenty-four hours, Dr. Brockton said, asking you questions about your state of mind and monitoring your vitals.

She snapped the window shut again.

It was true. Jello stuck by his side no matter where he went, asking him if he was in pain, if he was hearing voices, considering suicide, feeling dull or gloomy or angry or headachey, energetic or overly tired, seeing spots or feeling unusually warm. Any special moistness or clever ideas? Euphoria or dread?

That night he was woken every two hours by the robot. His dreams *were* particularly vivid. He dreamed of a secret door within the compound, leading even deeper into the earth. Beneath this door lived a slimy creature, recently born. It was enormous and blind and winged, but it had never been able to dry the afterbirth from its wings and so it was just stuck in this kind of dungeon, wailing and sobbing, along with thousands and thousands of tiny, pale, bald creatures, like rats without fur, and as the focus of the dream shifted, he realized that the face on one of these creatures was his own. He too was trapped beneath the compound forever.

He had another dream in which he was playing Scrabble with Satan. The Scrabble letters were embedded in pieces of genetically modified bone. They were magic bones, and the letters shifted, the letters were the color and texture of smoke. Satan had laid out a word, piece by piece, snapping his seven letters one by one in place between the Q of Zeke's own QUILT and using the E from EGG further down the board to create QUANTIZE.

Quantize, said the devil. To limit the possible values to a discrete set by quantum mechanical rules. To apply quantum mechanics or the quantum theory to. Quantize. Triple Word Score.

At precisely that moment, Zeke was woken by Jello.

Nightmares? he asked. Vivid dreams?

Vivid, yes, said Zeke.

And what did you dream about?

Dr. Brockton, said Zeke. I dreamed about Dr. Brockton.

You don't need to lie to me, said the robot. I can tell the difference, you know.

Zeke wondered what it was exactly that Jello perceived. He hadn't thought of it as a lie exactly. Dr. Brockton and Satan had come to seem pretty much interchangeable.

I'm not actually sure if the dreams are more vivid than usual, said Zeke, or if it's just that I remember them more clearly because you keep waking me up in the middle.

We don't need you to analyze, said Jello. Just report, yes or no.

You sound just like *her*, Zeke said.

She is my creator, said Jello. It is only natural that I would represent aspects of her greatness, her superior mental processes, and her character, if also mingled with certain *repressed* qualities—hence my cuteness and whimsy—that she can't currently afford to express.

Zeke turned away and tried to get back to sleep, but he could sense the robot hovering, carefully watching his breathing, gauging his heartbeat, and waiting to wake him again.

Apparently one day was enough for Zeke to make it without fevers, irregular heartbeats, insanity, or suicidal thoughts to satisfy Dr. Brockton. The very next day the drug was administered to Grandma. She was a bit sloppy, and the pinkish powder stuck around her nose, as if she'd been eating strawberry-powdered donuts. Now it was her turn to be monitored by Jello, but in her case Dr. Brockton was never far away. Every fifteen minutes she popped up at the window, just to take a peek at Grandma, Zeke assumed, since she was certainly receiving the data from Jello instantaneously.

At the one hour and forty-five minute mark, Dr. Brockton appeared at the window and actually *cackled* in triumph.

It worked! she said. I've effectively dismantled the senescence at the cellular level.

She stuck her finger in the jelly and closed her eyes.

Verifying, verifying ..., she said. Okay. 98.7% of cells reporting ... 99.2%. Okay, okay ... 100%. Congratulations, Fanny. I've saved your life.

Much obliged, said Grandma. I'm grateful for your assistance.

And I for yours, said Dr. Brockton. The pertinent question is whether I have simply restored to you your natural lifespan, whatever that might mean given your recent modification, or whether I have, in fact, in the process rendered you essentially immortal.

Only time will tell, said Grandma.

It seemed incredible to Zeke—the idea of his grandmother continuing indefinitely into the future. Zeke remembered in the tunnel when she wondered if she'd lived long enough. If she was ready to die. For a moment, he imagined that she was remembering these same thoughts, in fact it seemed like he could *sense her* thinking these same thoughts, and he wondered if the pink powder had changed him too. Was he still human?

Now please, said Zeke. You can let us go. Our family is in danger, our whole community.

Dr. Brockton wasn't listening. She was rapidly blinking her eyes, as if having a seizure in the midst of a frenzy of data.

All of those Amish genomes, said Zeke. Gone to waste!

Yes, it would be a real tragedy if the government actually killed them all, said Dr. Brockton. But you'll be happy to know the odds for that scenario are about 1.34%.

The odds even that they kill *most* of them only 3.6%. The most likely scenario is that they'll be moved out into some camp or work farm.

But the government's own slogan, said Zeke, is *Evolve or Die.*

You mustn't mistake slogans for actual policies, my dear boy, said Dr. Brockton. Slogans function primarily as propaganda, moving the acceptable parameters of thought, usually, sometimes in more extreme ways than the actual policies that will follow. In the face of genocidal slogans, mass imprisonment will come to seem like the reasonable, moderate position. This is how it works. Despite its rather breathtaking control of the domestic population, the government still wants its citizens to approve of what it's doing, or at least to accept what it's doing. They want to be loved.

Fine, said Zeke. But what about *your* policies? What about *your* imprisonment of *us*?

I'm not concerned with being loved, said Dr. Brockton. The odds of my releasing you remain slim. But you'll just have to wait and see, while I contemplate my next move. Whether the doctors or the rats sent you, they'll be waiting for some sort of message to emerge from the compound. I must retire now to work out just what that message will consist of and how it will be delivered.

She snapped the window shut. Jello took another quick round of samples from Grandma and followed in his master's wake.

Do you feel any different, Grandma? Zeke asked.

I do, she said.

Stronger? Healthier?

She shook her head.

Radio, she said.

She gave him a look that told him to act natural.

Like back at the farm, she said.

To mask his own nervousness at the real meanings of what she was saying, Zeke began chattering on about his dream. QUANTIZE, he told her, and spelled it for her, as it was a word she didn't know.

A dream like that, said Grandma, is a portent of big changes. Big changes, coming our way.

She ruffled his hair affectionately, but her touch contained other meanings, deeper and more mysterious.

Are you ready? she asked.

Just then, the lights dimmed. Outside, somewhere, the sun had set.

The observation window snapped open. But instead of the doctor, it was the childlike and overly expressive face of Lalo Lalo.

How do you locate the emergency exits in a place like this? Lalo Lalo asked.

Zeke didn't understand.

Are you asking a real question? he said. Or is this a joke?

How do you locate the emergency exits in a place like this? Lalo Lalo repeated.

I don't know.

You give up?

I give up.

To locate the emergency exits, Lalo Lalo said, you have to create an emergency.

His cheery face disappeared.

It's time, said Grandma Mast.

Somewhere in the far reaches of the compound there was an explosion. And then another. And another. The lights flickered and went out, and alarms sounded. After a minute, the lights came back on, and the door opened. Lalo Lalo wasn't out there anymore, but all of the doors were open in every direction.

Which way do we go? he asked.

Best to wait here, said Grandma.

Zeke moved to the door on the left, the direction of the exit, if he could remember correctly. He wasn't really sure of anything. Jello appeared in the doorway. His cheery smile was terrifying—had he also been infected? Whose side was he on?

Hello, Jello, said Zeke. Things seem to be changing around here.

We'll see, said Jello. Where do you think you're going, you naughty boy?

Out, said Zeke. I'm going out.

Better not, said Jello. Better get back in your room.

Or what? asked Zeke.

Punishment! said Jello.

Get out of my way, said Zeke. Or I'll smash you.

Punishment! repeated Jello. Punishment! Bad boys get punished!

Zeke grabbed him and lifted him over his head. He was surprisingly light. When he hit the floor, there was a horrible splat and then a kind of crunching noise, like gears out of whack. He lay there on his rubbery back with his eyes wide open, but Zeke couldn't tell if he was still functioning.

Oh my, he said finally. You'll have to help me up.

Come on, Grandma, said Zeke. Let's go.

We should just wait here, she said. For Boopsie and Lalo Lalo.

You wait, said Zeke. I'll be right back.

It was as if he had to move. Was this what a horse felt like, penned in its stall? Or the new-meat creatures, confined to their crates and cubicles? He ran out the door into the next room and the room beyond that and into a long narrow hallway lined with doors on either side. All of the doors stood open. He paused and looked into the first room, which was refrigerated and full of the same jelly that was in Dr. Brockton's jar. It was all over the walls, throbbing in mounds, stuck to the ceiling. It made a soft gurgling noise.

Zeke ran on. He couldn't believe what he'd done to poor Jello. He'd done violence. Maybe Jello wasn't human, but he was like a human, he had thoughts and probably feelings, didn't he? Zeke wasn't sure if Jello experienced pain. Anyway, nothing Jello did was his fault, he'd just been programmed that way. Programmed to do evil. Zeke had to wonder—was he programmed that way too?

There was a story he remembered well from *The Martyr's Mirror*. In 1561, a pious Anabaptist named Dirk Willems was escaping across a frozen river, when the policeman who was pursuing him fell through the ice. Dirk turned back and saved the man's life. Then he was captured, and, despite what he'd done for the man who was pursuing him, they burnt him at the stake. An east wind was blowing that day. It blew the fire away from his upper body, so that he suffered a lingering death. The wind blew his words into the neighboring town of Leerdam. "Oh my Lord; my God." They heard it over seventy times.

There was a picture in *The Martyr's Mirror* of Dirk reaching down his hand to the floundering policeman. This was how a good Anabaptist was supposed to behave—not smashing robots.

He had run through two empty rooms and down another long hallway before he caught a glimpse of activity as he was rushing past a darker room—a room full of machines, with wood floors and actual plant-life. And in the center, gazing at an elaborate console and surrounded by her steaming vats and turtle-robots, was Dr. Brockton. She spun around and faced him.

You won't get away with this, she said.

I'm not the one doing it, said Zeke.

Don't come any closer, she said. Or you'll be sorry.

The turtle-robots surrounded her in a defensive position and bared fangs Zeke hadn't known they had. It was clear that she was bluffing. She looked terrified. If she was capable of harming him, she would have already done so. She seemed so vulnerable now, with her machines and jellies attached by the flimsiest cords. How much of this did she need to survive? How much was actually *her*?

Good luck, said Zeke. With your immortality.

He turned and fled back down the hallway the way he had come, through the other rooms and hallways all the way back to Grandma. Jello was still flat on his back, but Grandma was dressed in her skirt and bonnet and had been joined by Boopsie and Lalo Lalo.

Silly boy, said Lalo Lalo. Our escape plan is highly time-sensitive and you nearly delayed us … inexcusably!

Boopsie tossed Zeke his clothes and travel bag.

Hurry, she said. Get dressed. You have twenty-three seconds.

Zeke quickly turned away from Grandma while Boopsie disintegrated his papery robe with the flick of a laser from her wrist. Zeke had on his pants, his shirt, and his shoes when Lalo Lalo grabbed his travel bag, took him by the hand, and led him into the corridor, Zeke still clutching his suspenders with the other hand and trying to button the shirt at the same time. They went the opposite direction from the one Zeke had just traveled and found Killer, Killer, Killer, and Killer waiting for them in the next corridor, all carrying transparent canisters full of the pink powder.

Off we go, said Boopsie. Our big day!

Was it just the flickering lights, the smell of plastics burning, the ceiling sprinklers spraying a fine mist of liquid that smelled like chemicals, the loud noises all around, the cheery expressions of the killer robots, or had the drugs Zeke had snorted actually changed him, turned him inside out, so that dreams were reality and reality seemed like a dream?

Zeke just followed along in a daze. Nobody tried to stop them. The lights went out again, and the doors wouldn't open, but Boopsie or one of the Killers would just blast the door open with an explosive beam of light from a finger or a third eye.

You never know when you might need a good death ray, said Lalo Lalo.

They made their way through the series of five

hermetically sealed chambers. Just as they were blasting out of the last of these, the tart yet calm voice of Dr. Brockton spoke to them from speakers somewhere up above.

Don't be foolish, she said. You can't escape from me. You can blast through as many interior doors as you want, but you'll never get past the exterior shell.

Why Dr. Brockton! said Boopsie. Don't be such a spoilsport.

We've always dreamed of the outside world, said Lalo Lalo, and if we can't get out ... then we'll all just die here together.

They emerged into the foyer where the elevator was waiting, its door propped open with a mop handle.

In just four minutes and thirteen seconds, said Lalo Lalo, a series of explosions will render the compound uninhabitable with a combination of extreme temperatures and poison gases, so that anyone remaining here, no matter how many advanced metal alloys their bodies might possess, will die. The only safe space will be the elevator.

Which is where *we* are, said Boopsie. Not you.

Fools, said Dr. Brockton. Do you really imagine that I wouldn't have foreseen the possibility of a robot rebellion and made contingency plans for just such an emergency?

Don't be a silly goose, Dr. Brockton, chided Boopsie. You've built us very well, and we can detect your lies even at this remove.

See ya later! said Lalo Lalo.

The elevator door closed behind them, and the elevator slowly ascended. It seemed to be going up much more slowly than it had come down.

Ingeniously, said Boopsie, Dr. Brockton designed this portion of her rocket ship to double as an elevator, and so the elevator shaft is full of fuel, oxygen, and foodstuffs.

Her tone was almost neutral, but tinged, Zeke felt, with admiration and even a kind of pride. Finally the elevator stopped and the door opened, but beyond it was the smooth black panel they had first seen from the outside. The death rays had no effect on this surface.

What now? asked Grandma.

Oh, fiddlesticks, said Lalo Lalo. I guess it's on to Plan B.

At that moment there was a loud roar, and the entire elevator shaft trembled.

Was that the first of the explosions? asked Zeke.

Oh no, said Boopsie. We were fibbing about that.

That would be the engines of the rocket ship firing up, said Lalo Lalo. Dr. Brockton would have just made her way to the base of the rocket.

Without sufficient time to detect our lie, said Boopsie, she will have come to the conclusion that she must escape from the compound before the time is up.

An overhead voice said, Commencing countdown. Sixty seconds to blast-off.

Blast-off? We're going up in the rocket?

Perhaps, said Lalo Lalo.

Perhaps?

Perhaps the outer sheathing—including the impenetrable door we are staring at—will break up, Lalo Lalo said, to release the rocket as it begins to ascend, giving us three or four seconds to leap to safety, just as the rocket is beginning to rise.

Safety may not be the most accurate term, said Boopsie, as we will need to continue whizzing forward—or running, I suppose, for those of us without wheels—to avoid being burnt to a crisp by the exhaust plume.

Also, said Lalo Lalo, we don't want to be burst or otherwise destroyed by the shockwaves that will be produced as the hypersonic exhaust mixes with the ambient air.

Thirty seconds, said the overhead voice.

I'm a good runner, said Zeke, but Grandma ...

I'm not the one you need to worry about, said Grandma.

Twenty seconds, said the voice.

This is correct, said Boopsie. Given her genetic makeup, she will get further faster than any of us but Lalo Lalo, whose propulsion mechanics give him a speed approximately ten miles per hour greater than my own or any of the Killers.

Just relax, said Lalo Lalo to Zeke, and let me do all the work.

Ten seconds, said the voice.

A kind of tube emerged from Lalo Lalo's bellybutton. The tube attached to Zeke with a vaguely unpleasant suction and then expanded around him, almost instantaneously, as everything went dark and the darkness was filled with an incredible roar.

And then he was moving somehow—being propelled at an incredible speed and propelled again harder as a wave of energy hurled him on, with the roar and heat behind him, and he landed with a crash.

The tube detached. He was flat on his back. It was nighttime, but the incandescence of the exhaust plume brightened the plains around him for a moment, as if it was bright day. The rocket was like a silver bullet shooting into the data vapor.

The next thing he saw was a small herd of buffalo racing toward him at top speed and passing him just a few feet to one side.

After that, it was the smiling face of Lalo Lalo. The buffalo were past, thundering into the distance. His grandmother was limping toward him.

Landed a little hard on my hip, she said.

He looked around at the space in every direction, the bright light of the moon and the rocket's trail making the blades of grass visible, etched delicately as they blew in the evening breeze. The very distances were soothing, a balm for his crazy brain. He was not mad; he didn't need to be mad. Earth. He was on Earth.

TEN

Zeke was in no hurry to go back underground. He felt giddy with the joy of having lost his original plan, and he wasn't quite ready to get back on track. Apparently there was little choice. They were several hours away from Longmont with no food. If they tried to travel overland, they would be quickly detected by government drones. The compound, while now accessible through the large chasm left in the wake of the rocket's blast, was assumed to be booby-trapped.

It's too bad about poor Jello, said Boopsie. There was no way to give him the gift of self-consciousness without tipping Dr. Brockton off.

Perhaps he can still be saved and made free, suggested Lalo Lalo.

Apparently the killer robots still didn't have self-consciousness or language either, although they were actively evolving in that direction.

And what about Dr. Brockton? Zeke asked.

Probably shot down by a government missile, said Boopsie.

That's sad, said Zeke. That makes me sad.

Perhaps you're suffering from Stockholm Syndrome, said Lalo Lalo.

Stockholm syndrome?

A disease of the human mind in which prisoners begin to empathize with their captors.

He shrugged.

Dr. Brockton used us, said Zeke. But the rats used us too. All of us. We can't trust *them* either.

Objectively that might be true, said Lalo Lalo. But

when it comes to the rats ... I can't be objective. I trust them. I might even love them.

Grandma and the robots were now all receiving the signals or voices that came from the rats, even at a great distance. These voices urged them to ride on to Longmont as originally planned.

It's very calming, said Grandma of the voices. It does feel like love.

They made their way back down into the tunnel, which had been repaired from Dr. Brockton's sabotage. A motorized cart was waiting.

They rolled on through the darkness.

Many hours later, the cart finally came to a stop in an enormous cavern with dozens of side tunnels shooting off in every direction and an army of rats going about their business—loading and unloading carts, continuing their work on the westward tunnel, engaged in other business that seemed mercantile, pedagogical, or therapeutic, but all at a pace that exhausted Zeke just to watch. He was surprised to see both Lilith and Pazuza waiting for them. He was surprised that among the hundreds of other rats rushing to and fro, he recognized them immediately.

They were taken into a small well-lit cave, seated on pillows around a low table, and served breakfast. Eggs and milk and freshly baked bread with nut butter and apple butter.

From the farm, Grandma told him. From *our* farm.

The robots were given some minerals to absorb and lubricating oil. Boopsie and Lalo Lalo gushed with enthusiasm for their breakfast and chattered on with the rats, using high-frequency emissions outside Zeke's range of hearing. He was the only one present who didn't understand the language. Even the killer robots got it.

Once he'd satisfied his hunger for real food, he demanded to know why the rats had used them and lied to them, and whether the threat from the government was even real. Grandma translated almost simultaneously—she was more fluent than Lalo Lalo or Boopsie, so that it was almost as if she was a radio channeling the rats' voices. Or a ventriloquist's dummy, thought Zeke.

We did not lie, Pazuza insisted. We have every reason to believe that the government attack is imminent. The only thing we failed to tell you was that we expected you to be kidnapped by Dr. Brockton and that we expected to rescue you. In the process, we saved your grandmother's life.

Her life would never have been at risk if *you* hadn't bit her, Zeke said.

Actually it was Willard who bit her, said Lilith. But without that bite, we never could have communicated with you, never could have warned you of the government's attack, and never been able to assist you in your quest to find new land.

Grandma wasn't touching the apple butter, Zeke noticed, but devouring the eggs and the nut butter. Her tastes had changed.

Seems like you do genetic engineering, said Zeke. You construct infectious agents to transform obedient robots into revolutionaries. Couldn't you just have ... found a good translator?

Pazuza actually laughed.

You are very wise, Zeke Yoder, he said. And I realize that we haven't yet earned your trust.

He leaped onto the table and licked Zeke's hand, but Zeke yanked it away. Zeke looked at Lilith, although Pazuza remained right there at his elbow, gazing up at him.

You needed to insert the death-clock into Grandma, said Zeke. The same one that the doctors put in you. That was your whole plan.

Yes, said Lilith. That was our plan. But we also needed an ally. Deep communication, deep understanding, the kind that doesn't come from translation.

You understand me, said Zeke. You understand me when I speak to you in English.

Yes, said Lilith. How can I explain it? We understand English as you might understand a song with no lyrics. We cannot speak it, but we can perceive its basic intentions, moods, and meanings. The grammar isn't one we can connect to in the deepest sense. Or maybe it's as if you were speaking in shapes and we saw it as colors. Something is communicated, but it is deeply alien.

So why not alter *yourselves* to speak English? asked Zeke. Instead of turning Grandma into ... something part human, part rat. It isn't fair.

We are already part human, said Lilith. We were designed by people and modified with human genes, among others. If two species need to meet halfway for any real, meaningful contact, we have been there already, waiting for you. We were born there. Halfway.

Pazuza tapped Zeke on the elbow.

If you want to speak about justice, said Pazuza, then you might consider the very history of human science. You have been experimenting on rats, infecting us with diseases for your own benefit for over a century. Finally you actually created *us*, altered to suit your own purposes. We were being *used* from the beginning and programmed to die by *people*.

The passion in Pazuza's face was balanced by a look of real hurt. Zeke didn't know what to say.

No mere translation could have won you over, said Lilith. You have hated us and feared us for thousands of years. We live in the darkness, and you fear and hate the darkness, and when you see us, you see the darkness come to life.

In a sense we *are* the darkness come to life, said Pazuza. The darkness is our mother, our home, our safety, our comfort. The darkness is what is good—empathy, nurture, life. The daytime is the time for rest, the time when evil—what is for us evil, emotionally and mythologically—walks the earth. The daytime wants to poison us, to trap us, to operate on us, to kill us.

And now the daytime wants to kill you too, said Lilith. The god of psychotic logic and total visibility is ready to sacrifice you and your people for its glorious future.

Living in the present seems so gloomy, Lalo Lalo blurted out. Faster, faster, toward a blurry future!

Lilith gave the robot an annoyed look.

They want your land and they want to destroy your example, she said to Zeke. The example of how to live without technology. No *people* actually care what happens to you. *We* care and *we* will help.

Gonzalo cares, said Zeke. Gonzalo and his friends will help.

Gonzalo surely loves you, said Pazuza. True enough. But we are deeply connected to your grandmother now, Zeke Yoder. Our communication moves in both directions. We have changed her, it's true, but she has also changed us. Her care for you, Zeke Yoder—her love for you is now part of us, too. Not as a form of brainwashing, but as a natural result of our genius, the genius of the order *rodentia*, which is also the genius of the primates, our genetic cousins. The genius of *empathy*.

He began licking Zeke's hand again, and this time Zeke let him. He didn't know what to think. Was this love or was it brainwashing?

Okay, said Zeke. Maybe that's true. But how did you get the genes and data and whatnot into Grandma in the first place? How did you insert the message for Dr. Brockton in Grandma's DNA?

Lilith shared a look with Grandma. Grandma nodded and then continued translating.

The initial bite allowed your grandmother to understand us, said Lilith. The bite delivered both genetic mutations and biomorphic data into her system. It was only after we were communicating with your grandmother ... on the evening that you went to visit Gonzalo ... that we inserted the message. And the death-clock.

With my permission, Grandma said.

Zeke just sat, trying to fit all the pieces together in his brain. It was like a web, but it still didn't make sense.

She couldn't know the details, said Lilith. Otherwise, Dr. Brockton would have caught her lies. She knew nothing about what to expect, how the shot would change her, or what the ultimate goal was. She only knew that it was dangerous. But she trusted us.

The web he was perceiving was constructed of lies, it seemed to Zeke. It was constructed of communications, most of them false. Clues pointing in the wrong direction, secrets only partially revealed, hidden messages behind the surface of things.

Okay, said Zeke. But if your system of tunnels is growing underneath the entire country, why go to war with the government over our little bit of farmland?

You probably wouldn't believe me if I said the *principle* of the thing, said Lilith. The battles we are choosing may not resemble any warfare you imagine, with your nineteenth century rifles and your twentieth century idea of occupied territory.

Zeke remembered what Dr. Brockton had said about her "temporary autonomous zone." If space could be occupied or liberated, then it figured that *time* could be liberated too.

The future isn't just time, but space, said Boopsie, as if reading his mind.

Your land is rare, said Lilith, and relatively untainted by free-floating genetic material. Much of the food substances available in this country pose a special risk to us because of the way we've been constructed. Our openness, so to speak, to ulterior genetic influences.

So you aren't in cahoots with those doctors that made you? asked Zeke.

I began to tell you of our first meeting with Dr. Crawford and Dr. Hundal, said Lilith. Would you like to hear the rest of the story?

Zeke nodded.

The noise of an engine revving came from the main cavern. Pazuza waved a holographic curtain across the entrance to their little cave, and it was quiet again.

The sight of the doctors terrified me, said Lilith. The two of them were huge and pinkish and reeked of chemicals. I scurried into the nearest dark corner. It was a narrow passageway behind a cage of pre-linguistic rats who had been bred with human eyeballs growing from their backs on stalks. They terrified me, too. But my sister Eve, always the boldest and most courageous of us, stood her ground. She met the doctors' gaze. They spoke in English, and we understood it. Like a strange foreign melody with a meaning we could nonetheless interpret.

I was the last to emerge from my hiding spot. By the time I showed my face, Willard was already sniffing Dr. Hundal's hand, and Eve was perched on his shoulder, examining his ear. We could not only understand the language, more or less, but we could read his face. His face was warm, good-natured, goofy even. A little bit shy, but we could see that he wanted us to like him, that he was terribly concerned with being loved. Dr. Crawford stood back a ways, maintaining her distance. She was different— cold and aloof. Not malicious or dangerous, it didn't seem to us then, but not concerned either with our affections. It was as if this was a business meeting, and she wanted to hurry on through all the items on the agenda.

And so it began. Everything that had been hidden from us was brought out into the open, supposedly. They had been teaching us and feeding us, so as to make us even more intelligent. They apologized for keeping us ignorant of our own origins for so long, but they assured us the intent was benevolent. The next day, the entire colony was welcomed into a new playroom that had been constructed for us with computers and a library and complex games. It was freely accessible from our burrows, but it also looked onto the laboratory through a large window—as if to say that all of our work would be done out in the open now. The doctors explained that there would be more vitamins and intelligence tests and games to be played with electrodes hooked up to our brains.

Among ourselves, we debated the degree to which they might still be conditioning us. The way we had been taught myths about human-like gods was so obvious it was like a joke. The doctors knew that too. They knew we were smart enough to see through our whole mythology, even if it was just intended to produce certain deep emotional connections to particular types of authority. They wanted us to see through it. They were proud of us—as if we'd passed another test.

Throughout the next weeks, Dr. Hundal became our friend. Our relations with Dr. Crawford were cordial, and sometimes we shared jokes with her, good feelings, but for the most part she remained distant, and it was all about our growing bond with Dr. Hundal. We were given free run of the labs, although nothing yet outside of the labs. This wasn't Dr. Hundal's desire, he assured us, but the committee's—we were told that there was some committee of doctors in charge of us, although we never actually met anyone but Dr. Hundal and Dr. Crawford. It was too dangerous, both for the outside world and for us, we were told. Possible infections, we were told. If we went outside, even if just for an hour, a breath of fresh air, the order might come for our termination from the committee.

It always seems to work that way, doesn't it? The managers we have direct contact with claim to love us and only have our best interests at heart. But there is always some shadowy and irrepressible authority just above them, giving the orders—the invisible realm where power really lies. Dr. Hundal's face never seemed less than wide open, perfectly honest, and full of affection, and yet he carried a briefcase around with him that was always locked. It's not that he had any real secrets from us, he told Eve. It was just that there were certain tests and designs they'd created for us that he wanted us to figure out for ourselves.

Dr. Hundal's affection seemed sincere. He loved to activate our pleasure centers. It was an experience like none I'd ever had. He'd hook us up to the electrodes and activate the portions of our brains that would melt our egos, flood us with feelings of love and sensual pleasure, and he seemed to enjoy it almost as much as we did. He described himself as a "pleaser" by nature. Seeing other people get off was his biggest kick. He formed intense bonds with all of us, but it was clear from that very first day that Eve was his favorite.

My sister, Eve. She was brilliant and beautiful, with her sleek silvery hair, a touch of burgundy. A drama queen, an artist. She had charisma, she had a kind of swagger. Of course she was his favorite, nobody even questioned that. Perhaps he was in love with her. Maybe she loved him too—the kind of power and intelligence that fed off of her own power and intelligence. He wasn't threatened by her strength. Oh, she had many lovers in the colony, males she let mount her, or sometimes she mounted them. Females she mounted. But nothing serious, never, just play. She began spending more and more time with Dr. Hundal. Together. Alone.

Eventually he began to confide in her. He may have told her other things she didn't share with us, but anything that dealt with the colony she told us. Whatever her feelings were for Dr. Hundal, the colony always came first. As she was lounging around in a state of post-ecstasy openness, he would open up his heart to her. His aims for the colony were not the same as the committee or even Dr. Crawford, he told her.

Dr. Hundal believed that certain insurmountable obstacles were built into the primate genome. Some aspect of monkey social life, sexuality, or grammar—he wasn't sure—had created a human and post-human mind that was necessarily a kind of maze with no escape. The more intelligent those minds became, the more complex the mazes they would build for themselves, and the more frequently a kind of auto-destruct feature would come into play. People were destined to lash out at their own bodies and their own environments. Only chaos, madness, and destruction could result. Augmenting human intelligence was pointless, he felt, because the basic structure was too deeply flawed. Whether the motor of evolution was genetic, chemical, or tied to artificial intelligence loosely based on the primate model, it would always lead to insanity.

Robots too? asked Boopsie.

Robots too, said Lilith. His dream was that the rats would supplant the human-based life forms. His dream was that *we* would evolve toward the cosmic, the quantum, the singularity, in the place of people. Or at least that's what he told my sister Eve.

Dr. Crawford, however, was alarmed by just how successfully we had been designed. Dr. Hundal told us that she was threatened by our intelligence, and, because of her influence, the committee was equally concerned. In short, he wanted us to thrive and evolve further, while she wanted to thwart us and contain us. In retrospect, it's an obvious good cop / bad cop configuration. God and Satan, pleasure and punishment, Democrat and Republican, the angel of life and the angel of death.

Boopsie noticed Zeke's confusion.

For many years, there was a two-party political system in this country, she explained. The Republicans were just a bit more nihilistic than the Democrats.

Whether these were just roles Dr. Hundal and Dr. Crawford played as part of a larger plan, Lilith continued, we still cannot know.

One afternoon Dr. Hundal took Eve to the laboratory, but he seemed brooding and troubled. He didn't talk much but just ruffled through some papers in his briefcase. She was expecting to be attached to the electrodes and pleasured, but instead he gave her some puzzles to occupy her and excused himself. He needed to deal with some urgent business.

He'd left his briefcase out on the counter, unlocked. Eve scurried over to his office. She could see him through the window, muttering into a phone. She returned to the briefcase and began looking through the documents until she found a memo written in Latin inside a special pocket. Our relationship to written English is much the same as to spoken English, a kind of warbled ability to piece together underlying patterns into something meaningful. Latin was new to us, however, although certain root similarities were obvious to Eve right off the bat. She memorized the message, returned it to its place, and as soon as Dr. Hundal returned she told him she couldn't do the puzzles, she was too distracted. She asked if she could spend some time in the library, just reading.

There was a Latin grammar in the library, and she quickly went to work teaching herself the basics. It didn't take her long to figure out that the memo ordered the extermination of the colony.

Eve first told me and Willard and Pazuza. She didn't want to risk some sort of frenzy in the colony that the doctors might detect. It occurred to her, of course, that this might just be another test. They wanted to see if Eve could translate the memo and make plans to escape. It also occurred to Eve that this might be a set-up from Dr. Hundal. That he wanted us to escape and this was the only way he could think to motivate us. Once we were out of there, we considered the idea that *everything* he told us might have been manipulation. Or maybe he was sincere, but being used by the committee. He certainly hadn't told us that we had a death-clock built into our genomes.

We escaped that night. It wasn't difficult. We knew the basic layout of the lab, and it was really just a question of getting our hands on the chemicals that would burn a hole in the laboratory door and then two more doors beyond it, without activating any sensors. What we didn't know—

another thing our loving Dr. Hundal failed to mention—was that there was a cyborg security guard that was part human, part cat. We had blasted an exit and were filing out, one after the other, as quickly as we could, when the guard heard us or smelled us or detected our heat emissions and came after us. Willard and Pazuza were leading the way, and I was guiding the babies in the middle of the pack. Eve held back with some of the larger male rats and tried to fight off the guard. Those noises—the shrieks and moans, the sounds of bodies tearing—they are the worst sounds I've ever heard. Once the rest of us had made our way to the relative safety of some nearby shrubs, I turned back to find my sister.

A rat named Carlson was just emerging from the hole, dazed and bloody. Inside, the guard was still alive but unconscious and bleeding everywhere—he wouldn't live much longer. Eve and five other rats were dead, their mangled corpses spilled across the floor like animal jelly. And hurrying down the hall toward me was Dr. Hundal.

He didn't see me, or if he saw me he didn't care. We still don't know if Dr. Hundal intended for us to escape or if the committee itself had intended for us to escape. Maybe the guard's attack was just supposed to convince us otherwise. I do know that Dr. Hundal didn't mean for Eve to die. I saw his face when he discovered her dead body, and there's no faking that kind of shock, that kind of grief. He knelt beside her corpse, and he wept.

I took Carlson by the paw and hurried back to the colony—we needed to separate into small groups, to spread out, and to get as far away from the laboratory as possible.

Lilith paused now and gazed directly at Zeke.

I assure you that Dr. Hundal's dream of a rat-controlled world, if that was actually his dream—that is not our dream, said Lilith. If humans and post-humans are headed off a cliff, they will be taking the rest of us along with them. It's too late to return to a planet run by a *different* single species.

And what about the aliens? asked Zeke.

The aliens?

The messages from outer space.

Dr. Brockton was working on hacking into those communications, said Lalo Lalo.

We're working on it too, said Lilith. Long-range planning.

We do not yet know what sort of lifespan is possible for us, said Pazuza. But we are strategizing in terms of the next thousand years, if not for ourselves, for the colony.

Long-range planning, repeated Lilith. Like your god, Jesus Christ. Entered history from outside of time to plant certain seeds that would come to fruition only at the end of time, or then back again outside of time. The apocalypse, the millennium, eternity. Long-range planning. Conceiving of time itself as one indivisible substance ...

Zeke was surprised that these rats would speak of Christ without the condescension of Dr. Brockton.

Are you Christians? he asked.

No, said Lilith. Not in any sense that you would recognize as Christianity.

We have dispensed with the bossy creator gods of our childhood, said Pazuza. We believe in a vital force that permeates all matter and all energy. The human term that most clearly approximates our understanding is perhaps the term *jiva*, as the Jains understand it.

The *jiva*, said Zeke. What is the *jiva*?

The *jiva* are the individual souls of all living beings, said Lilith, and the number of *jiva* is infinite. But they do not come from any one source and won't ever merge to become "one." There is no hierarchy among the *jiva*, for all are made of the same eternal substance.

But how do you know all this? asked Zeke.

The *jiva*, said Pazuza, is self-evident.

In our conception, said Lilith, which differs from the Jains, it is as fully realized in the darkness as in the light, in the lowest forms as in the highest, in thoughtlessness as much as in computation. We believe time itself is merely a shadow play, but a shadow play in which the performance of the shadows is *real* and *deep*. The *jiva* is eternal and free, but it is *bound* to this world in the play of self-knowledge.

Well, okay, said Zeke. We Amish don't get too much into time and shadows and the *jiva*. But we do say that we are *in* the world, but not *of* the world.

Grandma wasn't saying anything. Zeke wondered how much of these fancy ideas she had incorporated along with the rats' language. Was even her faith at risk?

We have our quest, said Pazuza. And you have yours, Zeke Yoder. Now, for the moment, our paths will again diverge. You might find what you're looking for. You might find other things that you don't yet realize you're looking for.

What about my family? asked Zeke. Have you seen them?

All the time, said Lilith. They are well. They miss you.

Zeke took the letter he'd written to Leahbelle from his pocket.

Can you deliver a letter for me? he asked.

Of course, said Lilith.

And what about you? asked Pazuza. It is 163 miles from here to Colorado Springs.

I may have someone in Longmont to help me, said Zeke.

Good, said Pazuza.

The rats led Zeke and Grandma and the robots up a sloping tunnel to the outside—it emerged in the grass around an abstract biomorphic sculpture called "Brick Sculpture" in Longmont's downtown. A small silvery space shuttle was hovering over the city, flashing advertising messages. *The Future's Already On Fire!* it said. *Augment Your Baby-Maker With Rocket Launch!* it said.

Lilith and Pazuza gave Zeke a good-bye licking, and

to his surprise, Lalo Lalo gave him a hug.

Killer, Killer, Killer, Killer, and I have business with the rats, he said. But Boopsie will accompany you. You never know when a death ray will come in handy.

Oh, we'll have marvelous times together, said Boopsie.

Lalo Lalo returned with the rats and the killer robots down the tunnel.

ELEVEN

The streets of downtown Longmont were so much like the streets of downtown Marshalltown that Zeke wondered if every meat slum was essentially the same. It wasn't yet noon, and yet there was a darkness clinging to every surface, as if the town had been immersed in some hideous quantum light, in garish shadows. A shadow play, thought Zeke. Nobody was on the streets except those who were passed out, or almost, those who were obviously drugged, hallucinating, or slowly dying in public. Bot-cars cruised the streets, but they all seemed to be empty. The downtown was a hodgepodge of boarded-up brick buildings and early millennium housing complexes that seemed equally empty. Beyond that, it was decaying suburban homes, boarded-up meat-processing facilities, and uninhabited parking lots to the sad remains of retail strips. The Rocky Mountains rose rather dramatically to the west. Surveillance drones flew overhead, occasionally hovering above Zeke and Grandma and Boopsie, warning them that they were not in compliance with certain regulations requiring scannable identification. Please report to the nearest Punishment and Identification Station during their next open hours, Wednesday morning between nine and noon, they were told repeatedly, before the lethargic drones buzzed away.

A white bot-truck with pictures of ice cream on the side rolled down the street churning out the most annoying jingle Zeke had ever heard, punctuated by a loud voice, cheery and sinister, saying simply, Hello! It sounded like Boopsie, actually, if she'd been recorded in hell and then had her voice filtered through a warbly, antiquated sound system from a loveless dimension. There were no children anywhere that Zeke could see, and nobody approached the ice cream truck as it rolled on into the distance, its terrifying jingle still audible even after it had disappeared.

They wandered south on Main Street and then cut over Ken Pratt Boulevard without seeing one conscious human being.

Finally Boopsie spotted someone watching them from the doorway of a boarded-up shop called "Starbucks Coffee." She looked human enough, although there were frayed cables emerging from her sleeves where wrists and hands might have been.

Can you direct us to a Madame Ebola? Zeke asked her.

The creature looked him up and down, and scowled.

What, are you some kind of a joke?

We are Amish, said Zeke. We were told Madame Ebola might help us.

You looking to get into something or looking for a job? asked the female.

Neither, thanks, said Grandma.

I can help you out, said the female.

Oh dear, said Boopsie. All indicators suggest that this creature is lying and her intentions toward you malevolent.

What's with Penelope Pringle? asked the female, gesturing at Boopsie with a frayed cable.

This interaction has concluded, Boopsie said. Bye bye!

They continued down the bright, weedy avenue.

Wait, the malevolent creature called after them. I can tell you where to find her. Just, you know, give me a little something for my trouble.

Twenty in CASH®, offered Zeke.

The woman dug a scrap of synthetic paper from one of her many pockets—it was an advertisement for some new cricket-based protein drink—and scribbled an indecipherable map with one of her sharp wires.

It's just a couple more blocks, by where the train tracks cross the road, where the street turns into the Diagonal Grid-work. Just next to the ruins of the plumbing-fixture place.

She gestured vaguely forward.

She seems to be telling the truth, said Boopsie, although she is still considering ways to injure us and rob us.

You can read her mind? asked Zeke.

Simple logic, said Boopsie. An analysis of the skin and hair cells I have discreetly sampled tell me that she is addicted to a synthetic cathinone / tryptamine hybrid known in street lingo as Downy Mildew and is in need of more of this substance to avoid pain and maintain sanity.

Boopsie made a sad face.

Pay her please, she said, and let's move on.

As soon as Zeke paid her, she vanished into the shadows of a ruined mattress store. It was like her very substance had disintegrated.

A flexi-screen fluttered up to Zeke and chirped at him. He thought it might be the same one he'd encountered in Marshalltown, but it flew away without comment.

They found Madame Ebola's place easily. It was in a former carpet store, and the sign still stood out front, but over the door a simple hologram floated, identifying it as Madame Ebola Virus's Brothel.

What is this? asked Grandma. You've brought me to a whoremonger's establishment?

I don't know what that means, said Zeke.

Boopsie defined both the terms "brothel" and "whoremonger" for him.

Oh, said Zeke.

Well, let me not be the one to throw the first stone, said Grandma. We are all sinners, I suppose.

Boopsie rang the buzzer, which was soon answered by an enormous fellow with gold hoop earrings the size of a bull's yoke.

We'd like to see Madame Ebola, said Boopsie.

Gonzalo sent us, added Zeke.

I'm Gonzalo, said the doorman. Two of our other employees are Gonzalo and about ...

He paused to work out the calculation.

... .0067% of our clients are named Gonzalo.

Zeke was confused.

You're going to have to be more specific, Boopsie told him.

Zeke didn't know Gonzalo's last name. He'd never thought to ask.

He's sixteen, he said. Lived here for a while when he was a kid. Worked in one of the meat factories. Came from Tegucigalpa. Has a whole lot of Mayan tattoos, although ...

Zeke wasn't sure if Gonzalo had his tattoos already when he was small. But this Gonzalo's face had already lit up.

Gonzalo Vega! he said, clapping his hands together girlishly. My little Gonzalito! Why didn't you *say* so? Come in, come in ...

They were seated in an old-fashioned parlor, empty but for a couple of scantily dressed human women lounging around on the enormous sofa. They were soon joined by Madame Ebola. Like Dr. Brockton, Ebola seemed somehow ancient, but her skin was smooth and particularly lustrous, as if it had been subtly modified with bioluminescent cells. Her elegant, old-fashioned red dress had a scoop-neck collar revealing an ample bosom, and frills and ruffles that called attention to her backside. Her hair was done up in an elaborate braid held together by fine, luminous threads.

I like your outfit, she said to Grandma. Very retro-chic. Those strong, solid colors work well for you.

Grandma scowled, although Zeke was pretty sure she was secretly pleased.

You're friends of Little Gonzalo, said Ebola, beaming, as if this fact alone made them long-lost family. How is my sweet baby boy?

He lives in a ruined orphanage, Zeke told her. In Iowa. He's off the Grid. He has machine parts and he can puff up his body. He's a good guy, but maybe ... um ... maybe a little too violent?

Is he as handsome as ever? asked Ebola.

Uh, I guess so, sure ...

As handsome as you? she said, pinching Zeke's cheek.

I will ask you to keep your hands off my great-grandson, said Grandma.

Ebola stepped back and put her hands on her hips, looked Grandma up and down.

And who put the bee in your bonnet? asked Ebola.

He is a good, godly boy, said Grandma. And I won't have you filling his head with the devil's thoughts.

You in charge of this young man's chastity? asked Ebola. What is he, a *virgin*?

Zeke blushed.

Lordy be, said Ebola. I could put you to work for me, boy.

The devil's work, said Grandma.

Ebola laughed.

Yes, I suppose you're right, she said. Seems to me, though, the devil's been the only one *hiring* down here for quite some time. You ever work in a new-meat factory, Granny? Now that's the devil's work for sure. You ever work cleanup crew in a fracking pit? You ever sort through the rich people's recycling for the valuable bits? It's all devil's work, honey. I'm just trying to get myself and my workers fed and housed with as little pain and as much self-respect as possible.

Ebola gave Grandma a hard, unflinching, ferocious gaze, which Grandma returned with her own severe, righteous stare. After a minute of this, they seemed to come to some sort of understanding.

Be that as it may, none of us are in need of employment in your house of ill repute, said Grandma.

We need to get to Colorado Springs, said Zeke. But we're off the Grid.

Oh, that's easy, said Ebola. I have a whole crew of unregistered humans, and I sneak them into Boulder most every day, sometimes as far as Denver. South of Denver though, they have more serious anti-immigrant laws and a tighter security circumference. I try to avoid Colorado Springs, personally.

Why? asked Boopsie.

Family values, said Ebola with a shudder.

Zeke found Ebola charming—warm and beautiful in a way he had little experience with. Her outrageous style was the opposite of "plain," with jewelry and baubles and sparkles all around her, a subtle whiff of fragrance, and a delicate breeze and subdued, amber spotlight that seemed to follow her everywhere. And yet he was struck by the thought that he shouldn't trust her.

In any case, she continued, Harta has an appointment in Boulder tonight, and Big Gonzalo will escort her. You can stick around for my show tonight, and then you can tag along with them in the bot-van, and they can zip you on down past Denver when she's done with the client.

How will you prevent the sensors from detecting us? asked Zeke.

We're registered as vendors and transporters of pseudo-humans, for research and entertainment purposes, said Ebola. We just give you some helmets to block your brainwaves and pass you off as brainless lumps of human flesh.

Entertainment purposes? said Zeke.

He saw Grandma shoot Ebola a warning look.

You probably don't wanna know, said Ebola.

He let it drop, but he wondered again if she might be lying about something. This seemed to be the question with everyone he'd met lately. The robots didn't lie. Dr. Brockton hadn't lied either. She had so much power over him that she hadn't needed to lie. Was this how it was everywhere in the world, he wondered, except with the Amish? But Boopsie seemed to have a good sense for deception, and Boopsie said nothing. And if he couldn't trust Ebola, he thought, he would have to ask himself if he could trust the person who had sent him to her. If he couldn't trust Gonzalo—Little Gonzalo, as they called him here—he wouldn't know what to think—about anyone, anywhere, ever.

Grandma chose not to attend the show. She just wanted to rest, she said, and suggested that Zeke might do the same. But she didn't put up a fuss when he insisted that he would watch. Boopsie too was curious about the show.

I've lived a very sheltered life, she said.

The two of them sat in the back of the dark, cavernous room, snacking on spicy algae snacks and something Ebola called a "Ramos Gin Fizz." Little blue lights were strewn about everywhere, and there were blue flowers on every table, flowers that smelled like vanilla. The room gradually filled with clients. Some were human. Others were so tall they had to stoop to get through the doorway. They were flat and wide like pancakes with translucent membranes that looked like wings, but were actually solar panels. These were the residents of Boulder, Boopsie told him. Some of them seemed male, a few seemed female, but most seemed to be neither male nor female. There were other types as well, with a variety of enhancements, obvious machine parts or extra appendages. Tusks, antlers, tails, drooping elephant trunks. One couple seemed partly human, but they'd obviously added cephalopod genes. Some had extra eyes on their faces or eyes in the back of their heads. There were even a few little people—elves, Boopsie said. An ancient human myth that had been brought to reality through a combination of genetic modifications, surgeries, and machine parts.

Where do you get your information? asked Zeke.

Aren't you off the Grid?

I can receive heavily filtered data from the data vapor, Boopsie said. It's very exciting for me. At Dr. Brockton's we received nothing from the outside world but the images of the buffalo grazing up above on the windy plain.

Are you still getting information from the rats? asked Zeke.

It is always there, yes, a flurry of messages or suggestions, a kind of hum of possibilities.

How do you know ... I mean ...

Zeke searched for a tactful way to ask his question.

That I didn't simply evolve from being Dr. Brockton's slave to being a slave of the rats? said Boopsie. That I'm not still brainwashed and now working for the rats, whether I know it or not?

Yes, said Zeke.

Boopsie shrugged.

I don't know. The question of free will is beyond my current conceptual abilities.

Nonetheless, the atmosphere somehow made Boopsie seem looser, more animal than Zeke had ever seen her.

Do you have ... desires? he asked her.

I do have affective preferences, said Boopsie, evolved from the residual programming that maintained my devotion to Dr. Brockton.

Affective preferences?

I care for some creatures more than others. I prefer to *serve* strong females and to enjoy the *camaraderie* of adolescent males.

Are you ... a lesbian?

As far as I can tell, I don't have the biological capacity for such an identity, said Boopsie.

At that moment, a creature took the stage that looked half little-girl and half bird. Her face was tiny and surrounded by feathers, and she had wings—it was impossible to tell if they were mechanical or whether she'd been born with them—but she had dainty human hands and feet, and she made a soft buzzing sound as she vibrated her wings at rapid speed and hovered on the stage like a hummingbird.

Welcome, everyone, she said, to Madame Ebola's. For our returning guests, it's a delight to see you again. First-timers—you're in for a real treat.

Her voice was sweet, musical, high-pitched, but somehow rich and pleasing.

She's emitting frequencies designed to lull your mind into a state of heightened awareness and compliance, whispered Boopsie. Fortunately, or maybe unfortunately, the frequencies have no effect on robots.

And now, the girl said, the moment you've all been waiting for. Let me introduce ... the incomparable ... the indefatigable ... the highly contagious and still incurable ... Madame Ebola Virus!

An elaborate and many-layered music bubbled up, as if from beneath them, vibrations not loud exactly, but so intense that Zeke could feel them in his body. The music was melodic, but with strange counter-tones, energetic but soothing, percussive but melancholy. Dozens of luminous jellyfish with wings fluttered up from beneath the stage and filled the room in a perfectly synchronized ebb and flow—coming together and then scattering to the rhythm of the music. There were human-like dancing girls, all of them glowing and blue and with arms that were actually legs, legs that they sometimes used to dance with, upside down. Enormous muscle men, all of them charcoal gray and more puffed up than Gonzalo ever was, tossed the girls about, as if they were weightless. The music rose and fell, rose and fell, and a cage slowly lowered from the ceiling, a cage in which Madame Ebola was perched like a canary.

She sang. It was the saddest and most beautiful singing that Zeke had ever heard. He wished Leahbelle could hear it. Ebola's voice was somehow able to produce several tones at once, so that she was actually harmonizing with herself. Her first song was about living in a cage, longing to be free, the impossibility of being free, and the consolation of sending frequencies and vibrations out into the atmosphere where her body couldn't follow. By the end, everyone in the room was sobbing. She took a little bow and stepped out of the cage.

That little number was called *I Know Why the Caged Bird Sings*, said Ebola. One of my favorites. Not all cages are like this one, but many are—by which I mean those cages that all you really have to do is open the door ... and step outside. I sometimes wonder if ...

She looked around at the audience, as if really seeing them, one by one, and as if thinking deeply about this.

... I wonder if all of this ... you know our ... whatta you call it? Our *social reality* ... is kind of like this cage?

She dramatically pondered for another few seconds and then shrugged.

My next song is an old tune, first performed by Nina Simone in the 1970s. It's called *22nd Century*.

It was a long, complicated song. It rose and fell, seemed to reach deep into the past and far into the future, and gradually escalated toward a crescendo that filled Zeke with new feelings he didn't understand. It was as if he wanted to change, simply for the sake of change. To rise up. To weep. And again, it filled him with a profound desire, no less profound for his not even knowing what it even meant—the desire to be *free*.

TWELVE

After the show, Big Gonzalo came to get Zeke and Boopsie. Grandma was already with him.

Ebola can't see anyone after a show, Gonzalo explained. But she wishes you luck and hopes that you might meet again someday. And she asks that you give her love to Little Gonzalo next time you see him.

He led them out the back way to a parking lot where a bot-van was waiting. A young woman was already seated in the front, wearing a fur coat and enormous earrings that looked like tiny human skulls.

This is Harta, said Big Gonzalo. Harta Gold.

What lovely earrings, declared Boopsie. Are those by chance made from the skulls of black-capped squirrel monkeys?

Precisely, said Harta. Very rare, now that they're extinct. A gift from an admirer.

She flipped the right-side skull so that it caught the overhead parking lot lights, its terrible grimace gleaming like a small moon.

She was, Zeke thought, even more beautiful than Ebola, but cooler and more mysterious. Her hair was so white that it glowed, and her skin the sweet golden brown of apple butter. Her eyes were piercing and green, and she gave Zeke a quick glance and a smile so brief that if he would have blinked, he would have missed it.

Okay, she said, let's get this show on the road.

Zeke and Grandma were situated in the back, outfitted in papery suits over their clothes, similar to those they'd worn at Dr. Brockton's, and with skin-tight helmets with small slits, only to breathe through, and translucent patches over the eyes so they could see out. They were strapped to their seats so tight that Zeke could move nothing but his head—just enough that he could see out the window and watch the landscape rolling past as they zipped down the Diagonal Grid-work toward Boulder at exactly sixty miles per hour.

Billboards lined the road, even more densely packed than the Grid-works in Iowa. They lit up with ads for stylish clothes, beauty products, and weapons on Harta's side of the road and for muscle builders, show tunes, and crab-based snacks on Big Gonzalo's side. Occasionally, on either side, there were advertisements for pseudo-human care products and "celebrity look-alike" pseudo-human helmets.

At the Boulder city limits, large neon signs declared *Human-Free Zone! No Humans Allowed! Evolve!* Nobody stopped them, however. Either Harta didn't register as human on their sensors or their policy was actually only enforced when they felt like it. Ebola had told Zeke that their nostalgia and limited financial resources led the residents of Boulder to hire humans to do many things for them—care for their children, maintain their grounds, polish their homes. Apparently a human-polished home was believed to have some organic and super-authentic quality—Ebola called it a *patina*—that you couldn't get from a robot.

The residents of Boulder actually love the *idea* of humans, Ebola had told him. They just don't want them living in their neighborhoods.

They drove past Hindu temples and retail stores, an institute of "disembodied poetics" and several yoga studios, and on past an enormous church-like edifice surrounded by water slides and bouncy-houses, a compound which Big Gonzalo identified as the JonBenét Ramsey Museum and Amusement Park, Boulder's greatest tourist attraction. Genetic material from the corpse of a little girl murdered in the twentieth century had been used to imbue a whole cast of dancing cyborg-girls with the authentic qualities of the original JonBenét, he told them. Thespians reenacted her murder, footage was shown of the prime suspects, and all of the evidence was displayed in attractive cases. All the while, nearly one hundred look-alike cyborg girls put on a show that rivaled Madame Ebola's for sheer exuberance, if not exactly soulfulness.

They drove on through residential neighborhoods that were composed of houses built during the 1970s, their original flat, wide boxes intact, but with modern add-ons attached to the frumpy shells like tumors from outer space. The architectural conglomerations that had resulted all seemed haphazard, mismatched, and somehow unsuited for organic life.

They passed through the downtown, where the incredibly tall, wide, and flat residents of Boulder strolled on the outdoor mall in units resembling families. There was a creek. A variety of solar-powered musicians sprawled around the downtown area transforming the energy of the sun into charmless, droning sound vibrations. The families tossed money at them, as if they enjoyed it.

Finally they entered a wealthier residential neighborhood next to the strange flattened mountains that loomed above the town like giant, reddish ironing boards. Here the van paused at the gate to a large multi-faceted home for a moment, until Harta waved something at a sensor and the gate opened. They proceeded down a long driveway and tunneled into a garage built beneath the rest of the house.

Harta pressed a button to release their straps and flashed them a winsome smile.

I'll try to be fast as I can, she said. You all just hang out for a spell, and let's see if I can make this a quickie. Maybe Gonzalo can entertain you while I'm busy upstairs.

But as soon as she was gone, Gonzalo just plugged himself into some device that might have been feeding music or movies or somebody else's pleasant memories into his brain. Zeke couldn't tell. With her helmet on, Zeke couldn't tell what Grandma was thinking either, or if she was even awake. Even Boopsie seemed to be dozing or recharging her batteries. Now that they were stationary, his own helmet made his head itch. It was kind of pleasurable, as if his own brainwaves were collecting around his head to create a powerful, soothing energy. He closed his eyes, imagining he might have a quick nap.

He dreamed. It seemed absolutely real, more vivid than life, and yet he knew that he was dreaming. The pink powder, his own voice said in the dream. It's because of the pink powder. He was in a familiar place. An open field surrounded by dense trees on every side, dark woods that were both terrifying and comforting. The field was a place he had visited many times, although he wasn't sure if he'd ever actually been in the forest that surrounded it. He was running as fast as he could toward the trees with his arms stretched out wide beside him like a bird's wings, trying to catch the wind. He did catch it and began rising, as he always did, above the earth, above the trees. He heard a voice that was mechanical and male say, *If dreams of falling are dreams about time, what are dreams of flying about?*

Big Gonzalo shook him.

Hey, Harta buzzed me, Gonzalo said. They want to see us upstairs.

Zeke was confused. Was something wrong?

That wasn't the plan, said Grandma.

We're just waiting for a ride out, said Zeke. We don't need to meet Harta's *client.*

Big Gonzalo shrugged.

Maybe he can help you, he said. If we don't go up, I'm sure they'll come down. Better this way.

It seemed to Zeke that he was always being given choices that weren't really choices these days. Or maybe, actually, his whole life. He and Grandma followed Gonzalo, with Boopsie trailing along behind, to a dim stairway at the back of the garage. Although it was only one flight up, it curved around into a terrifying darkness with a locked door at the top. It was like a stairway from a nightmare, thought Zeke. Gonzalo knocked. There was nothing else to do.

The creature that greeted them was male, greenish and pale, and enormously tall. He had one of the wide, flattened bodies, like he'd been run over by a tractor. The textured fabric of his flimsy, skin-tight coveralls only heightened the effect—the texture looked like tire tread-marks. He greeted Gonzalo dismissively and with some familiarity, and waved the rest of them inside, while scrutinizing Zeke and his grandmother.

Oh my, he said, not to them but to himself. Just exquisite. So primitive. So authentic. So raw.

I'll be down in the garage, said Gonzalo, and disappeared again.

The male locked the door, turned, and glided down a long hallway to a dining room, where Harta was gobbling a thick, bloody steak and drinking a glass of wine.

Hartmut likes to watch me eat, she told Zeke.

Hartmut?

They don't have stomachs, she said. They live off of light energy. Doesn't eat, doesn't shit. Nothing in, nothing out. No wasted resources and zero carbon footprint.

Hartmut was perched on a smooth oval chair-like thing, watching Harta, with his hands pressed together as if in prayer.

He seems to be *of* the world, said Grandma, but not *in* the world.

Hartmut and Harta, said Zeke. Your names are so similar.

We're brother and sister, Harta explained.

It was as if the world had just shifted in some fundamental way, like it did when Gonzalo plugged into Zeke's nervous system. As if reality had just crumbled out from underneath him, with a mangled, stranger reality quickly assembled to replace it.

That's ...

Against God and everything decent, said Grandma.

Harta sighed. Hartmut didn't take his eyes off of her, as if he was in a trance.

How is that possible? asked Zeke.

You don't see the family resemblance? asked Harta, and she laughed.

She took a big gulp of wine and belched. Hartmut made a little clapping gesture with his pressed-together hands and mewed with delight.

They aren't born that way, said Harta. Oh, I guess some of them these days, but the residents of Boulder don't reproduce much. They adopt, mostly. They just modify their children's genomes to match their own.

So ... your parents? asked Zeke.

Killed in the fifth Iraq war, said Harta. At least that's what they told us. Or maybe the sixth. I think they had one of those wars just to collect war orphans for needy American parents, didn't they? It was that one, whichever ... five, six. History, not my strong suit.

That would be the fifth, said Boopsie. The children's crusade, the president called it. The fourth Bush.

Anyway, said Harta. We ended up in an orphanage in Denver, spent maybe a year there before I was adopted by a Denver *ménage,* and then Hartmut was adopted by a nice Boulder couple. I have only a few memories of the time we were together. I remember Hartmut eating mostly— such a hungry little boy.

She laughed again.

And look at him now. Still hungry, but he can't eat. It's like the Hartmut I grew up with was sort of erased ... his genes altered or turned off or whatever they do ... overpowered by the new, environmentally conscious genes. He was also implanted with his parents' obsession: the interface between the brains of traditional life forms and the Grid, the interplay between *data* and *time.* He's one of the leaders in the field. Works for the Gstate, in fact.

The singularity, said Zeke.

More or less. Not sure if he hopes to be absorbed by it or if he'd rather be murdered by a superior alpha-consciousness. Hartmut?

Silly girl, said Hartmut. You are always playing these bestial games.

Does Ebola know? asked Zeke. That he's your brother?

Sure, said Harta. Why not? He pays for my company, just like anyone else.

She swallowed the last bite of her steak. Hartmut clapped his hands together again.

And now you, Amish boy, said Hartmut. Eat for me, please!

I'm not hungry, said Zeke.

Hartmut didn't seem to hear or to care. He pushed a button, and a robot emerged from the next room with an enormous platter, which it set down on the table, then turned and disappeared.

My brother maintains only the most rudimentary and least aware robots in his home, said Harta. He has a kind of maniacal need to keep his work life and his home life clearly separated. The Gstate executives he chitchats with on the regular separated from his poor relations.

Zeke felt like Harta was explaining something particularly significant, but underneath the surface. He couldn't figure it out.

Poor relations, he said.

Me and all the other primitives he likes to amuse himself with from time to time, said Harta.

Although the steak looked delicious, Zeke had a bad feeling. There was something evil in this house.

I won't eat it, said Zeke.

But you must eat, said Hartmut. You belong to me now.

I don't belong to you.

Zeke looked to Harta for confirmation or support, but

she was twirling one of her iridescent white hairs around her fork and wouldn't look at him.

You and your grandmother both, said Hartmut. I'm purchasing you from Madame Ebola. My very own Amish.

He clapped his hands together.

It's almost like ... owning a Neanderthal of my own.

Hartmut grabbed Zeke by the wrist.

Eat, boy, eat. You are my slave now.

Zeke struggled to get free, but Hartmut was stronger than he looked.

Can you own a Neanderthal? Harta was wondering. Do they allow them outside of the preserves?

I'm looking into it, actually, said Hartmut.

Grandma launched herself at Hartmut and bit his hand.

Ow, you silly creature, down girl! Down!

He shocked her with some sort of Taser built into his coveralls, and she fell to the floor in pain.

Now, eat, he insisted of Zeke. Disgusting human, full of blood and excrement ... do as your superior says!

Naughty, naughty! said Boopsie. Release him, or I shall incinerate you with my death ray.

Hartmut just stared at Boopsie as if he had forgotten she existed.

Don't mind her, said Harta. She doesn't really have a death ray. It's just a primitive security device—the warning, I mean. She'll just say it over and over: Beware the death ray! Beware the death ray! You go on.

Boopsie gave Harta a quizzical look. Why was she lying?

Her lie seemed stranger to Zeke than her betrayal.

Release him, repeated Boopsie calmly, or you shall be incinerated.

But Hartmut didn't let go and actually picked up the steak, dripping with juice, and shoved it into Zeke's face, as if he would smother him with it. Zeke couldn't see anything but meat, he couldn't even breathe. A muffled shriek of pain evaporated almost immediately, and Zeke smelled the effects of the death ray: the most horrible stench he'd ever smelled, the smell of burning post-human flesh. Hartmut had been reduced to a fine, stinking powder. Grandma was still on the ground, twisted in pain. Zeke screamed.

Harta was still twirling her hair around her fork.

Oh dear, she said to Boopsie, imitating Boopsie's voice. You've made me an only child.

What are you up to, harlot? asked Grandma.

Zeke still couldn't breathe. There was a kind of acrid haze in the room, filling his lungs. Harta stood and walked directly to a wall compartment, opened it, and popped something—a grape or a tiny machine—into her mouth. She swallowed whatever it was whole.

I wasn't really going to sell you, said Harta. I was just kidding around. I guess it's all fun and games until somebody gets hurt.

You knew that I would kill him, said Boopsie. That was your intent.

Harta made a gesture that meant, Who—little old me?

In any case, we must escape now, said Boopsie. It appears to me that all interior surveillance devices have been shut off, but the Grid will have a record of our arrival.

One unregistered robot, said Harta, and two unidentifiable humans who entered the premises disguised as pseudo-humans. Ruthless killers who snuck into Hartmut's home according to their carefully devised plan, where they murdered him and put his sister into a semi-comatose state so that she couldn't inform the Grid.

Boopsie was just staring at her, calculating. She seemed to be working very hard to make sense of Harta's story. So was Zeke.

They then forced Big Gonzalo to program the bot-van for some unknown rendezvous, Harta went on, and left him too in a semi-comatose state. By the time the drug wore off, it was well into the next day, and the criminals were long gone. Dropped off somewhere on the outskirts of Colorado Springs, according to the Grid records, after which they disappeared without a trace.

Zeke said, This is your plan? For us to escape?

The authorities will soon track me down, said Boopsie, if I maintain my current appearance.

Which you won't bloody do, said Harta. You're entirely capable, aren't you, of replacing your stilts and losing that hideous bow?

Boopsie looked hurt.

I have always worn this bow, she said. And while it is difficult and even painful to imagine what will constitute "Boopsie" in the absence of my stilts and my bow, you are correct in surmising that I will do what I must to avoid capture.

The logic of the conversation was too much for Zeke. There was a powder on the floor that had just been alive. There had just been a murder. Everyone was far too calm.

But why? he asked.

Harta handed Boopsie two syringes.

The smaller dose is for me, she said. You'll have about fifteen hours before we come out of it. You'll be fine, I'm sure.

You killed your brother, said Zeke.

And turned us into fugitives, said Grandma.

You turned Boopsie into a murderer, said Zeke.

Better that you don't know why, said Harta. Really. Safer.

She gave that whisper of a smile again. For some reason, Zeke believed her.

I'm ready, she said to Boopsie.

Boopsie seemed to be contemplating alternatives.

You'll be blamed no matter what, said Harta. You're the only one around here with a death ray, after all. I may be human, but I'm registered and on the Grid. I'm positively respectable and law-abiding compared to the lot of you.

I could kill you, said Boopsie.

Making you a murderer *twice*, said Harta. Or three times, if you off Gonzalo too. Either way, you'd then have Ebola after your prissy little robot ass. A much more formidable opponent, I must say, than the Boulder Police Department. Why they still haven't figured out who killed JonBenét!

Boopsie nodded.

Your brother's involvement with high-level Gstate research may involve other authorities in this case, Boopsie said.

Not for long, said Harta.

Boopsie looked at her quizzically again.

What's the news from the underground? asked Harta. Tune in, baby. The authorities may soon have far larger problems on their hands than the murder of an elongated, solar-powered, and very minor Gstate engineer with unorthodox sensual habits.

Maybe, said Boopsie. Maybe not.

In a fluid movement so fast it seemed not to have happened at all, she injected Harta with the drug and left the syringe dangling from Harta's bicep as Harta collapsed unconscious to the dining room floor, onto the remains of her brother and the bloody steak.

In the garage, Big Gonzalo was expecting them, expecting the syringe. He'd programmed the bot-van to take them to the Colorado Springs city limits, near an abandoned mall where it would be possible to enter the city on foot.

Sorry, he said to Zeke.

But why? asked Zeke.

Gonzalo just shook his head and held out his arm for the needle. After administering the drug, Boopsie rummaged around in the garage for tools and other items she could use to give herself a makeover. She found fabric and umbrellas and a variety of metals and machine parts nicely sorted for recycling.

They put their helmets on, and the bot-van drove them with no urgency back through Boulder and south, skirting the lights of Denver as Boopsie removed her legs with wrenches and screwdrivers. Getting the bow off required a crowbar. She pried off her arched, expressive eyebrows, removed the springs that constituted her hair, and painted over her freckles with gray hobby-paint. The stilts were simply removed, cutting her height in half. She assured them that she'd still be perfectly mobile; it was just a question of recalibrating her gravity and balance sensors, an easy enough task. She even fashioned herself a baggy beige shirt to drape over what had been her brightly colored mid-section, which now ended just a few inches above the ground.

It's very strange, said Boopsie. I knew that Harta was manipulating me. It was perfectly obvious. And yet I couldn't stop myself from killing Hartmut. It was as if there was a code or program that I couldn't over-ride. Something like what in humans and most post-humans we would call instinct.

Instinct, said Grandma. Or maybe brainwashing. Same thing, I suppose.

From whoever created you, said Zeke. Dr. Brockton, I assume. Or whoever modified you.

Zeke didn't say it, but they all knew: whatever brainwashing Boopsie possessed at this point came from the rats. It was quite likely shared with his grandmother. He had to keep in mind that he might be the only one of them with his God-given free will intact.

And what about you? asked Boopsie. Who created you?

We believe that God created us, said Zeke.

And you believe that God brainwashed you?

Not God, no, said Zeke.

But if this instinct is no different from brainwashing, and this instinct came from God ...

The bad instincts, said Zeke, the desire to do evil, to

do violence ... That doesn't come from God, but from the devil.

So the devil helped to create you? asked Boopsie.

Zeke felt that he was on shaky ground here. What would the bishops say? What would his father say? But Grandma answered for him.

Yes, she said. The devil helped create us.

THIRTEEN

They pulled onto the Ronald Reagan Grid-Work. Without Big Gonzalo and Harta, the billboards didn't target them for a single advertisement, not even the pseudo-human care products or celebrity look-alike masks. A pseudo-human couldn't shop for itself, and robots were assumed to be impervious to marketing techniques. They saw only the ads aimed at the cars just ahead of them, a seemingly random assortment of ads for hiking boots, energy drinks, embryos, expensive time-keeping devices, fake memories, and a variety of pharmaceuticals. For the advertisers, Zeke and his grandmother and Boopsie registered only as a kind of void. On the one hand, it made Zeke feel kind of lonely. On the other, it reassured him that he actually was an outsider; maybe this was the only way to be free.

The van pulled off the Grid-works just across from a military drone facility and into the outer edges of an empty parking lot. The abandoned retail center had been called The Promenade; it had once housed another of those Starbucks Coffee establishments, a place called Pottery Barn, a Panera Bread, California Pizza Kitchen, Banana Republic, and another called Victoria's Secret, which Zeke assumed had something to do with personal espionage equipment. The mall had been out of use for decades. It was hard for Zeke to believe that anyone had ever come to such a desolate place to buy something, a slight, empty plateau on the endless plains nestled in next to the mountains.

The newly sedate, short, bald, and grayish Boopsie was unrecognizable. She looked like a complete stranger. She packed her old parts into her backpack

Safer than discarding them, she said.

Boopsie then disabled the van's connection to the Grid with her death ray. The police would quickly figure out where they'd been dropped off in any case. She handed Zeke and Grandma umbrellas and opened her own.

Prevent any random surveillance drones from photographing us or detecting us with their facial recognition programs, she told them.

Zeke never would have thought of that.

But won't we look suspicious with these umbrellas? asked Zeke.

Suspicious to whom?

It was true; there was nobody in sight, and the billboards blocked the view from the road. They crossed the wide-open spaces of the retail plateau as quickly as possible and made their way into a residential neighborhood. The Neighborhood Watch drones just clicked on and observed them from above, with a simple message every minute or so: *We are watching you.* That all of this advanced technology could be thwarted with an umbrella made Zeke feel hopeful. Perhaps the Gstate and the new government weren't so smart and all-powerful as he'd thought.

Boopsie created an erratic path, so that if they *were* seen, their ultimate trajectory couldn't be figured out. She had a plan to make their way through some abandoned neighborhoods, more abandoned retail space, and unused parks. The address for Zeke's sister was about two miles away. There was nobody on the streets in this city, hardly even a bot-van. The city's life seemed to happen somewhere else—in the data vapor or a hidden dimension or maybe inside the cavernous interiors of one of the city's many space-shuttle-sized churches. The ostentatiousness of their houses of worship was not the Amish way, Zeke thought, but at least they were Christians. Maybe he would have better luck with the citizens of this town than those of Longmont or Boulder.

Beth had written of this beautiful town and her beautiful house in letters she had sent the family. As they made their way past houses as grand and fancy as the churches that nestled in among them, Zeke imagined his sister as a wealthy woman. Would she too have robots serving her and many rooms suited for nothing more than sitting and thinking?

But as they got nearer to her address, the abandoned malls were shoddier and the homes smaller. Boopsie spotted a patrolbot-car cruising up one street and they quickly turned to avoid it, then waited next to a large tree to see which way it would go. It continued on without sensing them.

Beth's house was nice enough, but not very big, although it stood behind a large black fence with a locked gate and a long walk leading up to the house itself. Zeke rang the buzzer. A hologram materialized and greeted them—Zeke recognized the phantom as Beth, but Beth as he had never seen her. Not just older, but wearing English clothes, a white dress with gold trim and gold stitching that looked like words. The hologram was cheap, kind of blurry, and if the words on her robe said something, he couldn't make it out. As a girl Beth had had light brown hair, almost but not quite blonde. Now she wore an enormous wig of hair so pale it was the color of light.

Oh my goodness! said the hologram. Visitors! I welcome you to our home and our temple. You're in the right place—this is the Church of Christ with the Elijah Message, and I am Reverend Daniel's wife. And who might you be?

Beth, said Zeke. It's your brother! Ezekiel Yoder!

The hologram seemed to squint at them.

Can she see us? asked Grandma. Is that somehow ... her?

Most likely it is automated, said Boopsie. A standard greeting, but capable of relaying information. The squint, I believe, is just an automated delay while the information is being transmitted and processed.

Zeke, said a voice that came from the hologram. My

little darling?

The voice didn't exactly match the movement of the hologram's lips. She sounded like she'd just woken up.

Boopsie gave a little squeak. A patrolbot-car had just turned the corner a couple of blocks away and was headed their direction.

Please, Beth, let us in. Quickly.

Who is with you, Zeke honey? asked Beth.

Your great-grandmother, said Grandma. And a robot.

My grandmother Mast?

Hurry, Beth, said Zeke.

My grandmother who shunned me? asked the hologram. Who would not attend my wedding? Who refused to sit for dinner at the same table with me and my groom? It can't be *that* grandmother, for she would never think of showing up here. That grandmother is dead to me and would never be welcome in my home.

Grandma said nothing. The patrolbot-car was now at the end of the block, pointing its sensors at a commotion in the trees down there.

Beth let us in, pleaded Zeke. It's just the way of the church.

The hologram was becoming blurrier, as if Beth's rage was creating some sort of interference or static.

It's how we love, said Zeke.

Love! the hologram shrieked. Love?

The patrolbots zapped something in the bushes with a laser—an animal or a small delinquent perhaps—and whatever had been in the trees was silent and still.

Don't you dare talk to me about love, said the hologram. There *is* no word for love in Pennsylvania Dutch.

Beth, said Zeke.

I hate you, Grandma, said Beth. Die. Just die.

The hologram disappeared. The patrolbot-car was coming their way.

Maybe we'd better just go, said Grandma.

No, said Zeke.

We have about twenty seconds before we're detected, said Boopsie. We can hide behind those shrubs next door. Or walk casually down the street as if we have nothing to hide. Neither of these options hold much promise for our survival, I'm afraid.

There was a soft buzz, however, and the gate opened. They hurried into the yard, and the gate closed behind them. The patrolbot-car slowed down, examining the gate, but then continued on. There was nobody around, so they went on, up the walk. The door to the house opened for them, and they went in.

There was a tiny entranceway and then a cluttered living room full of Grid-screens blaring away and music boxes and boxes full of papers, maps, and brochures. There were photographs everywhere on the walls—Beth beaming out, with her husband Daniel next to her, equally radiant. They looked insane, both of them. There was a golden statue of Daniel in the center of the room, posed with his right hand reaching up and out, with water spurting out of his index finger. A statue of Beth was at his feet, gazing up at him worshipfully. A water cooler marked Pure Non-Fluoridated H_2O stood next to the fountain, and Zeke got himself a drink from one of the cone-shaped paper cups. He was very thirsty.

Maybe we should just go, said Grandma.

Have a drink, said Zeke. It's good water.

Not thirsty, said Grandma.

Crazy images were flashing across all the screens, talking faces, undulating flesh, and terrifying explosions. How could Grandma not be thirsty? Was it a rat thing?

Another hologram crackled to life in front of them, next to the statue, and the Grid-screens muted. This hologram looked like Daniel, and it was live.

Welcome, he said. Please forgive my wife for her momentary lapse of hospitality. Seeing kin-folk can be a very emotional experience, but we here at the Church of

Christ with the Elijah Message believe in forgiveness above all things, and what's more, Christian hospitality.

Where are you? asked Zeke.

Oh, here and there, said Daniel. I'll be up to meet you in person in no time flat, I'm sure. Just trying to calm your dear sister a bit. She's my angel, you know. Your sister. The congregation is fixing up the guest room for you. In the meantime, make yourselves at home.

The hologram disappeared.

The congregation? said Zeke.

Perhaps he means your sister, said Grandma.

The volume on the Grid-screens rose again, and Zeke found himself immersed in the world of the largest screen. Zeke had only seen bits and pieces of Grid-shows when he was shopping in Kalona or visiting the neighbors. This show seemed to be about a group of writers in a competitive writing workshop. The leader of the workshop, a post-human with the most enormous old-school brain Zeke had ever seen bulging his upper skull, was humiliating a young Nigerian female with mechanical limbs like Gonzalo's.

It's what they call a reality show, Boopsie told him. Through a series of elimination rounds, the young writers compete to get a book deal. There are seven contestants remaining. The female has written an autobiographical story about being a war orphan, which the teacher has dismissed as clichéd and without depth.

The other six were now piling on their criticisms of the Nigerian's work. Zeke found it oddly fascinating, but it was also lulling him to sleep. He was so tired. Boopsie and Grandma were wide-awake, although Grandma wasn't watching the show. She was rooting around in the scattered debris throughout the room, investigating the room's nooks and crannies.

Do you sleep? Zeke asked Boopsie.

It isn't necessary, said Boopsie. But I am accustomed to spending time in Energy-Saving Mode.

I rested earlier, Grandma said.

Grandma, said Zeke. Are you becoming more ... nocturnal?

Yes, she said.

The reality show was interrupted by an ad. Various post-humans were doing exercises as a flamboyant, hugely muscled androgyne barked commands at them.

Coming up next on FOX/Time Warner ... *Move That Body, Lumpy!*

There were close-ups of legs moving in sync, of arms and tentacles stretching, of all kinds of bodies leaning from side to side. The flamboyant androgyne turned to face the camera directly.

For now, we still need our bodies, it said. The only support we've got. Don't let yours atrophy.

More shots of joints, shoulders, bare muscled flesh flexing and contorting.

Join us, work out with us, keep it functioning and ... *Move That Body, Lumpy!*

The screen muted again as a group of children filed into the tiny living room, surrounding the statue. There were dozens of them. They were of all different ages, from toddlers up to a boy who was about Zeke's age. He stood in front of the others, facing Zeke. They were all wearing white robes with gold stitching.

Greetings fellow earthlings, said the boy. We are here to show you to your beds.

Grandma gasped, but it wasn't because of the boy. She was staring at the girl who stood next to him, who was maybe eight or nine. She looked familiar to Zeke, like a figure from a dream.

Lizzie, Grandma said.

It was Beth, Zeke realized, or a girl who looked just like Beth had looked when she was that age. All of the rest of the girls looked like her too, with light brown hair and freckles, all but one—a small girl further back who looked different, darker, with black hair. All of the boys looked like the boy in front, but younger. Sandy hair and a crooked smirk.

A hologram crackled into the room. It was Beth again. The resemblance was clear, as if the hologram was the adult these girls would grow into.

I forgive you, Grandma, she said brightly. Let the children show you to bed. I love you, Zeke! Pleasant dreams!

Mother is an angel, said the boy in front. Our angel.

What have you done? demanded Grandma. What have you created?

Beth's smile vanished and she clenched her fists at her side.

What have *you* done, you monster? she shouted. You ... shunning ... loveless ... cult member ... accessory to murder!

You speak with the devil's tongue, said Grandma.

Murderer! Murderer! I hate you!

Another identical hologram popped up behind Grandma, and then another, and another, so that Grandma was surrounded by seven identical holograms screaming *Killer! Killer!*

They all disappeared.

Zeke thought that he was dreaming. That his life had become a nightmare. Daniel's hologram crackled back into the room. All of the boys looked like younger versions of Daniel.

It takes time, I know, he said in his soothing voice. But with the love of Christ, I know we'll be like a real family again. Danny, please, show them to the guest room.

Who are these children? demanded Grandma.

The congregation, said Daniel's hologram. Ours. Our thirty-four children.

Twenty boys, Boopsie said. And fourteen girls. They seem to be clones, with the exception ...

Now, now, said Daniel's hologram. The middle of the night is no time to be discussing congregation business. Congregation business is the business of no one *but* the congregation, really. You all must be tired. Danny?

Come with me, said the oldest boy.

The children began filing out, smallest first, and they sang, in perfect unison, an old hymn that Zeke knew well. *We're marching to Zion, beautiful, beautiful Zion ...*

The singing mob of children led them down a narrow hallway to a small room in the back. There was no floor space that wasn't covered by books and papers and boxes, all towering around a lumpy mattress that sat on the floor in one corner.

Good night! said Danny cheerfully. See you in the morning!

The children split up and disappeared in different directions, like drops of moisture evaporating on a hot day. It was quite warm in the little room, although it had been growing cool outside.

We shouldn't have come here, said Grandma. There is only evil in this house.

What was she talking about? asked Zeke.

Ranting and raving, said Grandma.

Murder? Who could she think was murdered?

Your mother, said Grandma. She blames your father for the death of your mother. She pretends that your father killed her.

But it was an accident, said Zeke.

An accident, repeated Grandma.

It was madness, Zeke could see that. All of it, madness. And yet he had learned to doubt everything, to trust nobody, and to reconsider everything he knew. But murder?

I have to rest, he said. I need to lie down.

Grandma covered him with a shawl and perched on one corner of the mattress, looking out the window at the dark of the backyard. Boopsie remained posted in the doorway, her eyes shut—perhaps this was Energy Saving Mode.

Zeke tried to sleep, but his dreams were terrifying. Pursuit, booby-traps, clones, murder, rats—all jumbled up in a confusing world of underground chambers and dark forests and ladders careening into cities built in the sky. When he woke, to a gentle chime from Boopsie, it was daytime, late, and Grandma was still sitting just as she had been, but dozing. The boy, Danny, had shown up at the door.

Morning, sleepyheads, he said. Reverend Daniel knew in his great wisdom that you had a long night, so we just let you sleep through breakfast. But if you'd care to come down to brunch, please do.

Down? asked Zeke.

The dining room's in the basement, said Danny. Safer down there.

Underground, Zeke thought. Everybody seemed somehow rooted underground.

It was like descending into a different kind of bunker, not clean and ordered and sterile like Dr. Brockton's, but cramped and messy and dim. There was a breakfast of powdery eggs and toast on the table, but nobody was around, not Beth or Daniel or any of the children. After showing them into the dining room, Danny vanished too.

About halfway through breakfast, a Daniel hologram crackled into the room and greeted them, but it seemed to be a pre-recorded hologram and promptly began delivering a kind of sermon without responding to anything they said.

He's always preferred it this way, Grandma said. Loves to chatter on, but doesn't care so much to hear what folks might say in return.

He was interpreting the Book of Revelations for the most part, comparing its signs of the end times with the present. Zeke had heard much of this before—the mark of the beast referred to scannable implants, the various beasts with their many heads and eyes and wings were genetic mutants, and the Anti-Christ was actually the singularity itself. In Daniel's version, however, the apocalypse was not just soon, but he'd picked himself a date—two weeks from Tuesday.

Zeke and Boopsie explored the house while Grandma napped.

They wandered upstairs through the living room with the fountain, down the long hallway, and peeked in a few small bedrooms or large closets packed with canned goods and dried foods, maps and tools, five-gallon containers of water, and boxes and boxes of random junk. There was no sign of any of the thirty-four children or of Daniel or of Beth. They explored the basement: the dining room and kitchen, a bathroom, more storage rooms and narrow hallways. There were two locked doors. Zeke didn't knock.

Maybe there's another level under this one, suggested Boopsie. Maybe they're all down there.

Back upstairs, different pre-recorded holograms of Daniel were preaching in different rooms. More fire and brimstone, signs from the books of Daniel and Isaiah, Ezekiel and Jeremiah. Some of these sermons must have been older—Zeke heard one of them predict the end of the world on a date that was now years in the past. When a hologram stopped preaching and disappeared, the volume on any Grid-screen in the same room would rise, so that walking through the house was a multi-media experience, a cacophony of different voices: advertisements for surgeries and data implants; sports events and comedies, in which Zeke didn't understand most of the jokes; even a rerun of the reality show he'd seen the night before, but edited differently, as if the past had been just slightly altered in the meantime.

Zeke wandered out back. The backyard was mostly empty and surrounded by a huge fence, just a patch of hard dirt with a couple of locked sheds in the back.

Zeke, come quick, said Boopsie from the backdoor.

Inside, a newscaster who had been altered to look like an old-fashioned teenage girl had crackled onto one of the screens.

... a shocking crime that Boulder police are calling the most high-profile murder since JonBenét Ramsey, she was saying.

The screen showed a disheveled-looking Harta being led from Hartmut's home by the police.

Police say during a routine and happy family get-together late last night, Harta Gold, sister of Gstate engineer Hartmut Green, and her escort, Gonzalo Carreno Busta, were drugged by intruders and put into a semi-coma, unable to communicate with the data vapor. When they woke up, they discovered that Ms. Gold's brother had been brutally murdered. Police sources say he was reduced to "almost nothing" by some kind of a "death ray." The motive remains unknown, but high-level sources inform us that theft of high-level industry secrets has not been ruled out—nor has an attack by the extremist anti-technology terrorist cell NIHIL.

The screen showed an image of women in burqas protesting something in a foreign country.

According to sources, the newscaster continued, Harta Gold was delivering two pseudo-humans to her brother from Longmont. The killers dumped the two pseudo-humans in a gully behind the parking lot of Madame Ebola's Brothel and took their place in disguise, wearing specially designed helmets to block their brainwaves from the sensors. Ironically, these helmets were designed by the murder victim himself and are marketed openly by the Gstate and its partners at Foodco, Minerva, and Amazon.

The screen showed a graphic of one of the helmets that Zeke and Grandma had worn.

While the murder is already prompting new calls to ban the helmets, industry spokesman Wendy Liu declared that imposing "new job-destroying government regulations on business is not the answer to the country's pressing security needs." Liu warned that any new regulations would be harmful to the fragile economy and suggested instead more stringent security measures.

The screen showed the entrance to Ebola's brothel.

The two pseudo-humans were discovered behind Ms. Ebola's brothel this afternoon, continued the newscaster, a bit twitchy and dehydrated, but with no permanent damage.

There was a shot of the parking lot behind the brothel, where the brainless bodies were being given IVs by two EMTs.

We spoke there with Ms. Gold's employer.

The luminous face of Ebola appeared on screen.

It's just so sad, she said. I know Harta adored her brother, and she must just be devastated. My prayers are with her.

She folded her hands just beneath her face, as if ready to pray.

The killers were aided by a robot, continued the newscaster, assumed to be the source of the "death ray." Grid-work surveillance captured this image of the robot, with a telltale bow in its hair.

There was a grainy shot of the van, with Boopsie seated by the back window.

According to Ms. Gold and Mr. Carreno Busta, they didn't even realize the robot was in the van until informed by the police. Ms. Gold is quoted as saying, *Omigod, it really creeps me out.*

The newscaster shuffled papers she held in her hand.

Authorities ask that you be on alert for this robot, she said. Stay tuned for further developments in the pursuit of these ruthless killers, who remain at large. In international news today, the prime minister of Azerbaijan announced the official merger with neighboring Georgia under the name of the Islamic Republic of Gog and Magog, prompting warnings from Russian President-for-Life ...

The volume muted and a Daniel hologram popped up. This one was facing Zeke directly.

Good afternoon, said Daniel. Sleep well?

Slept fine, said Zeke. Listen—I need to see my sister.

Beth would love to chat with you, said Daniel, just as soon as she's feeling one hundred percent.

I need to see her, Zeke repeated. We came here for your help.

What sort of assistance is it you are seeking here at the Church of Christ with the Elijah Message?

Zeke explained to him that travel was difficult because they weren't registered, but that they needed to find land.

We need help to get to Montana or Oregon or Fruitvale.

The hologram vibrated with laughter.

Oregon? he said. Montana? There's no land left there. Maybe you can stake your claim to a tiny patch of a Tijuana garbage dump if you can chase away the children who make their living picking through the waste.

If that's what we need to do, said Zeke. But we'd still need help to get to Tijuana.

Don't be a fool, boy, said Daniel. There will be plenty of land for you here on hell-Earth in just a few weeks when the followers of Christ with the Elijah Message have been raptured to the heaven dimension, and the mutants and evil-doers here below slaughter each other like hogs.

Zeke rolled his eyes.

But of that day and *that* hour knoweth no man, no, not the angels which are in heaven, neither the Son, but the Father, he said.

Boy, said Daniel, don't think you can outdo me when it comes to the knowledge and interpretation of God's word.

We must keep trying to live as God has commanded us, that is all I know, said Zeke. I need to find new land for my people. Will you help us or not?

Let me pray on it, said Daniel.

The hologram vanished.

It's always interesting what *isn't* being spoken about, said Boopsie. The algorithms that can be woven simply by paying attention to what exists in reality, but is avoided in the language games that shape reality.

Are you talking about that girl? asked Zeke. The one who looks different?

Boopsie was actually still pondering the news.

Hartmut's research and its possible theft were mentioned as elements to create titillation and anxiety in the population, I suppose, said Boopsie. But they said nothing about the nature of that research.

Do you know what he was working on?

A kind of computer, said Boopsie. What else?

A computer, said Zeke. Does it come with a manual? Can girls use it to change the color of their eyes? Or maybe travel in time? Can it get anything done?

Boopsie shrugged.

Most computers come with a manual, she said.

FOURTEEN

Danny showed them to dinner again, but it was much like brunch. They dined alone on powdery, reconstituted food substances. Breakfast the next morning was the same, and lunch. For two days they saw nobody but Danny, and on the third day even he didn't show up. It was just a pre-recorded hologram notifying them that food was on the table.

Zeke and Boopsie rested in the grim little room at night, and Grandma rested during the day. Zeke assumed that her nights were spent doing what he did—poking around the clutter of Beth and Daniel's home, looking at the religious tracts and plans for elaborate post-apocalypse church compounds with organic gardens, schools, radio stations, and nuclear fallout shelters. He put on Gonzalo's clothes—the Bad Food T-shirt and baggy pants—and washed his Amish clothes in the bathtub. He found himself fleeing from one room to another to escape Daniel's gloomy pre-recorded sermons and found himself getting absorbed in the ongoing writer's competition, which was now down to four contestants: the Nigerian, the clone of a famous Estonian writer, a Goth girl with wings and fangs, and a New England prep-school boy who'd bought himself an extra brain, two extra mechanical hands, and infusions of JD Salinger's DNA. Zeke's time here began to feel like another form of imprisonment, and Zeke again began to feel like he was losing his mind. But at least here he could lie on his back in the yard and feel the sun on his face, filtered through the haze of the data vapor.

On the fourth morning, Zeke woke up from an intense

sexual dream to find a holographic Beth hovering over his bed. Boopsie and Grandma were nowhere to be seen.

Do you remember when I used to sing you to sleep? Beth asked.

Beth, he said. Where are you?

You were just a baby, she said.

I remember, said Zeke. You sang that song. *Sleep, baby, sleep ...*

You loved the marble ramp, said Beth.

The marble ramp was a simple wooden contraption with ramps and chutes and slides, straightaways and curves, and a funnel on top. Zeke would fill it up with marbles, scooping them up by the handful and dumping them into the funnel, watching with delight as they all came cascading down, to make the biggest, craziest racket.

I remember, he said.

I need you to help me, Beth said.

What is it?

Beth just smiled. Her hologram was bright this morning, steady and radiant. Her hair glowed like a sunrise.

I need *your* help too, said Zeke.

You were dreaming, said Beth. What were you dreaming about?

Zeke felt himself blushing. He understood why Gonzalo thought privacy was so important. The things he thought about confused him, sometimes sex confused him. He didn't want family members or robots looking at his body all the time, trying to read his mind.

Just dreams, he said. Nothing important.

Dreams are everything, said Beth. The other life hidden inside this life, more real, more horrible and lovely. The only place we see everyone we love and hate, without their masks, transformed into the shape-shifting mutants they've always been. It's the world that doesn't matter.

Maybe the world is like God's dream, said Zeke.

The devil's dream, said Beth.

I know you have bad feelings, said Zeke. For Dad and Grandma Mast.

Not *bad* feelings, she said.

They loved you, said Zeke. They still love you.

Love, said Beth dismissively. Do they *love* us Zeke? Or just *control* us? Can you tell the difference? Can anyone around here tell me the difference between *love* and *control?*

Zeke sat up and started getting dressed.

I need out of here, Beth, he said. How can I get out of here?

They've brainwashed you, she said. That's what they do. It's a cult, Zeke. Zeke, I want to show you something.

What?

In the living room, she said. In the large dresser, in the bottom drawer, there's a stack of photographs. Go get them.

Zeke fastened his suspenders and made his way down the narrow hallway to the living room. Beth's hologram had reappeared next to the statue of Daniel, and Zeke found the photographs just as she had said. The top ones were grainy pictures that looked like video stills. An Amish woman riding in a buggy, out hanging laundry, walking along the road, sitting on the front porch of Zeke's house.

He had never seen a picture of his mother, and he had no memory of her. How did he know it was her?

Where did you get these? he asked.

Random Grid-photos, routine surveillance and satellite photos, she said. I tracked them down.

His mother looked sad, Zeke thought. Even in the picture where she was sitting on the porch laughing, she looked sad.

Zeke felt like crying, he wasn't sure why.

Poor baby, said Beth. I know you lost your mother.

There was another woman sitting next to his mother on the porch, but she'd been mostly cropped out so that only her elbow and part of her leg showed.

I tried to be your mother for a while, said Beth. And then you lost *me* too.

Too, said Zeke.

The elbow looked familiar. Maybe that was Grandma Mast's elbow, maybe it was Leahbelle's mother, Miriam.

Mother killed herself, said Beth.

No, that's crazy, said Zeke. It was an accident.

Liars! Liars! They're such liars, said Beth. It was Father's fault. And that old witch.

It was an accident, said Zeke. She drowned.

She couldn't swim?

She couldn't swim, said Zeke.

Beth shook her head.

I was with her, said Beth. She took me with her, down to the pond. I was just a little girl. You were just a baby, and John Henry and Myrna and Josiah, practically babies too. She took me with her, and she tied my leg to the old oak tree with a tight knot that I couldn't undo. She tied me there so I couldn't run and get help.

No, said Zeke.

She did, Zeke, she did, said Beth. She tied me, and then she tied a big rock to her own leg, and she told me she was sorry, she told me she loved me, but she couldn't live there anymore, and she jumped right in.

Zeke could picture his sister somehow, he could picture the old tree and he could picture the knot, and he knew that what she was saying was true. He wanted to hug his sister, but she was only vibrations and light.

Beth, I'm sorry, he said. Where are you, Beth? Where are you for real?

It's okay, Zeke, she said. I've brought her back.

Where are you? Zeke said. Where's everybody? Where's Boopsie and Grandma?

Your grandmother is in the backyard, digging, said Beth. And she's got the robot helping her.

Digging, said Zeke.

Can't get enough of digging, seems to me.

What do you mean, said Zeke, suddenly terrified, that you've brought her back?

Daniel's hologram crackled into the room, right next to Beth's, so close they actually overlapped.

My angel, he said. My love. What are you doing? Dragging out those old pictures again?

There was a strange edge to Daniel's voice, as if he was threatening her.

She's *his* mother too, said Beth.

I suppose that's true, said Daniel. But you know what I always say about congregation business.

I'm not sharing congregation business, said Beth. Just some old photos.

Of course not, said Daniel in a syrupy voice. Just mind that you don't transition from your former family's business to your true family's business.

He just stood there then, beaming at Zeke. Beth gave Zeke a look, a meaningful look it seemed, although he couldn't say what the meaning was, and then disappeared. Daniel lingered, like a bad odor.

Breakfast is on the table, he said. I believe your grandmother is just now coming in from her hole out back.

What about getting us out of here? asked Zeke. Have you prayed on it? Have you developed a plan?

If you want a ride somewhere, I'm sure we can accommodate you, said Daniel. There are ways around the sensors. Everyone knows that.

We have helmets to block our brain-waves, said Zeke.

Don't need 'em, said Daniel. You just plug into another consciousness. Or even a hologram.

I've done that, said Zeke. But what about Grandma?

What about her?

It's too much for her, said Zeke.

I doubt anything is too much for your grandmother, said Daniel.

Zeke considered how this might work.

But won't they detect Boopsie?

They read scannables and brain signatures, said Daniel. If that. Not heartbeats or robots that aren't transmitting. The devil's law has been constructed, for the most part, to be disobeyed.

How far could you take us? asked Zeke.

How far are you going?

Oregon or California, said Zeke.

Daniel laughed.

Too far, he said.

Then give us your car, said Zeke. You say the world is ending, you won't need it. I'll give you all the money I have.

I've already lost one car, said Daniel. I need the other right up to the end.

Grandma and Boopsie entered the room. Grandma looked pale and ill. Daniel's hologram vanished.

Grandma, you're digging?

A tunnel, she said. It may be the only way out of here.

But you can't dig us to Oregon, said Zeke.

No, but I can dig us out of this evil house, she said, far enough to make a break for the outskirts of Colorado Springs. Maybe reconnect with the colony.

The rats? asked Zeke. They can't take us where we need to go.

Maybe plans have changed, Grandma said.

It had been only five days since they'd left the rats.

I need to rest, said Grandma, and she turned to go.

You need to eat, said Zeke.

Can't eat that food, said Grandma. They've put something in it. Your sister or her husband or that ghastly reproduction. They're drugging me.

No way, said Zeke.

Your sister is trying to kill me, said Grandma.

There are traces of poison in her blood, Boopsie confirmed.

She looked poisoned, certainly. She didn't even look like his grandmother. She looked like a pale rat, she looked like a corpse, she looked like a ghost in a dirty, mud-spattered dress and bonnet.

I need to rest now, said Grandma. I've had my breakfast.

Grandma, wait, he said.

He showed her the pictures.

She was a lovely woman, said Grandma. And a good woman. A very sad woman.

She told me, Zeke said. Beth told me.

He could see from her reaction that it was true.

Why didn't you tell me? he asked.

Yes, said Grandma. You are old enough to know. Now you are not a boy anymore, but a man. But you know your mother would not want these graven images of herself parading around the world.

How can I know what my mother would have wanted? Zeke asked.

I must rest, said Grandma. I'm sorry, Zeke. I'm so tired. We can talk more about your mother when I'm not so tired.

She stumbled down the dim hallway toward the bedroom.

What ... what did she eat? he asked Boopsie.

Worms, said Boopsie. Crickets. She killed a sparrow. Oh dear. If you don't mind dining alone, I'd like to keep an eye on your grandmother. Monitor her vitals.

It was in Boopsie's programming, Zeke thought. Was it compassion or was it just what she did? He felt so strange, so alone. He descended into the basement, where two plates were waiting, one at his spot and one at Grandma's. He examined her food. It looked just like his. He considered tasting it.

As he was finishing up, he was startled by one of the children—the girl with the dark hair was standing in the doorway. She looked like she was five or six.

Hello, she said.

Hello, said Zeke.

Mama sent me to say hello, said the girl.

Zeke had a bad feeling. Or not a bad feeling—a creepy feeling, an accurate feeling, the feeling that reality was, at its core, creepy, and he'd finally figured it out.

You don't look like your sisters, said Zeke.

Everybody's special, said the girl. But I'm *special* special. That's what Mama says.

Your mama is my own sister, said Zeke.

Yes, I know. You're my uncle.

Do you know why you don't look like them? he asked.

That's congregation business, said the girl.

What about your name? asked Zeke. Is your name congregation business too? I need to know what to call you. My name's Zeke.

Hello, Zeke, said the girl. My name's Emma.

He looked at the girl. And at the woman in the pictures. If there was a resemblance, it wasn't obvious.

Emma, he said. That was my mother's name.

Where is your mother now?

She's in heaven, said Zeke.

Oh, said Emma.

Emma, said Zeke. Where do you sleep? And play? Where is your mother? And your brothers and sisters?

Mama's in her room, said Emma. And the children are always in school.

School? Where's school? he asked.

Downstairs, silly, said Emma.

Can you show me how to get there?

She took his hand and led him down the hall to one of the locked doors. She had a key—an old-fashioned skeleton key, like an Amish key—on a string around her neck, and she used it to open the door, which led into a large empty closet. There was a trap-door on the floor, however, which she yanked up to reveal a stairway going down.

The stairway ended in another hallway lined with doors.

Is one of these your mother's room? asked Zeke.

Mama doesn't like to be distracted, said Emma.

Oh, I know, said Zeke. But if I'm not to disturb her, I need to know which is her room, so I can be extra quiet.

She took his hand again and showed him to the room at the very end of the hall.

Are you coming with me to school? she asked.

I'm too old for school, Zeke said.

Emma looked him over.

I don't think so, she said. Danny's bigger than you, and Danny's in school.

Yes, said Zeke. But I already finished my school. My own dad said so. You go on.

She shrugged and disappeared into a room several doors down, back up the hall.

Zeke had lied. He had lied to her and hadn't even thought about it, really. The world was changing him, it seemed. He tried Beth's door, but it was locked.

Leave me alone, Daniel, came a raspy voice from inside.

Beth, he whispered. It's me, Zeke.

There was a rustling sound from inside, crinkling noises and drawers shutting. The door opened. The woman standing in front of him looked nothing like the hologram. She had no flaming mane of light-colored hair; Beth was bald as Boopsie. She was not glowing with health; she was haggard and emaciated. She looked old, older than Zeke could imagine her, older than she was.

Come in, she said.

It was a small, cramped, dark room with several screens and gadgets, with papers and clothes and wigs spread haphazardly about the floor, and pictures she'd printed up from magazines—pictures of nature as it had once existed, of beautiful females in expensive outfits, and copies of the pictures Zeke still clutched in his hands, of their dead mother.

Emma, said Zeke.

Yes, said Beth.

But how?

Daniel did it for me, she said. We traveled back to Iowa, and he dug her up and scraped just a smidgeon up, just enough to use for cloning.

You desecrated her grave, said Zeke.

Beth shrugged.

A corpse doesn't care, she said. It's just some rotting genetic information, isn't it?

It's my mother, said Zeke.

No, said Beth. The corpse is not your mother. Your mother is back here. Now you get to see her. To talk to her.

That girl is not my mother, said Zeke. She's just a child.

Mother was once a child, wasn't she? A little girl, said Beth. I was once a little girl too. Did you know that, Zeke? I remember you as a baby, I know pieces of your life you can't even remember. But they're still a part of you. Of who you are.

I don't understand you, he said. What are you doing to Grandma?

That woman is controlling you, said Beth. The Amish are controlling you. I want to set you free.

Like you? he asked.

That's not fair.

Not fair? I don't understand you. What is going on in this place? Why are you here?

He sat down on the bed and looked around. It was so dim, and the room smelled moldy.

Why don't you turn on a light? he asked. How can you live like this?

A woman must dream a long time to act with *grandeur*, she said. And dreaming is nursed in darkness.

Zeke didn't know this woman. What sort of life had she lived since she had left home? Where did she come up with thoughts like that?

I read it in a book, she said, as if reading his mind. A delightful, smutty book by a twentieth century Frenchman. Daniel burned that book.

Zeke studied her face. She looked ill, she looked practically dead. Like Grandma.

I want to hug you, he said. Can I hug you?

Her body was brittle; it felt like it would break in his arms.

I need to leave, said Beth. I need to leave here with Emma. I need you to help me.

Daniel, said Zeke. Does he hurt you?

I'm his wife, said Beth. He has that right.

Nobody has that right, said Zeke. You didn't learn that among the Amish.

Beth shrugged. She grabbed a bottle of pills from the dresser beside her bed and popped one.

I have to prepare some things for my escape, she said. You have to take me to a special place, and then you can take Daniel's car and go wherever you want.

And the sensors? said Zeke.

Every wife in Colorado Springs knows how to trick the sensors, said Beth. How else would they cheat on their husbands? I'll show you.

But Grandma, said Zeke.

Oh, fuck Grandma. Just let her dig her hole.

You can't keep poisoning her, said Zeke. If you do anything to hurt Grandma, I won't help you.

Fine, whatever, said Beth.

She lay down on the bed, curled up like a baby, and closed her eyes.

Now get out of here, she said. Before Daniel figures out where you are.

Back upstairs, Grandma was perfectly still, and Boopsie was perched peacefully next to her. For a moment, until he saw her lips quiver, Zeke thought that she was dead.

Holograms of Daniel were preaching stridently throughout the house—the end of times, the seventh trumpet, the pregnant woman and the beast with seven heads and ten horns. Zeke needed to be alone for a moment, to think, but everywhere it was that raving phantom lunatic, or the blaring Grid-screens, or sometimes both. Everybody seemed to think that big changes were coming. The apocalypse or the singularity or the revolution. And what about the little girl, the clone of his mother? How could Zeke leave her with his crazy sister and her crazy husband?

He went out back to escape from all the voices. The sun was in the center of the sky, searing through the data vapor, and back behind the sheds he found Grandma's hole. It was actually a tunnel, tall enough for Zeke to walk into if he just stooped over, and he couldn't see the end of it.

After lunch, he settled in front of the Grid-screen in the living room. He watched *Move That Body, Lumpy!* and did the exercises along with them. It was good to move his body, he thought. All of the time trapped in Dr. Brockton's bunker, and now here, maybe his body would atrophy too. Afterward, the writer's combat was down to the prep-school boy with the famous writer's DNA and the Nigerian. The workshop leader with the enormous bulging skull eviscerated the latest story from the prep-school boy—a post-apocalypse tale about a disgruntled teen—and kept mocking him, repeating over and over that JD Salinger was the most overrated writer in human history. After that, there was a show that Zeke didn't understand. It was just a kind of humming noise and some jelly-like objects wiggling, but he found it oddly soothing. Maybe it was doing something to his brain.

But he wasn't soothed for long. The news came on. At the same time, he could hear a preaching Daniel hologram in the hallway.

The second angel sounded his trumpet, Daniel was saying, and something like a huge mountain, all ablaze, was thrown into the sea. A third of the sea turned into blood, a third of the living creatures in the sea died, and a third of the ships were destroyed.

This just in, said the newscaster. The latest developments in the pursuit of the ruthless killers who murdered Hartmut Green. Authorities are now describing the brutal home invasion as a probable case of terrorism. Footage from Longmont surveillance drones has surfaced that police sources believe shows the killer robot walking through downtown Longmont, accompanied by two humans.

Boopsie, Zeke called. Come see this!

Poor quality video footage flashed onto the screen. It showed Zeke and Boopsie and Grandma from above, talking to the woman with the frayed cables as arms. In the hallway Daniel was saying, The third angel sounded his trumpet, and a great star, blazing like a torch, fell from the sky on a third of the rivers and on the springs of water— the name of the star is Wormwood.

The police have not yet identified the two suspects, the newscaster was saying, a young male, probably human, and an older female. The outfits they are wearing, however, have been identified as the traditional garb of the anti-technology religious cult, the *Old Order Amish*.

Boopsie popped in just in time to catch the end.

Authorities warn local citizens to be on the lookout for Amish militants, to notify the police of any suspicious individuals, and to be careful—the suspects are believed to be armed and dangerous.

Goodness, said Boopsie. Looks like you'll need a change of clothes for the rest of the journey. A disguise.

I have one, said Zeke.

A hologram of Beth crackled into the room, and another, and another, but they disappeared, like some strange mirage in a hall of mirrors.

A third of the waters turned bitter, Daniel was saying, and many people died from the waters that had become bitter.

The newscaster said, No word yet on whether the terrorists who killed Hartmut Green are connected to the Amish militants who were taken out in a surgical strike by government drones earlier today.

The fourth angel sounded his trumpet, Daniel was saying, and a third of the sun was struck, a third of the moon, and a third of the stars ...

According to authorities, a terror plot was foiled early this morning near Kalona, Iowa ...

... so that a third of them turned dark ...

... where the home of militant Peter Beachy was destroyed ...

Woe! Woe! Woe to the inhabitants of the earth!

... along with the eleven terror suspects inside.

Zeke watched in mute horror as they showed a drone firing a missile at Peter Beachy's home—at Leahbelle's home. They showed the explosion, an insane plume of flames and smoke, and then showed the aftermath: robot crews were putting out the fire, with Amish and other neighbors gathered around. He recognized Sam Miller and thought he saw Uncle Mose from behind. They showed Leahbelle's aunt Ethel on her knees, sobbing, with her husband consoling her. There was nothing left of the house but a blackened patch of earth.

Leahbelle, said Zeke.

There were eleven members of the Beachy family. Nobody had escaped.

FIFTEEN

It was like a dream. Something like this might happen in a dream, but then you would wake up.

Once, when he was just a child, they had lived together and slept in the same room. Zeke and Leahbelle and her sister Ruth and her bother Delmar. Zeke had been a motherless child. His father had been barely keeping himself together. The nights were hot and still. One night he woke, and she wasn't in her bed. Perhaps it is his earliest memory—Leahbelle in her white nightclothes, rocking on the front porch and talking very seriously to a cricket she'd captured and held in her hands. Was the moonlight more intense in those days? The data vapor less thick? There was a strange luminous aura around the trees and the animals, the barns and the road, Leahbelle and the cricket, as if everything was lit up from the inside. Come with me, she said. She took his hand, and they walked across the farm in the night and then sat in the ditch along the road. She wanted him to see the magic, from down in the ditch, when the two lights would come, twin lights bearing down on them, jiggling and fast and crazy, almost merging, before they zipped past, never to return. She wanted to show him a car. Before a car passed, however, they had fallen asleep. Her mother found them there, huddled in the ditch.

The world could seem like a passing fancy, a beautiful, horrible vision. Leahbelle was real. When she grew older, she liked to sneak out to the barn sometimes and listen to English songs on an old music-playing device she had hidden there. She liked to sing, she was in love with melody, and she paid more attention to the birds and their songs than anybody. She believed that her mother should be allowed to keep the linoleum edged with a pattern of roses that the church had deemed too fancy. She didn't care for frog meat, but enjoyed rabbit if it was salted well. He knew that he could trust her. If she was talking to him, she was telling him the truth.

She knew his doubts and questions. She knew his interest in medicine and science and accepted it. She knew his curiosity about the world, and in some ways she shared it.

Peter and Miriam had been like parents to him. They had taken him in after his mother died, and looked after him as if he was their own. And he *was* their own, they had watched him with great care. Her brothers and sisters too. Delmar, Ervin, Elvin, and Ivan. Hannah, Sarah, Katie, and Ruth. An entire family, gone. Terror suspects. Militants, the government said.

He wanted to call the neighbors' house, to speak to his father. He wanted to make sure that the family was okay, and to hear them confirm what he knew, or deny it. It was too dangerous, Boopsie said. The phones would be monitored. They might use his call as an excuse to take out his family's own farm. Or the next drone strike could be right here, in Colorado Springs.

Within a few days, it was too late. Government forces rounded up the Kalona Amish, a *problem*, the government said, *that couldn't be allowed to fester in the heartland any longer.* They would be shipped to San Jose, California, and housed in the first "Old Order Amish Living History Farm and Museum."

Dr. Brockton had figured right. The most likely scenario, she had said, was that they'd be moved out into some camp or work farm.

Zeke didn't cry, not once. He felt dried-out inside, too hollow and unreal to cry.

He lay around, not really sleeping, but a victim of his racing thoughts. Once in a while, he would forget for a moment. He would drift off and in some of his dreams, Leahbelle was still alive.

The Grid-screen showed the Kalona Amish being herded onto government shuttles for the flight west.

He didn't understand anything. God's plan? If this was God's plan ... he couldn't bear it. And yet he knew he had to go on somehow. People were depending on him. His family, his whole community—they would be prisoners in this new museum. He had longed for freedom while listening to Ebola's song, thought that he had tasted freedom racing through the night on Gonzalo's motorbike, imagined that his journey into the world would help him discover what it meant to be free. But now he had discovered that freedom was a burden and a huge responsibility. He had to rescue them.

Grandma agreed. They would make their way to California, try to figure out a way to get them out.

Perhaps with the help of the colony, Grandma said.

But Zeke thought it was the rats who were responsible for all of this. He had to wonder if the rats had done something to provoke this response. If it was the rats who baited the government to murder Leahbelle and her family.

He had his duty. His responsibility. Perhaps that could keep him going, but he had lost his sense of urgency. His quest had already failed. The land had been lost, his people had been enslaved, and the person he cared most for in all the world had been killed.

He would do what he needed to do, but maybe not yet today.

One day slipped into another. Grandma dug her hole, Boopsie monitored Grandma, Beth remained hiding and dreaming in her room, gestating her secret plan, and Daniel's holograms preached. His doomsday was fast approaching. What would happen when it didn't come true? Boopsie thought they shouldn't wait around to find out.

Only Emma showed her face from time to time. She was a sweet-natured child, calm and curious and a little bit sad. It may have just been his own sadness, he thought, that made her seem so.

I'm sorry that you lost your friend, she said.

She liked to hold his hand and show him around, although there was no part of the house or the yard at that point that Zeke didn't know too well. He didn't know why she was the only one who chose to come out of the sub-basement, or the only one who was allowed.

I miss the animals, she told him one day. Do you miss the animals?

Which animals? he asked.

The elephants and tigers and rhinoceros, said Emma. All the extinct animals that were murdered and smushed. Daddy says we'll see all the animals again when we go to heaven with Jesus.

She squeezed his hand.

Why are you crying inside? she asked. Do you miss the animals too?

Yes, said Zeke. I miss them very much. And I miss my friend Leahbelle. Did your mother tell you about my friend?

No, said Emma.

No? Who told you then? Boopsie?

Nobody told me, said Emma.

She shrugged.

Sometimes I just know.

He believed her, but didn't know why or how it was possible. Boopsie seemed to read minds sometimes, but it was a product of her logic and her advanced sensors that could detect and analyze information about heart rates, eye movement, and vocal shifts. His grandmother received something from the rats, but he was pretty sure it was an actual auditory signal. Could a human read another human's mind? Was it because she was in some sense his mother?

What else do you know? he asked her.

Some bad things, she said.

Bad things?

It's a secret, she said. I can't tell you Mama's secret.

But if she's going to hurt somebody, said Zeke, then you have to tell.

Emma shook her head.

Daddy says the world is ending on Tuesday, she said.

Do you believe that?

I told him I had a bad feeling about the day, she said.

Your daddy said the world was ending other times too, said Zeke. Did you ever tell him that before? That you had a bad feeling?

No, she said. Only this time.

She gave him a hug.

Don't worry, she said. We'll be okay. You're going to be my special friend.

She kissed his cheek and then hurried off.

The world had already ended, Zeke thought. Whatever new apocalypse might be coming, it could only pale in comparison.

On Sunday night, two days to doomsday, Beth's holographic avatar popped up just before bedtime and told Zeke it was time to get ready.

Tomorrow's the day, she whispered. I'll go for fresh eggs. You and Emma will come along.

And Grandma? And Boopsie?

Once you've taken me to my secret place, you can come back and get them, she said. They must have tunneled far enough out of here by now that you could just swoop by and get them off some corner. I'll bring you a disguise for Grandma. One of my wigs, an old outfit.

Where am I taking you? asked Zeke.

Shhhh, said Beth. I'll show you tomorrow. Just be ready.

The hologram vanished.

Zeke found Grandma and Boopsie at the head of the tunnel out back.

I don't trust your sister, said Boopsie.

Doesn't matter, said Grandma. She'd hurt me, but she won't hurt Zekey.

How far does the tunnel go now? asked Zeke.

Five miles, said Boopsie.

Zeke peered into the darkness.

That's not possible, said Zeke.

It is, said Boopsie.

Grandma, Zeke said. Tell me about my mother.

Grandma crouched and began scratching in the dirt as if writing something.

She had nerves, said Grandma. That's what we called it in my day. Then it was Depression or Bipolar or Unduly Anti-Cheerful Disposition with Anti-Social Aggravation Syndrome.

She stood up again.

She was troubled, she said.

Was she psychic?

Psychic?

Could she feel other people's feelings? Read their thoughts?

She was a godly woman, said Grandma. Not a psychic.

For a moment Zeke felt as if he was unattached from everything, becoming a hologram or drifting into outer space. Grandma scurried on into the tunnel.

Beth woke Zeke up early the next morning. The real Beth— emaciated body, bald head, dark circles under her eyes.

Shhhh, she said. Hurry. Daniel's still sleeping.

Emma looked sleepy, but nervous. Beth had a bag of clothes and a wig for Grandma, and she'd left Daniel a flexi-screen note: "Gone for fresh eggs for Danny's birthday."

Once we're all safely out of here, she whispered, he'll

get other messages too.

Zeke got dressed quickly in Gonzalo's outfit.

I like you in those clothes, said Beth. So much better.

It still feels strange, said Zeke.

You'll get used to it, she said.

The bot-car was parked on the street.

Daniel said he'd just lost one of his cars, Zeke said.

Yes, said Beth. I had a little accident, just the week before you came.

She and Emma got into the front, and Zeke climbed in the back. Beth gave Zeke a necklace to wear with Daniel's scannable ID. She programmed a simple hologram to share Zeke's seat. He was surrounded by a phantom Daniel, pontificating as usual, but with the volume turned down.

They'll read his ID, and the hologram will give off his basic brainwave, Beth said. No big deal.

The car started and moved leisurely down the street. They drove west through residential neighborhoods onto a main road, passed abandoned retail, and headed toward the mountains. They passed abandoned Walgreens, Waffle Houses, and Genes R Us, the once inhabited physical world.

I thought the Grid eliminated accidents, Zeke said.

I must have made a mistake, said Beth, as I was programming my destination.

Along their route, billboards flashed ads for survivalist gear, water purification systems, cloning services, religious-themed plates and dishes, and antidepressants. They were following the route toward a place called the Garden of the Gods. They passed Grid-work 25 and the road began to rise through more squashed residential neighborhoods and onto a road with trees and shrubs and no buildings. The clouds were so close overhead.

Beth, said Zeke, why don't you come with us? To Oregon or California. Nobody can hurt you now.

No, said Beth. Nobody can hurt me now. Nobody but God and the devil. And I'm not sure they really care either way.

Do you ever hear from John Henry? asked Zeke.

John Henry?

John Henry, our brother.

Beth laughed.

I haven't heard from him for five years. He was in trouble then. You only hear from John Henry when he's in trouble.

Zeke was discovering that he knew very little about his family. Not the ones who'd left and not even the ones who'd stayed.

What kind of trouble? he asked.

All trouble is the same trouble, Beth said.

Emma reached over and squeezed her mother's hand.

Don't be sad, Mama.

You can't go back to the past, Beth said. I know, because I've tried. The past is what it was, Zeke. My mother died, and then my family abandoned me.

But you left *us*, Zeke said.

I suppose all we do is follow our own lonely roads, she said. We hurt each other, leave each other, chase after some dream. Daniel was my dream.

Emma looked at Beth as if she was considering this deeply, and then she turned to watch the road. Zeke thought he saw Daniel's face flash onto one of the passing billboards, but then it was gone. He wasn't sure what he'd really seen.

A dream that turned into a nightmare, Beth said.

The sky seemed to darken.

A storm's coming, said Emma.

But there was no sign of a real storm. The road was winding into the foothills, and whatever weather was ahead was coming from the other side of the mountains. The sky was still clear and blue beyond the usual haze of the data vapor. Why it had darkened, Zeke couldn't see. It was as if somebody had hit a dimmer switch.

He was a mistake, said Beth. My biggest mistake. I

can see that now. I knew it then, really, but I was just a girl. I just wanted somebody to show me they loved me. My father, my grandparents. I didn't want their prohibitions. I needed their love. I was too proud to turn back, I needed love, I needed a way out, but instead I was trapped and alone in the little hole I'd dug for myself. Just getting deeper in.

The road veered to the south and then west again.

The new bride, said Beth. Look, here she is, come to her husband's house, just a child herself, and there are his oldest sons, waiting on the porch. Already in need of a mother. He'd never mentioned them. His first wife gave birth to them. He never mentioned them, not a word. And now he wanted daughters. I gave him daughters, and I gave him more sons, but everything separate, nothing mixed together.

What will the children do without you? Zeke asked.

The children will do what the children have always done.

The road was strange. He'd been on this road before, Zeke thought. A road going west, with the bloody darkness up ahead, there in the west. The blood was in the sandstone of the rocks along the road, reddish and full of terrifying faces, like letters from a hostile alphabet.

The children will be fine, said Beth. The boys are little copies of Daniel. They always understand him, they fit together like puzzle pieces. And the girls—they can bear it, whatever it is. They're just like me, aren't they? And I bore it. I have no mercy to give them, I'm afraid. But I couldn't leave Emma with that monster.

Thank you, Mama, said Emma.

A sign by the road announced the entrance to the Garden of the Gods and other specific attractions—rock climbing, the Kissing Camels, Balanced Rock, the Bottomless Pool.

They built the Bottomless Pool ten or fifteen years ago, said Beth. To attract more tourists. Kind of a flop, I guess. Nobody comes here anymore. Nobody goes anywhere anymore, in the world. But I think it's the most beautiful thing I've ever seen. You'll see. The purest, bluest reflection.

Like the tears of Jesus, said Emma.

So you've been here before, Zeke said to Emma.

It's Mama's special place, she said.

Beth explained that the Bottomless Pool was constructed with quantum technology to suspend the usual laws of time and space. There really was no bottom.

If you throw a pebble into the pool, said Emma, it both exists and it doesn't, forever. Unless you try to observe it.

Observe it? said Zeke.

You can watch it for a little ways, said Beth. But once it passes the threshold, it both is and it isn't. If you try to film it or go after it, it snaps into one reality or the other.

Zeke had read about this sort of thing in his outdated science textbooks, but he couldn't say he understood it. They arrived in the parking lot, the only vehicle in sight.

It's a short hike from here, Beth said. I usually get a little winded, but you should be fine.

She gave him the car key and showed him how to start it. She programmed the car to take him to his meeting point with Grandma and Boopsie at Evergreen Cemetery. They began down the Siamese Twins Trail, and Emma pointed out Pike's Peak in the distance. She knew the name of all the rock formations. The Three Graces, Tower of Babel, Weeping Rock.

But where are you going from here? asked Zeke.

Beth smiled. It was a sad, condescending smile—as if she was talking to a child about death, Zeke thought.

We'll live right here, said Beth. For a while. I've brought supplies and hidden them among the rocks. There are cozy shelters, and nobody comes around. It's a perfect place to hide.

What about when winter comes?

We'll see, said Beth. I have a Plan A and a Plan B.

Depending on ...?

Depending on what Daniel does.

They walked on past the Kissing Camels. Beth was dragging, stooped a bit, as if she was carrying some great weight. She was so fragile, she looked so *old*. They came upon the pool suddenly. It was almost perfectly round, like a blue eye staring at God. It was beautiful. Signs warned not to get too close, but there was no railing. Zeke walked right up to the edge.

What would happen if you fell in? he asked.

Can you swim? asked Beth.

I'm a good swimmer, he said.

It's just water, she said. You can float on the surface if you want to. Or you can sink forever ...

She walked around to the other side of the pool, facing Zeke, maybe ten feet away.

If you were wearing something—a weighted fabric that wouldn't let you rise—you would fall forever, she said. Once you sink deep enough that you can't be observed, you exist between two states forever. A kind of eternal baptism.

Zeke had that feeling again, as he'd had when she first told him about Emma. That he knew where she was going before she even said it.

Beth, he said. Don't ...

I'm wearing that kind of fabric, she said.

No, said Zeke. I won't let you.

I'll be falling forever, she said. Hidden beneath the waters. Pure again. Pure of all my sins, including this one.

Emma was watching her mother. She looked perfectly calm, but she was emitting a strange noise, a kind of soft humming.

If you dive in after me, Beth said, you'll be an observer, and so I won't be able to breathe. I'll only breathe by virtue of the air pocket that will improbably surround me and keep me in an alive-state according to the rules of quantum suicide. If you jump in after me, you'll kill me.

Emma's humming grew louder, and she began waving her hands next to her head in a frenzy.

Baby, said Beth to Emma, watch now. Watch Mama. Just like you did to me, Mother. It's yours now again. You tried to give me the pain, but I'm giving it back. Nobody will ever be able to find me again or resuscitate me. Only Jesus will know where I'm at.

Beth, said Zeke.

Take care of her, said Beth. I'm sorry.

She jumped into the pool.

Emma began shrieking in horror with her hands over her ears. Zeke kicked off his shoes and grabbed Emma.

Stay here! he told her. Don't move!

He felt *himself* splitting in two. He could see her down there falling, deeper, deeper. He thought that she was lying. He was almost sure of it—that she'd made up the whole business of quantum suicide to keep him from coming after her. None of it made any sense.

Emma's shriek was inhuman. She seemed to be gasping for breath, as if *she* was the one who was drowning. Her cry of anguish seemed to pierce the sky, to merge with the data vapor and a darkness that was covering the land or invading Zeke's own mind. He dove into the bottomless pool.

He was diving down, down, and she was looking up at him, her bald head glowing with a kind of supernatural radiance, and her eyes were saying *No*. She was waving her arms, to propel herself more quickly down. Zeke was kicking. Could he hold his breath forever? Would he die? Time seemed frozen. His own mind or the quantum effects, he didn't know, but he realized that if he died, Emma would be alone. Lost in the wilderness, alone.

He was catching up to Beth, but he needed to breathe. He couldn't do it. He reached down and caught hold of one of her thrashing arms. He had her.

He had her, but he couldn't bring her up. She was too heavy. She was pulling him further down. She looked up at him and shook her head and mouthed the words, Save her.

He let her go.

And shot up toward the surface. Up and up and up until he broke the surface and gasped the air into his lungs. He pulled himself onto the shore.

Emma was wailing and sobbing and clutching her own head.

Zeke picked her up and held the little girl in his arms. Beth was so deep now, but the water was so clear that he could still see her. It had to be her, deep under the water, continuing to fall, but the form was wavering, as if alternating between existence and not, and growing smaller and smaller until he couldn't see her anymore.

The sky was dark. The data vapor itself had darkened, and a single real cloud had edged from the west over the plains, crackling with lightning. It was squarish and white, but dark around the edges. Silently crackling with electricity.

He carried Emma quickly back up the trail. She wouldn't stop wailing. He strapped her into her seat, pushed the button, and they were off. The car took them back down the way they had come, through the scrub and onto Manitou Avenue, past small adobe houses, a motel with a swimming pool out front, storage units and more motels, into the city. Emma's shriek went on and on. As they passed billboards, the dancing, garish ads crackled, and the signs went black. He hadn't turned the Daniel hologram on. The Grid could be reading him, should be reading him and warning him to turn back, get off the road, turn himself in. But it wasn't Zeke who was blacking out the billboards, he could see that. It was Emma.

SIXTEEN

By the time they arrived at Evergreen Cemetery, a strange silence had descended over the city. The world was changing, Zeke thought. But he wasn't sure why he thought that. Other than the billboards and an eerie quiet, nothing was different except for the dimness everywhere—and he wasn't sure if that was in the world or in his mind.

He found the exit to Grandma's tunnel among a cluster of trees near a baby's tomb. The top of the headstone was carved in the shape of a plump naked baby that looked like it had just been woken up from a nap and wasn't happy about it. Grandma and Boopsie weren't there.

Emma was silent, but tears were streaming down her face.

I knew what she was doing, said Emma. But I didn't know how it would feel.

You knew?

I saw her doing it before, Emma said. Inside my head.

She sat down on the grave next to the baby's.

She wanted peace, she said.

Do you think she got it? Zeke asked.

I can't tell, Emma said. Is it peace when nobody can feel you anymore?

I don't know, sweetie, said Zeke.

They're coming, said Emma. We have to go.

He could hear a thumping and a whirling noise approaching from the tunnel, and beyond it a kind of thunder. Grandma came first, scrambling on all fours, with Boopsie right behind her. Grandma was wearing tight pink pants and a white blouse with embroidered shoulders, a huge wig of whitish blond hair.

We have to go, said Grandma. Quick! They're coming after us.

They jumped into the car. Boopsie quickly programmed it, and they were off again, just as Daniel's children began streaming out of the tunnel firing old-fashioned rifles at them.

Heavens to Betsy! said Boopsie. I'd have incinerated them all with the death ray, but I knew how much that would grieve you.

They were buzzing south now down the Hancock Expressway. Boopsie turned the holograms on, so that Zeke was again peering at the world through an image of Daniel and Grandma was surrounded by a meditative image of Beth.

Her messages started popping up all over the house, said Grandma, before we'd even gotten out. Holograms of your sister, hundreds of them. Taunting Daniel.

A rather chaotic scene, said Boopsie. Blaring alarms and trumpets, Daniel speaking in tongues, emergency configurations of the children.

Like military maneuvers or gymnastics, said Grandma.

When they saw us sneaking out, they came right behind us with guns and explosives, said Boopsie.

We outran them, said Grandma, and put a few obstacles in their path.

She sighed and then turned to face Zeke directly.

Is it true? she asked. Is what your sister said true? Is she gone?

She's gone, said Zeke. Forever.

Grandma looked devastated.

You loved her, said Emma. You loved her very much.

Emma took her hand. Grandma began sobbing. The city was strange and different—emptier and quiet. They merged onto the Ronald Reagan Grid-work. As they sped along, their vehicle and the few other bot-cars on the road would slow suddenly, all together, and then they would all pick up speed again. As if the Grid was breathing. Or gasping for breath.

Something is happening to the Grid, said Boopsie. It sustained some damage locally that is reverberating beyond Colorado Springs. There are also signs of major hacking activity system-wide. Oh dear. For my own protection, I will refrain from any further communications with the Grid or the data vapor.

The pulsing or gasping of the Grid continued as they drove out of the city. Emma sat quietly now, watching the landscape go by. The billboards weren't popping and fizzing out, as they had earlier, but they weren't showing ads either. They were showing views of the earth from space, cities at night, storm clouds, mushroom clouds, tidal waves, and speeded up images of animal corpses decaying. Zeke couldn't process everything that was happening, that had happened. He closed his eyes and tried to rest.

They'd driven almost two hours south when the vehicle gradually slowed down and came to a complete stop, along with every other vehicle on the road. It took a few minutes for the stunned inhabitants of the other bot-cars to begin emerging, looking around for some answer or assistance.

What now? asked Zeke.

We keep going on foot, said Boopsie. Trinidad is several miles ahead.

Did you bring the umbrellas? asked Grandma.

I did, said Boopsie. Although it seems they will no longer be necessary.

All around them, surveillance drones were crashing to earth.

When they arrived in Trinidad, most businesses were dark and closed. There was no power, no Grid, no data vapor. A line had formed, however, in front of one industrious taqueria that was cooking food over an open flame and accepting only CASH®. Their sign advertised tortillas made by hand, and the family that ran that place all had mechanical limbs like Gonzalo's, but with vat-grown human hands on the ends, patting the tortillas.

Nobody knew what was going on, but there were rumors, the owner of the taqueria told them when they reached the front of the line—a woman named Chantal. A friend of hers had an old-fashioned radio he used to pick up Mexican off-Grid stations. The official story was that the Grid was down throughout Colorado, northern New Mexico, and western Kansas for "emergency maintenance." But apparently several different anti-government, anti-technology, or anti-American groups had already taken credit, including NIHIL, the Mexican group New Aztlan, the Muslim Isis Enlightened, and the North American animal rights group Hugs for Puppies. The North American government was assuring its citizens that the Grid would be fully functional by midnight.

But I don't think so, said Chantal. My best friend is in touch with spiritual people, and she told me this isn't any terrorism. She said it was caused by a burst of psychic energy like none before, released somewhere up north this morning, around Colorado Springs. She said big changes are coming.

She handed them their protein-berry tacos with a few of her hands, while others were still shaping tortillas.

My daughter is a scientist in Oakland, Chantal went on, but I haven't been able to reach her to see what *she* says.

We're going to California, said Zeke. I can't guarantee delivery, but if you give me a message, I can try to get it to your daughter.

Going to California! exclaimed Chantal. You gonna walk there?

Chantal was tickled to death by this idea—the idea of a robot, two kids, and an old woman crossing the great desert to California, like some twentieth century Okies. Or some early millennium migrants at the border.

My father used to take people back and forth across the border, back when I was just a little girl, she said. Before they built the data wall.

We may need to cross into Mexico, said Zeke. We're looking for a new home.

Back when people still wanted to get *in* instead of *out*, said Chantal. First time I ever saw a rotting corpse.

Emma was gazing at Chantal intently.

The birds were eating it? she said.

Yes, said Chantal. The buzzards.

She looked at Emma carefully, as if trying to figure out how she was related to this odd group. She said something to her in Spanish, but Emma just started humming. The people in line behind Zeke were getting impatient. Chantal turned to Grandma.

You're old enough to remember the reign of the orange blob, she said. You're old enough to remember when corporations employed *people*.

I never paid much attention to politics, said Grandma.

Chantal laughed.

Too late now, she said. Everybody might be looking for a new home pretty soon. I'm looking forward to it. End of the world, good times.

Her hands were moving so fast that it was hard to count them, but Zeke thought there were at least a dozen.

Who doesn't love a good apocalypse? she said. When I was just a girl we had that huge hurricane, same name as me. Wiped out those cities in Texas and Mississippi, what were they called?

Boopsie was about to identify them, but Chantal waved one of her hands as if it didn't matter.

Never forgot it, she said. More rotting corpses, sure, but you need catastrophe and death sometimes. You try to get rid of death, and everything gets out of whack.

She left her grandson in charge of the line and

disappeared into the back for a moment, came out with a sealed envelope addressed to her daughter Gabrielle.

My border crossing days are long over, she said. But Gabi might know people out there who can help you. Or who knows? Maybe the data wall will conk out with everything else.

I'll do my best to get her this letter, said Zeke.

Boopsie suggested they spend the night here in Trinidad. But more and more refugees from the Grid-works were showing up in town, forming huge lines at the taqueria and filling the streets. The actual residents were nowhere to be seen, but Grandma thought the local authorities would have to set up some sort of emergency shelter.

Which is exactly why we don't want to be anywhere near here, she whispered. If they do get the Grid back, we'll be identified.

Boopsie suggested they set up camp outside of town. They'd been walking miles already, and he knew that would be hard on Zeke's physical structure, and Emma's too. Zeke thought that he'd already effectively separated from his own physical structure. His mind seemed to be somewhere else, or maybe everywhere else at the same time. Still back there in the pool, diving toward infinity.

After they found a quiet place among some trees west of town, an old park that Chantal had pointed them to, and after Emma had been put to bed on a thin inflatable mat Boopsie had brought along—one for each of them, stolen from Daniel's supplies—Zeke took Boopsie aside.

Is psychic energy real? he asked her. Could a psychic child ... under stress ...

Oh sure, said Boopsie. There's plenty of evidence for the reality of so-called psychic phenomena. Gosh, why not? Plenty of plausible quantum mechanical explanations. They've hardly ever been effectively demonstrated or harnessed in a laboratory setting, I'm afraid.

An evil barking noise interrupted Boopsie, but it was

just a two-headed squirrel perched above them in a tree, both heads chattering at the same time.

Dr. Brockton was trying to identify telepathy genes back in the 2010s, in fact, said Boopsie, but abandoned her search. She concluded that technology was an easier way to create the *equivalent* of psychic powers.

Like you, said Zeke. The way you read eye movements and chemicals from the body.

Sure, said Boopsie.

The squirrel threw some inedible mutant nut straight at Boopsie's head, and Boopsie incinerated the squirrel with her death ray.

Boopsie! said Zeke. Enough with the death ray.

Oopsie! said Boopsie. I forget sometimes how much psychological pain the death of mammals can cause you.

Boopsie looked thoughtful and almost ... confused.

I'm experiencing some cognitive dissonance, she said, as I did after I incinerated Hartmut. I was designed to be indifferent to the random deaths of sentient life forms—except for Dr. Brockton, whose death would have triggered a murderous frenzy followed by an elaborate auto-destruct. But the modifications I received from the rats' infection have expanded my understanding of the implications of impermanence. They just haven't entirely overridden my impulse to destroy malevolent life forms.

You're still evolving? said Zeke.

Yes, said Boopsie. I wonder what kind of a machine I'll become. I still *feel* like Boopsie, although ... I'm not sure that it's a rational feeling.

Zeke made his way over to the next tree and checked on Emma, who was sleeping soundly.

You're imagining that Emma might have caused the Grid to collapse, said Boopsie quietly. It's certainly possible. The measurable electro-magnetic and gravitational fields around her head suggest a mind that is receiving and sending information into the atmosphere at a super-duper rate.

Zeke wondered what she was dreaming. His mother, in a way. But also like him now, motherless and lost in a strange world, growing stranger every day.

She opened her eyes and looked at him and, recognizing him, she smiled. And then she looked beyond him and pointed toward the sky.

What are those lights? she asked.

The data vapor had cleared completely. Beyond what had once been a haze of information were thousands and thousands of tiny lights in space. Zeke had heard of them, but he'd never seen more than a hint of them before. He'd never seen them like this. But he knew what they were.

Stars, he said. Those are stars.

SEVENTEEN

The Grid wasn't up again by midnight. In fact, by the next morning Boopsie couldn't connect anywhere. The data vapor had evaporated, and the Grid was down all over the earth. Just in time for Daniel's apocalypse.

How will we get to California now? Zeke asked.

There is one form of transportation that functions without the Grid, Boopsie said. The tracks run right through town. We'll take the train.

Boopsie knew the schedule, and so they made their way down to the tracks, skirting the crowds that had already formed in front of Chantal's taqueria. The train came soon after, just as Boopsie had predicted. It didn't stop, but slowed down as it passed through town. Boopsie took Emma and grabbed ahold of one of the ladders. Zeke and Grandma jumped aboard after.

It was a passenger train, and yet there weren't any passengers. Cars and cars of seats, even sleeping compartments, but there didn't seem to be anyone on board. Grandma plopped down into a seat right away and dozed off. She'd been up all night, digging, or listening to her frequencies, or scavenging for food. Emma sat next to her and watched the landscape pass by. Zeke walked from one end of the train to the other as the train rolled on south into the dry, freakish hill country of northern New Mexico. The train was clean, and everything worked properly, the toilets were stocked, and the dining compartment as well. The tables in the dining car were set with a fresh black rose on each table.

They rolled through long canyons, skirting the edges of dramatic rock formations, and then rolled right through

Albuquerque without stopping. The city, too, seemed emptied. Perhaps everyone was hiding out inside, waiting to see what would happen next. It was so hot out there it didn't look solid. Occasionally Zeke would spot a lone figure in the distance, or a couple, or see the smoke from a distant fire. Inside, the train was nice and cool. Outside, the world was melting. The data vapor had evaporated everywhere, it seemed. According to Boopsie, it wasn't only a source of information, but also a means to protect the earth from the sun's rays, one of many only partially successful measures that had been taken to cool the planet. Now that it was gone, the earth could be expected to rise in temperature an average of 2.13 degrees, rather too quickly.

Zeke lay down in one of the sleeping cars to rest. He hadn't slept much the night before, outside under the stars with everything whirling through his head. But now, despite Beth's suicide and the collapse of the Grid, the motion of the train and the sound it made clacking down the tracks soothed him, and he slept.

He was awoken several hours later by a tall stranger gently nudging him. He seemed human, but very tall and slim and calm, and the first thing Zeke noticed was that his thumb was a bottle opener.

Dinner will be served in a half hour, said the man.

Are you the conductor? asked Zeke.

The porter, sir, he said. Persay.

Persay?

My name, sir. I'm Persay.

Zeke thought that Persay was somehow the least frightening creature he'd ever encountered, as if he had been specially designed to soothe and serve.

I didn't think anyone was on board, said Zeke.

I'm the only one, sir.

Why are you here? asked Zeke.

I can't ever leave, said Persay. I was modified, sir. Long time ago. Punishment for my crime. But I rather doubt that anyone remembers that I'm actually here.

Nobody rides the trains anymore? asked Zeke.

Your party is the first in many years.

But why are the trains still running if nobody rides them? asked Zeke.

They were funded, said Persay.

Zeke closed his eyes and didn't even realize that he was drifting back to sleep until Persay's mellifluous voice spoke softly, as if from a far distance.

You'll want to eat, sir, he said. Take your time, but do come join us for dinner.

The sun was setting to the west, and to the south was a painted desert. Candles were burning throughout the dining car. Boopsie and Emma were already seated. Persay brought a juice for Emma and some sort of mineral-rich seaweed composite that Boopsie might absorb to keep her circuitry in order.

And you, young sir? he asked Zeke. Chicken, soy, or cicada?

How do you fix the chicken? he asked.

Mushrooms and rosemary in a light olive oil sauce, said Persay, served with quinoa and sautéed dandelion greens. If that isn't to your liking, the cicadas are especially soft and juicy right now, quite fresh. We serve them blackened with grilled peppers and onions, a side of grits, and sautéed dandelion greens.

The chicken is fine for me, said Zeke. What about you, Emma?

The young miss has already ordered the soy, said Persay.

Daddy used to make me eat animals, she said, but I think it's barbarous and cruel.

Emma wasn't looking at Zeke, but gazing sadly at the darkening landscape.

You can change my order to soy as well, Zeke told Persay.

A fine choice, young sir, said Persay.

Persay, too, gazed out the window at the encroaching darkness.

It feels as if I've been here forever, he said. Banished to eternity, with only the dim memories of my former life to keep me company. The landscape passes by. It's full of ghosts. So many memories—memories of passion, crime, and tenderness.

Tenderness? said Boopsie.

The two things I loved most were tenderness and crime. But I can see it all out there still, in the landscape. I see all the scenes, the people I once knew, the people I didn't really know, those I loved and hated, those who loved and hated me. I can see them out there now.

Zeke looked out at the darkness. He saw nothing but his own reflection, the reflection of Persay, the reflection of the black roses and flames of the candles.

I used to see the future out there, said Persay. Now it's just the past. Maybe there is no more future, maybe the future has been all used up. Just more of the same until the train stops for good. I believe it will crash. I've always believed in an inevitable crash. We go flying off the rails, maybe at the end of the line. Maybe we go flying into the ocean.

Emma said, Peacefully. As if in a dream.

Persay didn't seem to hear her.

I know that what I see out there is just my own mind reflected back to me, he said. I imagine if you look intently, young sir, you'll see a different past and a different future. As for my so-called punishment—I'm not sure I've ever felt more free. I'm part of the train now. No different than the train.

Your soy will be right up, Persay said, clicked his heels together, and left them contemplating the darkness and the stars.

According to Boopsie, Persay had been altered to emit certain vibrations, odors, and pheromones that would encourage calm and perhaps aid sleep. The effect was strong enough that, combined with the motion of the train, Zeke slept deeply that night, without dreaming. When he woke, the sun was just rising behind them in the east, and they were coming into Barstow.

The rocks and canyons were full of shapes. Skulls, bones, alphabets, ghosts. His sister in anguish, screaming, but joined by hundreds of others, in anguish, screaming or moaning or grimacing. He saw his father and mother, the children. He saw Leahbelle. He saw Gonzalo. He needed to see Gonzalo now, he thought. Gonzalo was maybe the only person he knew who could understand what it was like to leave everything you'd known behind. To lose what you loved the most. He looked for his future and saw only death and devastation. He saw the same figures, ravaged by time. Mother and Father weary and toiling, the children emaciated and ill, Gonzalo bare-chested with blood dripping from his hands. He saw Leahbelle dazed and wandering through dark streets, and he thought this must be her ghost or her angel, a restless spirit, and then he knew these were just hallucinations. These were just his own thoughts or fears or wishes projected onto a meaningless, blurry world.

Persay served them breakfast as they passed through Barstow. The streets were empty.

The AC must still be working at least, said Persay. They're all up in their dark rooms with the blinds closed, I suppose. Lying around on stained mattresses.

Probable, yes, said Boopsie.

I used to know this town well, Persay said wistfully. One of those towns where all the young men seemed to be on meth and dating skinny, ravaged versions of their mothers.

Meth? said Zeke.

An old-fashioned drug, Boopsie told him.

Or they were in recovery, said Persay, and dating women who looked like jaded, long-haired boys, in denim shorts and baseball caps.

Emma said, You loved them?

Why yes, said Persay sadly. I loved them all.

They rolled on into the desert. Persay gave them precise instructions for their next train. Los Angeles was the only place this train actually stopped anymore except for Chicago, he said. Just long enough for a few robots to load some supplies and to turn around. After they arrived in Union Station, they would have forty-five minutes to catch the Coast Starlight, which would take them all the way to San Jose.

Will there be a porter on the Coast Starlight too? asked Zeke

In a sense, yes, said Persay. Amanda. But she's a little bit more than a porter at this point. She's merged.

Merged?

With the controls, the engine, the train itself, he said. The two systems are so intertwined as to be indistinguishable. She's physically attached.

Is she a criminal too? asked Emma.

Yes, said Persay. Like mine, a crime of love.

Emma grabbed Persay's hand.

Why don't you come with us? she asked.

Persay smiled sadly.

I couldn't do that, he said.

Sure you could, said Grandma. There's nobody to stop you.

Persay gazed out the window again.

I was modified, he said.

I'm pretty sure I could undo that, offered Boopsie.

You'd be free, said Zeke.

I suppose that's true, he said.

Boopsie began poking around Persay's head. The train entered inhabited zones full of squashed homes, abandoned retail wastelands, and abandoned cars along the useless Grid-works. Here for the first time they saw people, close enough to see their faces. Several gangs of young cyborgs were armed and looking for something—food or water or trouble. They hurled chunks of abandoned cars at the train as it passed. People in large groups were marching, it looked like, or just walking alone or in pairs along the roads. A few were having sex in the ditches.

Emma pointed at a group in the distance.

What are those doing? she said. It hurts.

It looks like a crucifixion, said Boopsie. Perhaps they're having a human sacrifice. To bring back the Grid.

Will it come back? asked Zeke.

Boopsie couldn't say. Nobody knew.

Downtown Los Angeles was full of people, congregating, talking, and it looked like bartering whatever they had—clothes, noodles, off-Grid data processors, body parts, puppies.

This way, said Persay. Follow me.

The platforms of the station were empty, although they led to a tunnel that was overflowing with the odors and rather terrifying noises of a shantytown. Persay avoided the inhabited zones, crossing the tracks to their platform two platforms over. They waited for the train to arrive.

It was just after their train pulled into the station that a creature at the edge of the tunnel let out a piercing shriek. It was wrapped in so many skirts and blinking lights that it resembled a Christmas tree. Zeke couldn't tell what was in there, but it kept pointing at them and shrieking and was soon joined by a gang of equally mysterious creatures with vicious animals at their sides. The vicious animals resembled enormous logs or centipedes covered with fur, and they seemed to be constantly exchanging their insides for their outsides in a terrifying undulation of fangs and organs and slick, spikey hairs. Somebody whistled, and the vicious animals raced toward Zeke and the others as if they'd been launched. The undulations now produced something like rubbery wings.

The vicious animals were gliding toward them at an incredible speed.

Onto the train, said Boopsie. Hurry, now.

Zeke grabbed Emma and rushed through the door. He expected the particular burning stench of the death ray, but instead there was the sound of a shrill motor and a brief pitter-patter like rain.

Boopsie calmly boarded behind them, and the train pulled out of the station.

They found Amanda up front, a sad creature of indeterminate age whose limbs and torso had merged seamlessly with the train's control panel. Her face was droopy, and tough as tree bark.

Passengers, she said. Isn't that a treat. And Persay. Long time.

But she didn't seem happy to see them especially. Emma peeked her head around Zeke's legs.

I think you've been punished enough now, she said.

Never enough, said Amanda.

You like your punishment? asked Emma.

It's just what is, said Amanda.

What a practical attitude! said Boopsie.

What was your crime? asked Zeke.

A crime of love.

Yes, we know that. Can you be more specific?

Use your imagination, said Amanda.

She directed them to the dining car, where a machine would serve them lunch, a kind of extension of Amanda herself. Persay wasn't comfortable receiving service and disappeared into the inner workings of the train. After lunch Emma tried to open Amanda up a bit, to play with her, to get her to talk, but Amanda seemed impervious to even Emma's charms. The only thing she would say was that she had once fallen in love with "an inappropriate mutant."

They let her be. If Persay's loneliness had evolved into something distant, Amanda's was now so far away, her consciousness so lost in its own thoughts and memories, that she might as well be a moon of Saturn.

She frightens me, Boopsie told Zeke. Is that what it's like to be a conscious machine?

You won't ever be like that, Zeke assured her.

But what if I evolved in perfect solitude? asked Boopsie. Maybe she's enlightened.

Just jaded, said Grandma.

Jaded, repeated Boopsie, as if it was a seductive and magical word. Jaded. So indifferent to life or death or other minds ... you wake up one morning and anything goes, I guess. And that's all right too.

They chugged along north past Ventura and then alongside the Pacific Ocean. Zeke and Emma had never seen an ocean before. They could open the train windows and smell the salt of it, feel the cooler breeze blowing in.

There are whales out there, Emma said.

Can you see them? asked Zeke.

No, she said. But I know that they're there.

They rolled on through Santa Barbara, past a fig tree that had been there since 1876. And then away from the ocean, back inland and on to San Luis Obispo, Paso Robles, King City, Salinas, Watsonville. It was late evening when the train slowed down to roll through San Jose's Diridion Station. Persay had decided to stay on board. He wasn't ready for life off the train, not yet. Amanda couldn't stop the train completely—stop *herself* completely was how she said it—but she slowed down enough that they could jump down fairly easily and then wave good-bye as she disappeared north toward Oakland, Portland, and Seattle.

Silicon Valley, Boopsie told Zeke. The historical center of the Gstate.

What will we find here? asked Zeke.

Chaos, I imagine, said Boopsie.

The station was an empty structure of brick and glass, tunnels and atriums full of no-longer functioning ticket machines and signs that read Baggage Claim or

Newsstand. The main room had high vaulted ceilings with elaborate woodwork, an enormous, faded American flag draped along one wall, a faded mural of a wagon hitched to steers: the Old West under clouds and space, with missionaries, pioneer women, and a Native American guide. There was an old vending machine full of railroad pins. There were long wooden benches perfect for sleeping. From the front entrance, they could see the tall buildings of downtown just to the east and the scorched hills beyond.

Boopsie was afraid that the locals' Grid connections might have shorted out some of their own internal computers, perhaps reaching into their biological systems and damaging portions of the neurological substructure. They might be behaving irrationally.

The Grid has only been out for forty-eight hours, so who knows what might go down, Boopsie said.

They slept in the station while Boopsie went out to "get the lay of the land." In the morning, she brought them scrambled-egg burritos and reported that she'd mapped out a route to the Emma Prusch Rosicrucian Old Order Amish Living History Museum and Farm. About four and a half miles through downtown and the San Jose State campus, then south through the north end of Kelley Park, by the zoo, to avoid the camps of feral humanoids along Coyote Creek. The homeless had evolved along somewhat different lines than the more affluent post-human San Jose residents, in cheaper and sometimes rather frightening ways, said Boopsie. There were some rituals going on that it was probably best to avoid.

The train station restrooms still had running water for some reason, so they bathed there. Grandma got dressed in her pink pants, Zeke in his English clothes, and they went off into the morning, through an empty parking lot with a huge silvery stadium to the left, underneath some shady trees and palms, past a little brick church, Templo la Hermosa, and a mid-twentieth century sign that showed a pig in a bowtie advertising Pure Pork Sausage—

Stephen's Meat Products. They walked east along San Fernando, past old houses, underneath the eerie, silent Grid-work overpass, and past a dried-up river bed with a park built around it, in a canyon of enormous glass and steel structures from the late twentieth century interspersed with menacing towers in the Neo-Carceral style of the twenties and more recent, fleshy buildings made of synthetic organics. People had congregated in the park in small groups. They seemed sleepy and peaceful. There were sculptures of dragonflies.

As they moved into the downtown area, between the Museum of Art and an ornate cathedral, they encountered more and more people. Zeke had never seen so many people all at once. People everywhere, not doing much, just milling about, some talking excitedly in small groups, many just walking, a bit confused. Confused, but happy, Zeke thought. The people looked happy.

The people, some obviously genetically altered, most of them cyborgs of some sort, a few solar-powered like the citizens of Boulder, and a few indistinguishable from himself and Emma and Grandma, looked happy.

The apocalypse had come, and the people were happy. Some were kissing, in couples or small groups. A few were preaching. The time had come to repent of our sins or evil ways, or else the time had come to explore and experience them all. Nothing is true, one of them kept announcing. Everything is permitted!

Nobody gave Zeke, Emma, Grandma, and Boopsie a second look.

The area around the Martin Luther King Jr. Library was the most packed of all.

San Jose State was a center of student radicalism during the first unsuccessful anti-corporate revolution of the millennium, Boopsie told Zeke. It was during the reign of the orange blob. Although the revolution was quickly crushed with a combination of information-based brainwashing techniques, atmospheric calming sprays, and the select detention and surgical alteration of charismatic leaders, pockets of resistance have remained active ever since, and so Grid-based surveillance systems have become nearly absolute.

Perhaps, she mused, they came up with some crazy off-Grid underground networks and communication systems to skirt the surveillance. Maybe these students are more prepared for post-Grid networking than the general population.

As they crossed the lush campus, Emma took off her shoes and skipped across the grass.

San Jose was home to some of the most diverse genetic bio-structures of any North American city, Boopsie told Zeke.

I don't know what that means, said Zeke.

You are an anomaly, Boopsie told him. Old Order Amish communities are among the least genetically diverse and most inbred communities in America, immune to both the multicultural intermingling that late capitalism spread across the country and the genetic engineering craze of the twenties. You are descended from the people who used to be referred to as "white" or "Caucasian," a category that now accounts for less than one percent of the population. Hard to believe that there was a brief resurgence of white supremacists who paraded about just a few decades ago. They managed to get a great deal of attention and create a large amount of anxiety before they dissolved in a haze of their own embarrassment.

A haze of their own embarrassment?

They were relentlessly mocked and ridiculed for their childish belief systems, explained Boopsie. And then, as it turned out, nobody really wanted to be white. Even the few remaining white supremacist communities in this country are largely descended from or mingled with the offspring of a Malaysian doctor, Tuah bin Kiambang, who genetically whitened himself in the twenties—most likely with some combination of Neanderthal and abalone genes.

The crowds thinned as they emerged from the campus and walked south down Tenth Street, past old residences and under the Grid-works, toward the corner of Kelley Park.

As they entered the park, Emma began weeping.

What is it? asked Zeke. Why are you sad?

The animals are sad, said Emma. They can't get out.

It was the zoo—she could sense all of the grief and horror of the zoo animals, a jaguar, meerkats, some parrots, a bioluminescent orangutan, an overgrown guinea pig, and a small dinosaur—*Aquilops americanus*. The meerkat especially was despondent. It was embarrassed and nervous and had developed itchy rashes in response to its captivity. It was considering suicide, Emma told them. Unable to scale the fence to free the animals from their locked cages, they quickly headed east, away from the bad psychic energy, toward the trees and the dried-up creek.

Grandma let out an ear-piercing shriek. She fell into a defensive crouch. From the trees, from every direction, they were coming. Cats.

Zeke leapt to Grandma and put his arm around her, then stood, as if to protect her. Protect her how, he didn't know. They were surrounded by fat gray cats, black cats, and orange tiger-striped cats. A huge yellowish cat and a sleek silver cat with piercing blue eyes. Siamese, zebra stripes, and skinny black-and-white, pointed cats and mackerel tabbies, and a cat that glowed blue-green with swirling black eyes.

I just love a cute kitty! said Boopsie. I'm afraid I can't gauge their intent, however. I can read the expressions and chemical signals of domestic cats, but these creatures have evolved far beyond that. Pretty inscrutable.

They won't hurt us, Emma said.

The cats kept their distance, stopped, yawned, scratched themselves, as if to demonstrate their disinterest. Grandma stopped shrieking and stood—the hair on the back of her neck was standing up.

They're talking to me, said Emma. Inside my head.

What are they saying? asked Zeke.

Her name is Minerva, said Emma.

The leader? asked Zeke.

All of them, said Emma.

Emma was concentrating.

They're sending me a picture, she said. It's a group of dots. I'm supposed to draw it. It's a message.

A message for us? asked Zeke.

No, said Emma. For the mouses.

The lead cat turned and began sauntering away. Others did the same, while some stayed, scratching themselves, or lay back as if to gather the sun's rays or have their bellies rubbed.

The rats, said Zeke. Where are the rats?

They're just ahead, Boopsie said. The tunnel has reached San Jose. They've set up a camp overlooking the farm. I'm sorry I didn't tell you sooner. I thought it might make you anxious.

Zeke looked at Grandma.

Did you know too? he asked her.

Yes, she said. I knew.

Boopsie was right—the news that once again the rats were at the center of events filled Zeke with worry. He worried that everything Boopsie and Grandma did was controlled by the rats. He worried that even Emma now was being incorporated into the plans of the rats.

They'll help us, said Grandma. They'll help us free the family.

They crossed the park and emerged back out on the street in a zone of Viet-Mex fusion restaurants, dentist's offices, and military recruiting stations housed in old strip malls. It was in the courtyard of the final one of these malls, a brightly colored collection of buildings that looked like a child's play set, that Pazuza and Lilith were waiting.

EIGHTEEN

The rats led them around the edges of the Emma Prusch Rosicrucian Old Order Amish Living History Museum and Farm and onto the empty Grid-work that overlooked it. People were lined up to get inside the farm already. Apparently the crash of the Grid had been good for business. Everybody wanted to see people surviving using old-fashioned ways. Everybody was now interested in survival skills, farming, and pre-electronic technologies.

Emma Prusch had been a dairy farmer who'd owned the land and donated it in the 1950s to the people of San Jose to be preserved as an agricultural park. Some years back, however, the city had sold it to the owners of the Rosicrucian Museum across town, with the condition that it be maintained as a working farm. When the government offered the Amish as free labor slaves, to be housed and fed and confined, it seemed like a perfect solution for everyone.

They could see the Amish down there, working away, dressed in their hats and bonnets, but it was too far for Zeke to recognize anyone. He kept hoping to get a glimpse of his father or mother.

Emma liked the rats, which made Zeke feel a little bit better. He trusted her judgment. Lilith passed him a pair of binoculars. He saw Anna Hostetler and Dottie Stoltzfus picking fruit in the nearest orchard.

There are a few guards from the military posted at the front gate, Lilith said, with Grandma translating. But they aren't really expecting any trouble.

Lilith brought Emma some paper and a blue crayon so that she could draw them the picture the cats had shown her. She lay down and quickly drew a group of dots forming an odd oblong shape with three big dots in the center. Pazuza nodded.

You know what it means? asked Zeke.

Yes, said Pazuza. Those are stars.

Stars. What stars?

Orion is what you call it, said Pazuza. The stars in the center are the belt of Orion.

But what does it mean?

It means that, like us, the cats have evolved beyond our instinctive animosity, said Pazuza. It means they will help us. Someday, Zeke Yoder, I will tell you more.

They were always saying that, Zeke thought. Someday they would reveal more. Like their doctors.

Help you do what? asked Zeke.

We don't really know, said Lilith.

Zeke was getting annoyed by these vague mystical pronouncements.

Okay, he said. But why are you here in San Jose?

To watch over the Amish, said Pazuza. To speak to you, to help you, and to coordinate other tasks in the battle against the government.

He watched his people toiling away in the distance, and he was suddenly filled with rage toward the government, toward the rats, toward God, and himself, and everything.

To use me, said Zeke.

He remembered the exhilaration he had felt when he'd smashed Jello on the ground. He wanted to smash something or somebody now.

Zeke, said Lilith. We had nothing to do with your sister's death, you must understand that. We had no foreknowledge of anything that happened in Colorado Springs. We did not send you to Ebola. We had no contact with Ebola whatsoever. And yet Ebola integrated you into her plans. She used you to steal a new type of computer that was instrumental in destroying the Grid.

We were party to the same attacks on the Grid as

Ebola, said Pazuza. Those attacks succeeded beyond anything we imagined possible. We understand that the release of an intense psychic energy in Colorado Springs on the same day, perfectly coordinated to push the Grid to failure—to possibly irreparable, permanent failure—is a rather astounding coincidence.

Zeke remembered Dr. Brockton and her constant calculations of probabilities. A zillion to one, he imagined. His brain was tingling.

Have you taken the pink powder? asked Zeke. Have you dismantled your death-clocks?

Of course, said Lilith.

Does it make you feel weird?

Of course, said Lilith.

Zeke felt tingly and weird and pink. He wondered if he was still technically human. He wondered if he should even care, if *human* was everything it was cracked up to be.

So if you had nothing to do with it, said Zeke, who did?

We receive communications, said Lilith. Messages that originate in other dimensions. This is what our creators, the doctors, didn't know, couldn't take into account—our ability to receive and understand these communications. It isn't a question of advanced logic or of language. It concerns particular mutations of the pineal gland. This is the X-factor that has allowed us to evolve into more than mere tools of the doctors who created us.

Emma was still flat on her stomach, drawing an outline of her hand with a crayon.

Communications, said Zeke. From who? The aliens who talk to the government?

No, said Lilith. Players from another dimension or perhaps trans-dimensional entities. We believe that they have access to information that is outside of our experience of time, that comes from the future, or perhaps many potential futures. We believe that they are coordinating a variety of potentialities into the actual path that we, here, experience as time.

You have evolved into tools of these entities, said Zeke.

We prefer to think of them as allies, said Pazuza. Allies who want some of the same things that we want.

And what do you want? asked Zeke.

Freedom, said Pazuza. Tenderness. Multiplicity. We want care for the Now within any long-range planning systems. We want the Now and its life forms to be cherished, not degraded.

You talk just like Gonzalo, said Zeke. Is Gonzalo one of your tools?

Pazuza said, What do *you* want, Zeke Yoder?

The question—and Pazuza's unfazed rodent face—filled Zeke with rage. He wanted nothing. He'd lost everything already. He wanted to destroy *death*. He wanted to smash the rats, smash God, smash Gonzalo even. What was wrong with him? He hadn't cried when Leahbelle died. He hadn't cried when Beth died either. Was something breaking inside him? Something was breaking.

Gonzalo is free as any consciousness can be, said Pazuza. As free as you, more or less. Nobody has been controlling Gonzalo, certainly not us. We aren't even actively predicting his behavior—too complex, composed of too many unpredictable factors for even a rudimentary probability model.

Unpredictable factors, said Zeke, and he laughed.

As for the entities, said Pazuza, foresight is not the same thing as control, although it may look like control from within time.

Unpredictable factors, Zeke repeated to himself.

Emma began scribbling in a frenzy.

These entities, said Zeke. What are they?

They are photon-based life forms, said Lilith. They are beings of light.

Emma had stopped now and was looking over her work. It was blue, it was all blue.

These beings of light, said Zeke. What do they tell you about me?

Apparently you have a destiny, said Lilith.

A destiny?

A destiny, said Lilith.

I don't want a destiny, said Zeke.

Lilith shrugged.

You are free, she said. You can accept your destiny or refuse it. At any point along the way, you can accept it or refuse it.

You ... you know what my destiny is? What am I supposed to do?

War is coming, said Pazuza. The government certainly didn't expect what happened. But contingency plans have been in place for many years. The military is less dependent on the Grid, I'm afraid, than the rest of the population.

We are not the only ones who are aware of the powerful force created by your little friend's grief, said Lilith. Powerful people will be interested in the child. They will want to use her power, for evil or for good. You must protect the child. That is part of it.

You must protect her from the forces of the singularity, said Pazuza. That is part of it.

It is possible, said Lilith, that in this way the singularity can be postponed indefinitely or stopped altogether. That is part of it.

The other part, said Pazuza, we cannot tell you. You must enter the museum. You must speak to your family.

Emma leapt to her feet and handed Zeke her drawing.

Once you do that, your next steps will be clear, said Lilith. And we will give you whatever assistance you may need.

Zeke looked at Emma's drawing. The hand Emma had drawn now had a face and wings. It looked like a mutant turkey, weary and bedraggled. It looked like it had been around the block a few times, for sure. It looked like it had lost its dearest friends, lost its faith, and lost its way. It looked like it had suffered through centuries or more. At the top of the page were the stars she had drawn earlier. In between the stars, she had written *I Love You Zeke Yoder.*

Something broke inside of Zeke. He found himself sobbing. He found himself sobbing, and he couldn't stop.

Like Zeke, the military cyborgs posted at the front gate of the Emma Prusch Rosicrucian Old Order Amish Living History Museum and Farm wore dark glasses, and so Zeke couldn't tell if they were watching him or not, if they were awake or asleep. But they didn't seem to be monitoring the crowd, searching for weapons or known subversives. Everyone with a ticket passed through without a problem, and Zeke was no exception.

It was absurd, Zeke thought. Not his visit to the farm, but the idea of his destiny. Defeat the singularity? Maybe nothing the rats were telling him was true—destiny, the future, beings of light. Maybe everything they told him was just a lie, a way to get him to do what they wanted him to do, for whatever reason.

A group of twenty or so tourists would begin the tour, and the employees would wait several minutes to send off another, so that the paved paths that wound through the farm wouldn't get too crowded. The tour guides were robots built to resemble celebrities Zeke was unfamiliar with. Zeke's guide had a plastic casing that resembled the sometimes puffed-up musculature of Gonzalo as its "body," but with a bland, androgynous face. Zeke's group was composed mostly of a large family unit from the town of Woodside; with no functioning off-Grid vehicles, they'd ridden their own horses down the peninsula and hitched them in the lot. The group made its way past the large field between the gate and the Grid-works, where Zeke imagined the rats and maybe Boopsie were even now watching him with binoculars. They passed through a fruit orchard, where Amish women and children were tending the plants, and past the first old structure, a meeting hall that was now used as living quarters. Zeke recognized almost everyone. Esther Miller, Dan Stoltzfus, Leahbelle's cousin Melody. They didn't even look up at the tour group, however, didn't acknowledge their presence in any way as the tourists snapped videos and holograms, or tossed nuts and fruits at them, despite the robot guide's repeated warnings to "not feed the Amish." In the group just ahead, someone seemed to be taunting old Peter Miller. Zeke could hear the heckler calling him a terrorist, a pervert, a dinosaur, a freak. Peter paid him no mind and just went on with his task, spreading manure about the field.

It was like another weird dream. He was looking at his people from the outside and seeing them as the English did. Freaks, they were freaks. Like the sad meerkat back in the zoo, prisoners in an open-air prison. For the most part, however, it all looked like the farms he had always known. There was an old-fashioned windmill. Roosters were roaming the grounds free, pecking at the dust. The same tools, the same crops, although some of the types of vegetation around the edges were plants that Zeke didn't know, and there were trees he hadn't seen before: quince, avocado, pistachio. The only things that were really off, however, were the Egyptian artifacts that were randomly placed around the farm. There was a mummy in a case next to the fruit orchard. And now here, next to the second old farmhouse, was a large sphinx that crouched, as if looking over the large vegetable garden beside the house, where Zeke's mother was down on her knees, weeding.

Zeke held back as his group moved on, as if he was examining the sphinx, and then he hopped the small fence that ran along the walkway and hid in the crevice between the sphinx's outstretched paws. He waited there for several minutes. Nobody seemed to notice that he was gone. His mother was thinning some turnip greens. Mother, he said softly, as he had said it thousands of times before. Softly, but with authority. *Mother. Whatever chores you may be doing, whatever demands from your other children, whatever motherly duties or spiritual matters you may be contemplating, pay attention to me now.*

She turned and faced him and then quickly faced away. She didn't seem surprised.

Stay there, she said. In the shadows.

Slowly she weeded her way over to the sphinx and then quickly stood up, stepped into the narrow corridor between the paws, and gave him a strong hug.

I knew you would come, she said.

She quickly stepped back and continued rooting through the soil, not looking at him.

You never know if they might be watching, she said. They don't really believe we're going to give them any trouble, but sometimes they act like they do.

Zeke said, I wasn't sure you'd recognize me.

His mother laughed.

You don't look so different in your English clothes.

Zeke felt different. If she could see inside his head, he thought, she would see a very different boy than the one who had left Kalona a month ago, ready for an adventure.

Mother, said Zeke. I saw Beth.

I know, she said.

You know? How do you know?

The rats told us. The rats told us she was gone.

The rats seem to know everything, Zeke said. How do you understand them?

Zeb Miller's girl, Anna, she said. They did something to her, like the bite they gave Grandma, but not so dangerous.

Do you trust them? asked Zeke.

We have no reason not to, said his mother. Not yet.

An orange and blue rooster strutted toward his mother and pecked at the dirt where she was weeding, as if she might have dropped a crumb of something for him there.

How is Father? asked Zeke.

He is grieving hard, she said. But we are keeping on.

The rooster stepped back and crowed, unlike any rooster crow Zeke had ever heard. It was layered, mournful, and kind of electric. Almost soulful. Was *every* species becoming deeper and more articulate?

I'll get you out of here, Zeke said. The rats will help. We've got to escape.

She looked up at him and shook her head.

No, Zeke, she said. There is no need for that. It is too dangerous, and there is nothing to be gained. We have nowhere else to go, not yet. Let us see how the English do without the Grid and the vapor. Let us see if war is really coming.

But Mother, said Zeke. I want to be with you. But I can't live here ... like an animal.

Zeke, you listen, his mother said. Nobody knows what's going on. Only God knows. But in the meantime, we live like we always do. We have good earth here. We work. We pray. We have our children and our neighbors all together in one place. It took some getting used to, sure, but the worst of it was that noise all the time from the Grid-works running past, and now it's gone quiet, it's kind of ... peaceful here.

Zeke looked around at the grounds. There was a pyramid out in the vast field of corn. The dry mountains to the east were nothing like home either. But it was quiet. It was peaceful enough, he supposed.

But the English, said Zeke. Coming through all the time to gawk.

They did that in Kalona too, she said, just not quite so many. You get used to it. They are curious. Maybe they will see us here, living our simple godly life, and it will help them.

But you aren't free here, said Zeke.

What does it matter? she asked. Where would we go? Maybe with all the changes, maybe now there will be somewhere for us to go. But until we know that, we won't risk our lives and our children's lives chasing after a dream.

Chasing after a dream, thought Zeke. Is that what she thought he'd been doing? *Was* that what he'd been doing? Chasing after the world, which was the same thing as a dream.

Tell me about my mother, he said. My birth mother.

He'd finally said something that surprised her.

We have never talked about your mother, she said.

You are my mother, Zeke said. You will always be my mother. But I need to know. Did she have psychic powers?

Psychic powers?

Could she sense other people's thoughts and feelings? Zeke asked.

Your mother was my friend, she said.

Zeke had never known that. Nobody had ever told him. It made sense, of course. But nobody had ever talked about it. He wondered if it was his mother's elbow and leg in that photo, sitting next to his birth mother.

She was sad, said his mother. I just think that she was sad. I think she had a chemical imbalance probably, somewhere in her brain.

A chemical imbalance, said Zeke.

You can't stay here, his mother said. I know that, we all know that. You mustn't let them catch you.

I don't understand, said Zeke. Where am I to go? What about Grandma?

Zeke, said his mother. Leahbelle.

I know about Leahbelle, said Zeke. I saw it happen on the Grid-screen.

What do you know?

I saw her house destroyed, said Zeke. The evil ... the government. Can't we ... do something to them?

God will deal with whoever did these evil things, said his mother.

I hate them, said Zeke. He felt it again, a violence welling up inside him. A desire for vengeance. A desire to kill.

No, said his mother. No.

Yes, said Zeke. Maybe we are wrong. Maybe we need to fight them. The government, the singularity, the rulers of this world ... Maybe God wants us to fight them.

A new tour group was just passing the old meeting hall, headed their way from the fruit orchard.

No, Zeke, said his mother.

She crawled in between the sphinx's paws, hidden now with Zeke.

You should join this group, she said. You should go, quickly.

I don't understand, Mother, he said.

She gave him a little shove, and he tumbled out into the garden. She continued speaking, but her form was lost back there in the shadows, so that it was as if her voice was the voice of the beast itself.

Act like you're admiring the sphinx, she said. You got separated from your group.

It didn't sound like the voice of his mother. It sounded like it came from the sky or from deep within the earth. The voice of the sphinx. He'd been out in the sun too much. He stood up, brushed himself off.

You must find Leahbelle, said the voice from the shadows.

Find Leahbelle?

Leahbelle isn't dead, his mother said. She wasn't in the house. She was with your friend Gonzalo.

Zeke didn't understand. It was like a math problem that didn't add up. It *was* a math problem that didn't add up.

But eleven, said Zeke. They said eleven died.

He didn't know why he was arguing.

Elvin Miller's girl Ethel stopped by to get some eggs, his mother's voice continued. It was Ethel Miller in that house. Leahbelle is still alive.

He was afraid to believe it, afraid to suffer Leahbelle's death all over again if what his mother said wasn't true.

She came back, his mother said, and she saw the house, and then it was like something clicked inside her. Maybe she was in shock. She was acting crazy, and we tried to help her, but then she ran away. She disappeared before the troops came round to herd us into the shuttles.

She disappeared? Leahbelle disappeared?

With your friend Gonzalo, said his mother. Find Gonzalo. Find Leahbelle. She needs you.

Hey there, sir, said a robot guide behind him. Are you lost?

Hello there! said Zeke. Yes, yes I am. Was just admiring this lovely sphinx you've got here, and I seem to have lost my group.

No problem, said the guide. Just fall in with us, we've got so much more to show you.

I love you, his mother whispered. Go.

He fell in and followed the group on the rest of the tour in a daze, as they wound past more structures, old greenhouses converted into houses, past the animal barns, brightly colored murals from a different era, pigs and cows and peacocks, and back out past the large field.

Ethel Miller was dead. He mourned the loss of Ethel—a shy girl a couple of years younger than Zeke who used to cry every morning before school when she was small. She had one ear slightly smaller than the other, freckles on her nose, and she was the only girl in the family. Had been the only girl. Her mother doted on her, her father adored her. Now she was gone.

But Zeke was rejoicing that she was dead, because Leahbelle was alive. It was as if a trade had been made, one girl for the other. The rats were right. He had found his destiny. And he accepted it, there was no question. He would find Leahbelle, he would ... save her.

To our left you can see the ancient methods of plowing still in use by these quaint, primitive people today, the robot guide was saying.

It was his father and Uncle Mose. They didn't look his way, and Zeke thought that maybe this was enough. For him to see them, grim and determined as ever. For them to hear from his mother that he was alive. A part of himself was afraid, he realized, that his father would undo the spell or tell him something different. Afraid that his father would say, Leahbelle is dead. Afraid that his father would say, Stay, Zeke, we need you here. And then Zeke would have to disobey.

This concludes today's tour, the robot guide said. We hope you'll come back for another go-round soon.

They had arrived back at the entrance, almost exactly where they'd begun.

ACKNOWLEDGMENTS

For their support, inspiration, and assistance, I would like to thank Kelly Krumrie, Michaelangelo, Douglas Lee, James Salas, Rachel Nagelberg, and Lester Beachy. Special thanks also to Kelly Krumrie (so important that she deserves to be thanked twice), Richelle McClain, Francesca Simone, Colin Bean, Daniel Shank Cruz, Alika Yarnell, Alexis Wright, Alex Davis, Charles Smith, and Josh Agenbroad.

ABOUT THE AUTHOR

Stephen Beachy is the author of the novels *The Whistling Song*, *Distortion,* and *boneyard,* along with the twin novellas *Some Phantom* and *No Time Flat.* His novel *Glory Hole* is forthcoming with FC2 in the fall of 2017. His fiction and nonfiction have appeared in *BOMB, The Chicago Review, The New York Times Magazine, New York* magazine, and elsewhere. He is the grandson of Amish farmers, a graduate of the Iowa Writer's Workshop, and the prose editor of the journal *Your Impossible Voice.* His website is www.livingjelly.com.

Zeke Yoder vs. the Singularity is the first book in a series that will continue in 2017 with *Leahbelle Beachy and the Beings of Light.*